THE JAPANESE MOB GETS CLOSER.

The door clicks closed. I shiver, despite the stifling air. The *yakuza* are still on the loose. Fujikawa must be furious about being set up and not getting his painting. It's only a matter of time before he seeks revenge or sends his henchmen to harass the Yamadas.

I wish I really were Kimono Girl. I'd wrap the Yamadas in my magic robe and whisk them away, into the print. And my dad, too. If that rock through his window was an attempted break-in, and if his paintings were destroyed because someone expected to find something among them, he must be on their radar.

Somewhere along the way, the *yakuza* got bad information. Why else would they think my dad or Skye or Julian had any idea where the lost van Gogh painting would be? Now the Japanese mob is barreling down the wrong path. Full throttle. And we can't get out of the road.

OTHER BOOKS YOU MAY ENJOY

Battle Dress	Amy Efaw
Black Mirror	Nancy Werlin
If I Stay	Gayle Forman
Incarceron	Catherine Fisher
The Killer's Cousin	Nancy Werlin
Legend	Marie Lu
Looking for Alaska	John Green
The Outsiders	S. E. Hinton
Prodigy	Marie Lu
Sapphique	Catherine Fisher
Tales of the Madman Underground	John Barnes
Three Days	Donna Jo Napoli

TOKYO HEIST

DIANA RENN

TOKYO HEIST

speak

An Imprint of Penguin Group (USA) Inc.

SPEAK
Published by the Penguin Group
Penguin Group (USA) Inc.
375 Hudson Street
New York, New York 10014, U.S.A.

USA / Canada / UK / Ireland / Australia / New Zealand / India / South Africa / China
Penguin Books Ltd, Registered Offices: 80 Strand, London WC2R 0RL, England

For more information about the Penguin Group visit www.penguin.com

First published in the United States of America by Viking,
a member of Penguin Group (USA) Inc., 2012
Published by Speak, an imprint of Penguin Group (USA) Inc., 2013

THE LIBRARY OF CONGRESS HAS CATALOGED THE VIKING EDITION AS FOLLOWS:
Renn, Diana.
Tokyo heist / by Diana Renn.
p. cm.
Summary: After a high-profile art heist of three van Gogh drawings in her home town
of Seattle, sixteen-year-old Violet Rossi finds herself in Japan with her artist father,
searching for the related van Gogh painting.
ISBN 978-0-670-01332-6 (hardcover)
[1. Art thefts—Fiction. 2. Gogh, Vincent van, 1853-1890—Fiction. 3. Fathers and daughters—Fiction.
4. Seattle (Wash.)—Fiction. 5. Tokyo (Japan)—Fiction. 6. Mystery and detective stories.] I. Title.
PZ7.R2895Tok 2012   [Fic]—dc23   2011043364

Speak ISBN 978-0-14-242654-8

Printed in the United States of America

1 3 5 7 9 10 8 6 4 2

The publisher does not have any control over and does not assume any responsibility
for author or third-party websites or their content.

In memory of my grandmother, Esther Bruketta,
who never went anywhere without an intriguing mystery
tucked away in her purse

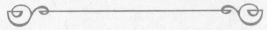

PART 1 SEATTLE

1

The wind, the rain, my soaked Converse sneakers: I blame it all on my dad. It's his fault I waited in front of Jet City Comics for over an hour before hopping a bus to Seattle's Pioneer Square. Now I'm slogging downtown through a rainstorm, dragging my suitcase through puddles.

Most of the art galleries are already closed for the day, but the Margo Wise Gallery glows with cool light. I duck under the awning and wipe my steamed-up glasses. Through the gallery window, I scan the crowd. Well-dressed men and women gather around paintings, eating off tiny plates, but I don't see anybody whom I know. A jazz trio plays in a corner. Everyone will stare when I go in. I don't look like an artist's daughter. I look like a runaway trying to score food.

But I was invited! I take the damp, creased postcard from the pocket of my leather jacket. GLENN MARKLUND, MADRONA GROVE: PAINTINGS FROM ORCAS ISLAND. ARTIST RECEPTION THURSDAY, JUNE 26, 6:00–8:00 PM. My name, Violet Rossi, appears on a label above my mom's address. The other side shows one of my dad's paintings: a lone madrona tree on a bluff, its bark a collage of mottled browns, its leaves dark green and waxy.

Its trunk sways to the left, like a woman sticking out her hip. The tree radiates *chikara*, my favorite Japanese word. It means "confidence" or "power."

I could use some *chikara* right now. I suddenly don't know if my dad mailed the card himself, or if a computer just randomly spit out my name. *"Ganbatte!"* I whisper to my blurry reflection. That's Japanese for "hang in there." Characters are always saying that in manga and anime. My friends and I say it to each other at school. It will take a whole lot of *chikara* to walk into that gallery and put myself on display.

I twist my frizzed curls into a bun, which I secure with two lacquered chopsticks. I straighten my yellow kimono scarf, pick up my luggage, and step into the light and the laughter.

People surround my dad. A photographer snaps pictures of him. No wonder I didn't see him at first. His normal uniform is a plaid shirt slung over a T-shirt. Paint-splattered jeans. Crooked glasses. His shoulder-length hair, pulled back in a ponytail, always looks oily. If you didn't know he was an artist, you might think he'd spent a week living under the Aurora Bridge. In a cardboard box. Which, for all I know, he does. It's not like I've actually *seen* his new house in Fremont, even though he's been living there for almost three months.

But this evening, he wears crisp, black jeans and a black V-neck sweater. His blow-dried hair hangs loose. Maybe he didn't pick me up after work because he was too busy styling his hair.

The gallery turns into a surrealist painting. Everything stretches and blurs. What if my dad doesn't want me spending the next six weeks at his house? My mom flew to Rome this morning for her summer research fellowship. Two grad students are subletting our North Seattle condo. I have no doting relatives to take me in. As for friends, in a week, Edge will be at film camp. Reika is in Tokyo with her aunt and uncle. And I already told everyone that I'm spending my summer in the city, in the artsy Fremont district. How can I say my dad blew me off?

Breathe. Maybe when my dad sees me, he'll slap his forehead and apologize, like he does when he's late to meet me at Romano's Macaroni Grill for our roughly-every-other-month-dinner thing.

My sneakers squelch on the floor as I shove through the crowd.

But before I can get to my dad, a tall woman strides toward me, blocking my path.

Thunder rumbles outside. Maybe this June storm colors my view, but this woman would make the perfect villain for a *Kimono Girl* episode. My hand twitches with the urge to sketch her. Her silver, bobbed hair is cut razor sharp, her thin lips stained deep maroon. Draped over her black pantsuit is a purple scarf with intricate geometric patterns. I could call her the Scarf. Her scarf might possess magic powers. It could make things disappear.

"Can I help you?" the unsmiling woman asks me.

"Uh, that's okay."

"We don't allow bags larger than a purse in the gallery."

"Sorry. Do you have a coatroom?"

"We do not." She nods at a guy standing by the door.

The short, scrawny man in a gray suit walks rapidly toward us, head tipped to one side. His thinning hair is combed back and stiff with gel, a scraggly goatee looks like the site of a botched hair transplant, and his mouth hangs open. He makes me think of the sockeye salmon we studied in biology this year. And I suddenly get a vision of how I could use him as a character, too. As a shape-shifter named Sockeye, who can transform from man to salmon. Yes! He travels Elliott Bay as a fish, then springs from the water as a man to commit heinous crimes!

"What's going on, Margo?" Sockeye asks.

"Julian, would you kindly escort this young lady and her wet bags to the door?"

Reality hits. The Scarf is Margo Wise, my dad's new art dealer, the gallery owner.

"Wait," I say as Julian steps toward me. "I'm here to see my dad. I'm Violet Rossi." As they both look doubtfully at me, I add, "Glenn Marklund's daughter."

Margo glances at the door. "Really? Are there more of you?"

"No. Just me."

"Well." She looks me up and down, like I'm a sculpture that didn't turn out right.

I shouldn't be shocked I'm breaking news. My parents never married. I'm the offspring of two college students who dated briefly, then called it quits. My mom didn't see a future with my dad, so she raised me on her own, even though it meant taking twice as long to get through college and an art history PhD program.

I'm proud of her. If anyone has *chikara*, it's my mom. But I think her determination to do it all on her own wiped out any trace of my dad in me. I have her height—five foot nine—and her Italian features: a round face, dark curly hair, and curves that I prefer to hide with oversize T-shirts and hoodies. I didn't get my dad's angular, Scandinavian features or his Nordic blue eyes. I can see why Margo and Julian are struggling to connect the dots. Still, it seems like my dad failed to mention my mere existence. My thoughts curl up in a fist.

"I'll get Glenn," Margo says. "Julian. Move the child's luggage behind your desk."

Sniffing loudly, Julian picks up my bags. My duffel bag leaves a wet splotch on his leg.

I look around the gallery, trying to act like I belong. I pretend I'm Kimono Girl slipping into a painting. In *The Adventures of Kimono Girl*, the manga-style graphic novel I'm working on, Kimono Girl (KG for short) has an enchanted vintage kimono. It allows her to slip into works of art. Inside the art, she can hide and observe people on the outside, or she can explore the worlds in the paintings. At work this week, I've storyboarded the whole sequence of how she first finds the robe in a shop. The shopkeeper tells her that it once belonged to a Japanese artist. KG gradually discovers its powers. I'm already up to page ten.

I'm sure KG would love to zoom into my dad's enormous canvases. Fuchsia flowers dot the bluffs, and teal waves glimmer in the distance. Trees in every shade of green pose like models, more like tree portraits than landscapes. I walk up to the tree from the postcard. That tree has serious attitude. A stay-out-of-my-way tree, alone on a bluff.

Imagining I'm Kimono Girl hidden in those branches, I steal a look at the crowd. Most people are just here to see and be seen. But a Japanese man in a dark gray suit commands my attention. Silver hair. Gold watch. Black shoes. Wire-rimmed glasses. Everything about him seems to catch the light and gleam. Edge and Reika would say I only notice him because I'm a total Japan freak. But I don't think that's why. I'm drawn to his look of intense concentration. He stands in front of a canvas, swaying slightly, as if the painting is playing music only he can hear.

What would it be like to have someone look at my graphic novel that way?

"Violet? What brings you here?"

I spin around to face my dad. "Seriously? You were supposed to get me after work."

"No, I'm getting you tomorrow at three thirty. Friday."

"Mom left for Italy today. I waited for two hours. I left you four phone messages."

He slaps his forehead. "Gosh. I'm sorry, kiddo. There's been some stuff going on lately on top of this show that's sort of distracted me. And I've misplaced my cell phone again, can you believe it? So I didn't get your messages." He glances at a photographer hovering nearby and puts up one hand. "Um. So. You're here. That's terrific! You hungry?"

I shrug and follow him to a banquet table.

"Margo had this catered by Wild Ginger, and—oh, excuse me a moment? There's someone I promised I'd touch base with. Just real quick. Then we'll catch up. Okay?"

I load up a plastic plate with vegetable spring rolls and steamed *gyoza*. As I dig in, I notice I'm being stared at by a pale, thin woman with close-cropped auburn hair. She watches me through narrowed eyes. I turn my attention to my plate.

My dad returns. "Great turnout, huh?" He points out some big-time art collectors: media people, high-tech tycoons, investment bankers, venture capitalists. I recognize only the weatherman from Channel Four. "And over there? My two newest collectors." He points to the silver-haired Japanese man a few yards away. He's now standing by a Japanese woman. They are discussing a painting.

The woman—his wife, I assume—looks at least a decade younger than him and has the air of a former model. She wears a white cocktail pantsuit with gold, strappy sandals and carries a gleaming, gold clutch. Her hair—jet black with one artful gray streak off her forehead—is smoothed back in a twist and secured with a pearl comb. When she smiles, I notice her teeth are crooked, which startles me at first. But the rest of her beauty overpowers this flaw.

"Kenji and Mitsue Yamada," my dad whispers. "They're serious collectors. They live mostly in Japan, but they own a house here in Seattle and come a few times a year for business. Kenji's with the Yamada Corporation. Heard of it?"

I shake my head.

"It's one of the biggest construction companies in Japan. They have offices in cities all over the world. Kenji's the CEO."

"I thought you hated business. When did you start worshipping the corporate gods?"

My dad pours a cup of seltzer. "Kenji's not your typical

businessman. He's retiring this year. Wants to be a dedicated patron of the arts. And his wife curates an art museum in his Tokyo office building."

"Looks like they're big fans." I watch the couple exclaim over details in my dad's painting. In Studio Art, no one looks at my class work with awe. I "show promise" and have "great ideas," but there are always a hundred things to fix.

"Guess so," my dad agrees. "Not only are they taking four of my paintings for a show at their museum next month, they commissioned a mural from me for their lobby."

"In their Seattle office? Cool."

"No, no. Company headquarters. In Tokyo. I'm flying there in August, after you go back to your mother's."

I stare at him. Awesome. Now I've got one parent jetting off to Italy, and the other zooming away to Japan, while I get to spend my entire summer working at a second-rate strip-mall comic shop, taking money from snotty kids and forty-year-old men who need showers. Plus, it's my life dream to go to Japan. One of my best friends is there all summer, and I would kill to be there with her. And now my dad—who won't even touch sushi with a ten-foot chopstick—is the one who gets to go. This is so not fair.

The auburn-haired woman comes over and snakes an arm around my dad. She fixes her cool, gray eyes on me. "Hello," she says, then looks at my dad. "Who's your friend?"

My dad's neck is turning red. "So, uh, Skye, actually this

is Violet, my, um, daughter. Violet, this is Skye Connolly. My, uh, girlfriend."

Um Daughter and Uh Girlfriend shake hands. "Nice to meet you," we lie in unison.

Okay, somebody has to say something to break the stare-down contest.

Skye wears a black sheath dress, and her right arm sports a tattoo of a black bird with a long neck shaped like a question mark. "I like your tattoo," I tell her. "Black swan?"

"Cormorant." She looks at the characters I copied in white ink on my black leather jacket: the cast of *Fruits Basket*, every character a zodiac sign. "Cute. You're a manga fan?"

"Sort of." *Cute.* My dad said that once, last fall, when I showed him some rough ideas for *Kimono Girl*. That's the last page I ever showed him.

My dad laughs weakly, as if relieved the two of us have found some spongy common ground to flounder on. "Are you kidding? Violet devours manga. Reads it in all her spare time."

"No, I don't." Actually I do. But I'm not a hard-core *otaku* or anything. I don't do cosplay, or post fan art on the Internet. I go to only one con a year. But I feel pretty much done talking to Skye. She's made it perfectly clear that she doesn't get manga. Or me.

Coming here this evening was a huge mistake. I don't fit into my dad's world at all. And I don't think he wants me to. Now he's talking to Skye in a low voice. I've gone from a weird blot on the scene to invisible.

I turn to go. But Margo's striding toward me again, this time with the Japanese art collectors, and I'm caught in their curious stares.

2

"It is a great pleasure to meet you, Violet," says Kenji Yamada, after Margo introduces me. His English is precise, his accent Japanese mixed with something else. British, I think.

"Yes, very nice meeting you." Mitsue's voice makes me think of tea swirled with honey. She admires my damp kimono scarf. "Is this made from a kimono?"

"Uh, yeah, so there's this store in the international district? They have a bin of vintage kimonos with rips, for ten bucks each, and I use those to make scarves and headbands and stuff?" My mom is always yelling at me about ending sentences with question marks. I wish I could talk about art—or anything—with confidence. With *chikara*.

"How creative!" Mitsue exclaims.

"You must be an artist, like your father," Kenji says, his eyes twinkling. Then he shakes my dad's hand. "Glenn. Congratulations to you, my friend. Wonderful show."

"Thanks. I'm so glad you could make it. Considering everything that's going on."

Mitsue bites her lip. "We are happier here. I do not feel so

comfortable in our home right now. I cannot sleep at night."
Her jade teardrop earrings shudder.

"Yes, but life must go on. Our art was stolen, not our
spirit," Kenji says. "We would not miss this reception for anything." He sounds cheerful, but his smile falters and he looks
down.

"You had art stolen? What kind of art?" I can't help asking. I love mysteries. My favorite mystery/paranormal manga
series is *Vampire Sleuths*; I've devoured all forty-two.

"A portfolio containing three van Gogh drawings," says
Mitsue. "It was taken last Wednesday evening from our
Seattle house. Skye had just finished some restoration work
on the drawings, and we were supposed to deliver them to
the Seattle Asian Art Museum the next day, for their upcoming exhibit." She sighs and twists the strap of her clutch.

"What were the drawings of?" I ask.

"Three studies of a bridge," Kenji explains. "Inspired by
a Japanese woodblock print by Ando Hiroshige called *The
Moon Crossing Bridge at Arashiyama*. The museum was going
to display them alongside the Hiroshige print that we own."

I didn't think regular people could own van Goghs. Then
again, I'm getting the impression the Yamadas are not exactly
regular people.

"I understand you're working with the FBI and Interpol.
Any leads yet?" Margo asks.

"A few, perhaps," Kenji says. "The investigation is still in an early stage." He turns to my dad. "Actually, detectives will be contacting you, Glenn. Margo, Julian, and Skye, too. They must talk with anyone who knows our collection. I apologize for the inconvenience."

"It's to be expected," Margo says. "They're just doing their job. Besides, all they have to do is review our security camera tape to see that Julian and I were here at the gallery at six o'clock last Wednesday evening, planning Glenn's show."

"Yeah, I already got my summons," my dad says. "I'm going in Monday morning. But they won't waste much time with me, either. I teach at the Art Institute on Wednesday evenings."

I wait for Skye to offer up an alibi, but she just stands there, eating cheese cubes.

Kenji pats my dad on the shoulder. "Let us return to happier topics. Glenn, I should have wished you double congratulations. I heard about your—"

And then Skye has a Category Five choking fit. She's doubled over. My dad puts a hand on her back. Everyone looks worried. In thirty seconds, the fit is over. Margo fetches Skye water.

I watch Skye carefully. That fit seemed staged. Was Skye trying to create a distraction, to stop Kenji from completing his sentence? What didn't she want him to say?

"So, Glenn," Kenji says when things have calmed down, "my nephew, Hideki, would like you to begin work on the mural earlier. I'm afraid that means flying to Japan a bit sooner."

"Oh? How much sooner are we talking about?"

"We would be leaving in one week's time. A week from today."

My dad shakes his head as if he has water in his ears.

"I know it must seem sudden," Kenji apologizes. "We suggested to Hideki that an acceleration of the project schedule would cause you too great an inconvenience. But as you know, my nephew is soon to be CEO, and he is technically in charge of the mural commission. He has some . . . fixed ideas, we can say. He feels strongly that the work must be done by the end of July. Executives from a partner company will be visiting headquarters on the first of August. He hopes to impress them with our lobby art."

"But . . . but . . . starting in a week?" my dad splutters. "We haven't even agreed on the design. I've barely started the preliminary sketches. I don't want to do a rush job."

I clear my throat. *Hello? See another problem with this trip?* But my dad doesn't seem to notice this giant thought bubble hovering above my head like a storm cloud.

"Well, if it has to be, it has to be," my dad says, looking dazed.

"I do not wish to cause stress," Kenji says. "We would be happy to meet with you in our home, perhaps this weekend, to talk through some of your concepts."

"Hey, does that mean I'll stay at your house alone this summer?" I ask my dad. That's not such a bad consolation prize. I could invite all my friends and screen a Hayao Miyazaki marathon. Maybe Edge would come back from film camp for that. Maybe he'd stay the night!

My dad pulls the plug. "You can't stay in the city alone for three weeks. You're fifteen."

"Sixteen!"

"Violet's spending the summer with me," he explains to the Yamadas. "Her mom's in Italy."

"There is a simple solution." Kenji smiles. "Of course, Violet must come to Japan."

My dad scratches his neck. "Yeah, uh, I don't think I can swing that right now, financially. She'd need her own hotel room. And the day-to-day stuff—a friend of mine went to Japan, and he said prices are really high. He said a cantaloupe can run you eighty bucks!"

"But I don't even like cantaloupe," I whisper.

Kenji waves my dad's worries aside. "We will take care of any extra expenses."

"Thank you! Wow!" I turn to my dad. "Please?"

"Well, hang on. What about your job at the comics store?"

"I can quit." The fact is, I've been working part-time at Jet City Comics since September, and I've been thinking of quitting. Aside from the 10 percent employee discount, the job sucks, due to the crappy location in a strip mall and my boss's complete lack of interpersonal skills.

Mitsue turns to me. "If you need a summer job, I could use help in our museum archives, with a print-cataloging project. You work in a comic shop, so you must have experience handling paper."

"I do! I help take care of the collectible comics. Your job would look great on my college applications. Mom would love that." I look at my dad. "Mom's been on my case about college."

"I'll talk to your mother. If Angela says yes, you can go."

I pump a fist in the air. "Yes!"

"I assume you'll still require my services with this accelerated itinerary?" Skye says to the Yamadas. "Because I'll need to make arrangements with my other clients."

"Ah. To be honest . . . your services will not be required on the trip after all." Kenji brushes an invisible thread from his suit sleeve and avoids looking at her.

"What? Wait. I don't understand."

"We will discuss the details at another time."

Skye stomps off to the banquet table. As she narrows her eyes at me and downs a glass of wine, I get the feeling that I have just made her list of Least Favorite People. No wonder the Yamadas could slot me into this trip so easily. I'm probably going to Japan in Skye's place.

3

I text Edge. HEY. I JUST MET ART HEIST VICTIMS AND WON A FREE TRIP TO JAPAN. WHAT'S UP WITH YOU? But the text won't go through. Following a hallway, I discover a back door that leads outside, into an alley. Next to a Dumpster, my signal shows two bars.

The Dumpster lid is flipped open. I crouch beneath it for shelter from the rain and send my text again.

I look around while I wait for Edge's reply. The sky is more November than June, charcoal-smudged clouds all bunching together. A dying streetlight flickers and buzzes above the gallery door. Where is Edge? Why hasn't he replied to my texts all afternoon?

At the end of the alley, a green Prius parks. Two men get out. Latecomers to the party, I assume.

I check my phone. Maybe Edge is so tired from working on his demo video for film camp that he fell asleep. I call, hoping the ringer will wake him. Voice mail. After a few jazzy notes, I hear his resonant voice. "Hi-de-ho, Hep Cat. Edge Downey's voice mail. You know what to do."

I press the phone to my ear, pouring his voice into my

head. I adore his outdated slang. He's always digging up expressions from old black-and-white films.

If it sounds like I'm crushing on my best friend, Edgerton Downey, I am. Fortunately, Edge has no clue. According to a lot of the *shōjo* manga I read, it's actually *more* romantic to hide your feelings.

"I'm at my dad's reception. Major stuff is going down. Where *are* you?" Then I stand up, glancing at the two men. They've opened large umbrellas and are leaning against the Prius. I can't make out their faces this far away, but I get that weird feeling of being watched.

Maybe they're not going to the party. Maybe it's a good time to get out of the alley.

Suddenly, the gallery's back door opens, emitting a pool of yellow light.

I duck back under the Dumpster lid and drape myself in shadows.

Sockeye—I mean, Julian—comes outside. He puts up a limp, broken umbrella, then whips out a cell phone. The rain muffles his conversation, but I can hear parts of it.

"I understand, but it's a trip to Tokyo. For *business* . . . yes, but the person they were going to send can't go now, so it's up to me to oversee the transport and installation and—what? . . . God, no. Why you are always so down on my job?"

So I'm not replacing Skye. Julian is.

"Fine, Mother. Fine. I'll talk to you later when you can actually listen." He hangs up.

My phone slips and skitters into the alley. *Chikuso!* (My favorite Japanese swear word.)

Julian whirls around, pointing his umbrella in different directions. "Who's there?" he shouts. He opens the gallery door wider until the pool of light shines right on my face.

I step out from under the Dumpster lid, my hands raised.

Julian shakes the umbrella at me. "What were you doing? Dumpster diving?"

"It's the only place I could get reception. Could you put the umbrella down, please?"

He retracts it. "Sorry. If I seem jumpy, it's because a couple of Margo's clients had some art stolen last week. We're all on high alert."

"I know. The Yamadas, right? I just met them." Wait. If the Yamadas are Margo's clients, and Julian works at the gallery, Julian must know something about the heist. Maybe I could learn something to help spark ideas for *Kimono Girl*! "Are there any leads on the case?"

"There's an investigation underway. And Mr. and Mrs. Yamada just put up a hundred grand in reward money. Hopefully, someone will come forward with information soon."

One hundred thousand. Dollar signs dance in my eyes. What if *I* found the drawings?

People always say I'm good at finding things. Car keys, bills, papers, glasses. Those aren't the same things as lost art, but still I drift into fantasy, imagining myself finding the drawings in the alley Dumpster, then presenting the grateful Yamadas with the missing portfolio. They'd write me a check. I'd give some reward money to my mom for my college fund. I'd buy a car, so Edge and Reika and I wouldn't have to take the stupid bus everywhere. I'd pay my own expenses in Japan. And I'd load up on top-notch art supplies, so I could get my manga looking sharp. Then maybe I'd have the guts to show my drawings to people.

"So what would a thief do with the art?" I ask as Julian ushers me back inside.

Julian shakes out his umbrella and puts it in the stand in the hall. "Usually art thieves aren't the brains. They're doing dirty work for someone higher up. So the thief will probably pass the drawings on to some head honcho. Maybe he already has."

I open my mouth to ask another question, but he says, "Look, kid, it's been fun chatting, but I have to get back to the party."

"Sure. Thanks for the info. Hey, can you tell me where you put my bags?"

Julian leads me over to his desk, behind a partition that screens it off from the gallery.

"Mind if I use your desk for a while? I have a project I'm working on."

Julian grudgingly shifts a few binders out of my way. Then he leaves me alone.

I take out my black, spiral-bound sketchbook and a mechanical pencil. Julian's desk displays only binders, auction house catalogs, a computer screen, and random Euro-style office supplies. Also a notepad with Margo's gallery logo at the top.

In *Vampire Sleuths* 37, best friends Kyo and Mika break into the school principal's office at night (which is the only time they can sleuth, being vampires). Searching for clues to solve a computer-hacking case, they find a blank notepad. Kyo puts a sheet of paper on top of it. He rubs that top paper with a pencil until a numeric code emerges. Mika deduces that the code was written on a previous sheet of paper on the notepad; the pen left the imprint on subsequent pages. The code turns out to be a password for the school's computer system.

Maybe that rubbing trick works in real life. And I'm curious about what Julian might take notes on, since I'm using him as a character study for Sockeye. I take a piece of tracing paper out of my backpack, lay it over the notepad, and rub it with my pencil. Imprints of letters and numbers appear. I pick out the words in slanting handwriting:

PICK UP SUIT!
CALL MOM

KAZOO 6:30
2535554612

Most of the notes seem obvious, except "kazoo." Is he taking some adult education class like "How to Loosen Up and Be a Fun Person"? That string of ten numbers intrigues me, though. It might be a phone number. Two five three is a Tacoma area code. Who would Julian call there? Feeling daring, like a professional sleuth, I pick up the phone and dial.

"You have reached Pierce County Realty. Please leave a message, or call back during our regular business hours, which are . . ."

I hang up fast and shove my notepad rubbing into the back of my sketchbook. What am I doing? Sleuthing? No. *Snooping.* And totally procrastinating on *Kimono Girl.*

I open my sketchbook and review my storyboards so far. The first panels focus on Kimono Girl alone. She looks a little like me, but slimmer and minus the black frame glasses. She browses racks of kimonos and tries one on. She crosses the right lapel over the left as she stands before a bad painting of a farmer and sheep that hangs in the dressing room. She fades away from the real world and falls into the world of the painting, landing in the farmer's field.

At first, feeling trapped, she panics. Then she tries crossing the lapels left over right and ends up back in her world, in the shop. She buys the kimono. The next few panels show her practicing her skill, increasing her speed and confidence, with paintings in her parents' house and then in art museums. Once she gets her bearings in the art, she can train her eyes to see out into the world she's left. That's when she decides to help solve a rash of art crimes that are plaguing Seattle galleries and museums.

I've been stuck there in my story, trying to figure out who would steal art. Now I recall how I hit the villain jackpot tonight. "Bad guys coming," I whisper to my heroine.

First, I do a rough sketch of Margo—the Scarf— exaggerating details to make her look sinister. Pointy angles, arched eyebrows, elongated legs. Art dealer by day, evil magician by night. She knows people willing to buy black-market art. She can use her scarf to whisk away stolen goods and deliver them to clients.

Could the real-life Margo be a suspect? She might know where the Yamadas kept the van Goghs. But she was here at the gallery at the time of the crime.

I turn to a new page and do a rough sketch of Julian— Sockeye—exaggerating his fishy features. I then show him shape-shifting: leaping out the window, turning into a salmon midair.

Could the real-life Julian be the thief? He works closely with Margo, so he probably knows something about the Yamadas' collection, too. But he has the same alibi as Margo:

Plus, he seemed anxious about the crime, playing security guard around the gallery.

That leaves Skye. I sketch her, starting with her long neck and stooped shoulders, which mirror the shape of her bird tattoo. A cormorant. I'll call her character the Cormorant. I give her beady eyes, a sharper nose.

My thoughts drift to the real-life Skye. She worked for the Yamadas in some way. She got bumped from the Japan trip. She didn't offer an alibi. She staged a choking fit to stop Kenji from speaking. Kenji was curt with her.

I gnaw the end of my pencil and stare at her emerging portrait. Am I fascinated by her because she'd make the perfect thief for my story? Or because she *is* the perfect thief?

eaving the reception an hour later, my dad and I find Julian by the front door.

My dad claps him on the back. "Hey, Julian. You have fun tonight, man?"

Julian flinches and pulls away. "Fun? I am *working*. I don't have time to have fun."

"Jeez, what's with him?" I ask my dad once we're outside.

"He's Margo's assistant. The guy started out as an art handler, a total nobody, schlepping boxes and hanging art for exhibits. Margo saw something in him and showed him the ropes. Promoted him to assistant a couple years ago. You'd think he could show a little gratitude."

"Does Julian know Mr. and Mrs. Yamada?"

"Oh, sure. He does all Margo's computer work, maintaining client records in the database. I don't expect him to win any awards for customer service, though."

We come to my dad's ancient Volvo wagon parked on a side street. I slide into the front seat, shoving aside CDs, fast-food bags, paint rags, and empty Venti Starbucks cups. "I guess you really like coffee," I say, kicking aside five cups as my dad gets into the driver's seat. There's so much I don't know about my dad—his friends, his girlfriend, his daily habits.

Just as he starts up the car, Skye appears, backlit by the red neon sign from a bar behind her. She taps on the car window. "Hey. Can we talk?"

My dad rubs his forehead. "Oh, boy. Here we go." He gets out, and they walk a few feet away from the car.

I just want to get out of here. Once we're at my dad's house in Fremont, my summer can finally begin. For weeks I've imagined this time with my dad. Maybe it would be like when I was little. Until I was nine, I used to visit him on Capitol Hill, in this big house he shared with other artists. He'd come up with projects for me, like potato-stamp prints or tissue-paper collages. He'd let me organize his brushes. He'd introduce me to all his roommates and friends.

And often—my favorite—we'd play the Frame Game. We'd go outside, each holding an empty picture frame. Like miners panning for gold, we'd scour the scenery for images until we found one we liked. "Find a different perspective," he'd sometimes tell me, coming to my frame to see. "The trick is to make someone view an ordinary thing in a new way." Or, "That's a great composition, kiddo. Now *that* picture tells a story."

I don't know why my dad moved out of that house, or why we stopped playing the Frame Game. I don't know why we mostly just meet at the Macaroni Grill now. I don't know why he hid my existence from his art dealer, his girlfriend, and who knows how many others.

I look at my dad and Skye, deep in conversation. I hurl imaginary ninja weapons.

Skye crumples as if a weapon actually hit her. She buries her face in her hands.

My dad shoves his hands in his pockets and stares at the ground.

Uh-oh. Big Issues. I crack the window so I can hear.

"We wouldn't have had much time to hang out in Tokyo anyway," my dad is saying. "Between the art show and my artist talks and the mural, my time just isn't my own."

"I don't care. I have unused vacation days. I'll pay my own way."

"How are you going to afford that?"

Skye lifts her pointy chin. "I'm getting a little cash windfall soon. I'll put the trip on my credit cards and pay it off when my money comes through."

My skin prickles. *Cash windfall?* From the sale of some stolen art, perhaps?

"Skye, it's just not a good time to—"

"Stop pushing me away!" Skye explodes. "When are you going to let me into your life? If I don't go on this trip, it'll damage our relationship. It's too much time apart."

"Hey, I'm not the one who decided you can't go to Japan! Don't pin that on me!"

"What, you think it's my fault I'm not going? You know it's crazy they're even looking at me in the first place. You know that, don't you?"

My dad hesitates, then nods.

"Of course it is," Skye says fiercely, taking a step forward. "Think about the facts. Kenji discovered that portfolio in his office archives in February. I told him to keep it quiet, at least until he got the pictures insured. But he made this big deal of loaning the art to the museum. All those interviews. I mean, the *Today* show? Come on!"

"His nephew encouraged him to do the interviews," my dad says. "Both Hideki and Kenji thought it would be good press for their company."

"Still, Kenji could have said no or delayed the public relations stunt. So what happened? The news of his little treasure trove gets all over the Internet. As I predicted. I even told him to update his security system. Did he? Nope. I mean, the guy might as well tape a big sign on his back saying 'I'm a clueless rich guy moving van Goghs around the world. Come and get 'em!' I tried to help. Now they point a finger at me."

"It's not fair," my dad agrees. "But you're going to look like a flight risk until your name is cleared. You shouldn't go to Japan. That's the reality. It's not my fault."

"Yeah. You're always blameless, aren't you? Must be really nice. Listen, I'd start looking for a lawyer if I were you. Don't assume you're off the hook."

"What do you mean?"

"The detectives are going to look really closely at anyone who knows the Yamadas and their collection. Even if the Art Institute confirms you were teaching last Wednesday night, investigators are going to see if you played some kind of back-stage role."

"Oh, Skye. I can't take the drama right now. It's late. And I've got a kid in the car."

"Right. A kid." Skye smirks. "So you don't like drama. But you decide to tell me about your kid by just having her show up here tonight. Oh, no, that's not dramatic!"

"I should have given you a heads-up about her. I'm sorry."

"A 'heads-up'?" Skye takes another step toward him. "We've had how many conversations about kids? All you ever said was you didn't want any!"

He didn't want any kids? Did that include me?

Their voices rise and fall like waves. Ugly words crash down. I don't want to listen anymore. I roll up the window and sink into the seat. I hold my hands up to my face to block out my dad and Skye. Then I turn my hands into Ls. Frame Game. I scan the surrounding area out the window, opposite my dad and Skye. Suddenly, I catch an image between my fingers.

It's that green Prius. It's moved up a block. The two men with umbrellas are standing outside of it again.

"Fine! Just walk away!" Skye shouts. "You'll be sorry! I'm

the best thing that ever happened to you, and you know it! There is not one other woman who'd put up with your crap!"

My dad gets back in. He slams the door and starts the car. He grips the wheel hard. Through the passenger mirror I see her receding figure, waving her arms and shouting. Crazy.

We drive by the two men, pausing at a stoplight right by them. Under the streetlight glare, I can now see both guys are Asian. One guy is short and thin, with spiky hair and a square jaw. The other is stockier and taller, with thick hair. They both wear sporty blue raincoats and carry oversize Seahawks umbrellas. Probably just tourists, in town for the ball game.

The light turns green, and my dad drives on. I look at his grip on the steering wheel. What really scares me is that my dad is going to be questioned on Monday about the stolen van Gogh drawings. I catch my breath. If he's been involved with that crazy lady Skye all these months, maybe he does have some connection to the crime. I sit up straighter. I have to find out more about this art heist and about Skye.

"So, uh, Skye was supposed to go to Japan?" I ask, trying to sound casual.

"Yeah, for professional reasons. She's an art conservator." His voice is clipped.

"Cool. My art class went to the Seattle Art Museum last month and toured the conservation labs." I loved that field trip. The people who worked there were like magicians, using tools and brushes to restore paintings to their original brilliance. Patching tiny rips and wormholes. We even got to see how shining an infrared light on a canvas could reveal a pentimento, a drawing or painting beneath the top painting, which showed where the artist changed his mind. Beneath an oil painting of flying cherubs, we could see four ghostly arms that the artist had tried out before settling on their final outstretched position.

"So does Skye work at SAM?"

"No. She's at a small firm in Belltown. The Yamadas hired her to rehouse their print collection. She was also supposed to oversee the transportation of my paintings for the art show."

"And she's a suspect because she worked with the Yamadas' collection?"

"She worked in their home. She had direct access to the stolen portfolio." My dad sighs. "Violet, do you think we could just have some quiet? It's all been . . . a lot."

"Sure." I stare out the window, blinking back tears, and as he stops for gas, I let a few fall. We cross the Fremont Bridge over the ship canal, and I gaze at the statue of people waiting at a bus stop, at the funky cafés and vintage clothing shops. When I pictured arriving in this neighborhood for the summer, it was always a happy image. I thought I'd be talking art with my dad and going to museums and swanky parties with him. Skye dropped a bomb on all that. I almost hope she really is an art thief. Then they'll just lock her up.

My dad turns up a steep hill just past Fremont Center. He parks in front of a small house with peeling yellow paint. Sagging concrete steps lead up to it from the street, overgrown with tangles of blackberry bushes, like thousands of strands of dead Christmas lights. "Home sweet home," he says.

But then, as we climb the steps to the porch, he stops short and swears under his breath. The window to the right of the door is shattered. Jagged shards cling to the frame.

5

"Stay outside." My dad picks up a stick of driftwood from the porch, unlocks the door, and goes in, brandishing the stick. He stomps around inside, opening doors, flicking on lights.

I hug myself while I wait and try to picture where my mom is in Italy right now. Unpacking her suitcase in a dorm room. Throwing open shutters on a tall window. Biting into a fresh tomato while someone sings an aria in the market square below. I take out my cell phone, wanting to call and hear her voice. Then I slip it back in my pocket. I'm sure my mom never imagined a scene like this when she made my summer arrangements. I can't worry her now.

After a few minutes, my dad pokes his head out the broken window. "Coast is clear. Watch your step," he adds as a coat tree heaped with plastic bags topples behind him.

Inside, I step over art magazines, art books, blank canvases. I walk around boxes filled with driftwood, twigs, rocks, bird feathers, shells, and moss. My stomach lurches at the smell. It's as if a stew of paint thinner, rotting fruit, and old socks has simmered on the stove all day. I'd give anything right now to walk into my own home, to smell my mom's famous pasta sauce and to hear her sing out, "Hey, V, where's my hug?"

I can't take my eyes off the mess. "Oh my God, your place got *trashed*."

"No, no. Except for the broken window, it always looks like this. I'm still unpacking. And the place needs work. Used to be a pretty nice old Craftsman bungalow. Drug dealers lived here, and let it go to pot. That's a joke," he adds. "Sorry. Maybe you're too young to get it."

"I got it." I join him in the dining room, where he kneels to pick up glass. Just beneath the broken window, surrounded by glistening shards, sits a big, ugly rock. It looks totally out of place, even in the crazy dining room with the leaning card table and mismatched folding chairs.

"Aren't you going to call the police?"

"Naw."

"Why not? They could fingerprint that rock."

"Not granite. The surface is too uneven."

"They could send a cruiser to check things out. Look for footprints and stuff. What if the same people that broke into the Yamadas' house did this to your window?"

"No. There's been a rash of petty vandalism in the neighborhood lately. Besides, no one's going to steal my art. I'm no van Gogh. Look, the fact is, I hate to call the police with this investigation going on. I don't want a bunch of police and reporters sniffing around here."

"Really? Why not?" I stare at him. He never mentioned his girlfriend to me. Does he have something else to hide?

"Because I have to focus on my mural commission, now that Kenji's nephew has moved the trip date up. This chit-chat with detectives on Monday is enough of a disruption. I need to not think about things that don't concern me. Like punks throwing rocks through my window." He picks up the rock and hefts it to the entryway. "Hey, at least I got a fine doorstop. Don't worry. I'll board up this window. I know a glass guy who owes me a favor. He'll come by tomorrow and replace it. And here's the dead bolt. See? Solid. But if you're uneasy, I'll call the cops."

I am deeply uneasy. But if he wants to focus on his work and not report this, I guess there's nothing I can do. Maybe it is just a coincidence anyway. "I'll be okay." I look past him, suddenly aware of the living room walls, which are covered, floor to ceiling, with elaborate murals. "Wow. Your walls are amazing."

"Thanks! My friends call them my frescoes. I like to work out ideas on the walls."

I walk into the living room, grateful for a distraction from the broken glass, from my whole shattered illusion of staying with my dad. The pictures seem alive. My eyes can't fix on any one spot. One image leads me into another, and another, and suddenly I'm just rotating, trying to take everything in. So this is what it feels like to stand inside a painting.

"I started out covering up some water damage I couldn't afford to fix. Then I just kept going." My dad points to a train disappearing into a mountain tunnel, above a bookcase. The tracks follow a crack in the plaster. His finger traces a cluster of glacial lakes, which I now see are painted around bubbling plaster and brown water stains. "And these cracks here were from the last earthquake." He traces them over the fireplace mantel, showing how a web of cracks has been transformed into a tree. The tree sprouts vines, curling to the next wall, where green, orange, and yellow-and-brown birds perch: cockatoos, partridges, parrots, and doves. Owls with wide, staring eyes. "See? If you can't repair something, you can turn it into art."

Lugging my bags, my dad leads me down a short hallway painted with explosions of rhododendrons and outlines of madrona trees. We come to a small room off the kitchen, furnished with an old drafting table and a sagging, plaid loveseat. The white walls are bare except for one tendril of ivy, drawn in pencil, that snakes in from the hall. "Sorry, there's not much in the kitchen," he says, and at first I think he's talking about the wall art. "Mostly I eat takeout. But help yourself to anything you find." He unfolds the loveseat, revealing a hide-a-bed. "The Ritz it is not. Apologies."

"It's fine. I could use some sheets, though." I try to sound casual, but inside, I'm smoldering. He hasn't done one thing to prepare for me.

"Good idea. I'll hunt some down. Then I'd better get cracking on some mural ideas."

"You know what? Forget it. I'll sleep without them. I'm going to turn in. I have to take two buses to get to the comic shop tomorrow, and my shift starts at nine. I'd better get up early."

Then I notice something on the armrest of the hide-a-bed. A woman's black sweater.

We both stare at it for a while, as it if might hiss and attack us.

There's no sign of *my* existence in this house. No school photos, even though I've given him a picture every year. And yet. This sweater.

My dad picks it up, opens the door to the basement, and flings it down the stairs.

"Skye doesn't live here, does she?" I ask.

His laugh comes out like a bark. "Nope."

"Does she come over a lot?"

"I don't think you'll be crossing paths here. As of tonight, she's not in the picture."

"You guys broke up? Tonight?"

"We were on a collision course. It's getting late. Sit tight. I'll rustle up those sheets."

I lie down. Springs creak beneath me. I'm relieved Skye's

out of the picture. But that also means finding out her connection to the art theft will be that much harder.

After my dad fails to come back with sheets, I get ready for bed, then dial Edge again.

No answer. I feel seriously sick.

I've never had a real boyfriend. But I've read a ton of *shōjo* manga, and listened to Reika's ups and downs with her Boyfriends of the Month, older guys from other schools.

I don't have anyone else like Edge. He's been there for me every day since we met in seventh-grade French class, on a day when I felt totally alone in the world. We had to write and perform a skit together, and he made me laugh so hard with his ideas I actually fell out of my chair. We've been best friends ever since. If I confessed I liked him as more than a friend, and he didn't feel the same way, it could wreck the friendship.

That almost happened this fall. We were at Deluxe Junk in Fremont one Saturday, trying on vintage clothes for a short film Edge was working on. I came out of the dressing room in a flouncy gold prom dress from the eighties. He emerged in a powder-blue tuxedo with ruffles down the front. We cracked up, looking at ourselves in the mirror. "The seventies? Wrong decade," I told him, since he usually dresses like he's from a 1940s film—trousers, a waistcoat, the occasional gray fedora.

"It's good to branch out now and then," he replied.

An old Michael Jackson song came on the radio, and we danced. Edge did disco moves, his honey-brown hair falling into his face, and I tried out some robotic 1980s dance moves.

"There's this homecoming dance next weekend," he said while boogying my direction.

I walked like an Egyptian. "Yeah. It'd be so funny if we showed up in these clothes."

"Together?" he asked. Suddenly, the mirror version of Edge stopped dancing and looked directly at the mirror version of me, and I stopped dancing, too.

For a moment, I could picture us walking boldly into the decorated Crestview High gym, to the center of a dance floor, hand in hand, not caring who looked at us. And suddenly, that gold dress felt too tight. "Of course not. We don't go to lame school events, remember?" I laughed.

He looked down. "Right. No. Of course not. I was just kidding, too."

Something had shifted, or the air had changed, and our mirror-selves didn't look at each other. We didn't dance anymore. We changed back into regular clothes. Things stayed weird for a whole week, until homecoming passed, and then we were fine.

That one weird week was enough to make me realize I had to keep my feelings for him bottled. I felt like I could lose him. I already know what it's like to lose a great friend.

But right now, I just have to hear his voice. I call his house. Edge's mom answers.

"Hi, Mrs. Downey, it's Violet. Can I talk to Edge?"

"He's still out. He's not answering his cell?"

"No. I thought he was staying home to work on his video."

"He was, but then he went over to help someone with a demo, someone who's going to the same camp. Wait, I have their home number. Let me find it." Paper rustles.

I'm not surprised his services are in demand. A few months ago, Edge shot this amazing, short film-noir spoof. It followed staff members at our school—the parking lot attendant, janitors, bus drivers, cafeteria workers. He made it seem like they were all up to something suspicious as they carried out day-to-day tasks. When he posted it online, it went viral. In the last month of school, our lunches at school were interrupted by people coming up to congratulate him. Suddenly, Edge was *visible*. I felt proud, sure, but scared. I wanted to grab his arm and yank him back into our circle of friends and never let him go. I wasn't ready to share him.

"Here it is. He's at Mardi Cooper's house." Mrs. Downey reads me the number, but I don't write it down. That's the last place in the world I'm going to call.

6

Early in the morning, I slip out of the house and catch a bus back to North Seattle while my dad's still snoring away. I lean my throbbing head against the bus window. I barely slept last night. The paint fumes got to me, and I had to get up and open my window. Then I was thinking about the rock through the dining room window, and how now I was basically opening a portal for any aspiring robbers or vandals to enter through. And lacing through worries about my dad and the mystery were my new worries about Edge and Mardi.

Around midnight, I ended up turning on my laptop to distract myself. First, I emailed Reika about the mystery and my upcoming trip, so we could try to meet up in Tokyo. Then I did an Internet search on the Yamadas and the missing van Goghs. I read articles about them and watched video interviews of Kenji until almost two in the morning.

Now, unable to doze on the bus, I take my sketchbook out of my backpack and draw what I learned, in manga-style panels, to try to make sense of it all.

In a panel labeled *February*, Kenji Yamada sifts through a box in his Tokyo office. He finds the portfolio of drawings mixed in with old blueprints.

In the next scene, Kenji has the drawings appraised by a top art expert and a team of van Gogh scholars. "Congratulations," the appraiser tells him. "Though unsigned, these are authentic van Gogh drawings, in good condition, worth two million dollars."

Kenji appears on the *Today* show. "My brother, Tomonori, bought these drawings, with a corresponding painting, from a small art dealer in Paris, in April 1987."

An incredulous Matt Lauer asks, "Are you saying you had van Goghs in your Tokyo office for *decades*? In a box of old construction blueprints?"

Kenji replies: "We didn't know they were van Goghs until a few months ago. Back in 1987, appraisers told my brother that the unsigned drawings and painting were old, but imitations of van Gogh. Tomonori put them in storage— we didn't know where—and when I found them a few months ago, I immediately had them reappraised." A new panel, with Kenji's voice floating above an appraiser with a magnifying glass. "Thanks to advanced technology and more knowledge of van Gogh's style today, appraisers could now properly authenticate them and attribute them to the great Dutch master."

Matt Lauer leans forward. "And there's a painting that

goes with these studies? If it's a van Gogh, too, and in reasonable condition, it must be worth millions more."

A close-up of Kenji, his eyes brimming with emotion. "Yes. My brother told me he had put the painting somewhere separate from the drawings, for safekeeping. I never had the chance to learn where. My brother took his own life just two weeks after returning from Paris in 1987."

Flashback panel. The back view of a man in a suit on a Tokyo subway platform, one foot dangling over the edge. A bare foot. I know from a manga series I read that Japanese people usually remove their shoes and socks before committing suicide.

Last night, I also read an article that came out a few months before all this van Gogh business, about how the Yamada Corporation is in a ton of debt. And financial troubles aren't the only thing that's been plaguing them since February of this year. There've been accidents. Some real doozies. I turn to a fresh page and list them now:

1. Scaffolding collapsed on three building sites.
2. Equipment exploded in a tunnel.
3. A mini-excavator on an office park construction site went into reverse instead of forward, and the driver plunged into a ravine, narrowly escaping death.
4. Last month, a bridge the company is building in

Kobe collapsed, killing two workers, injuring a
dozen more.

I stare at my sketches and my list. Images and words swirl together but don't form a picture that makes sense. Tomonori hid a painting that wasn't known to be valuable. He separated the painting from the drawings. He didn't tell anyone where the art was, not even his own brother. And he committed suicide just two weeks after buying this amazing art. Why?

I'm so lost in thought that I miss my bus stop and have to run back four blocks.

By the time I get to work, I'm ten minutes late. Still, I dash into the 7-Eleven next to Jet City Comics, buy some yogurt and a bagel for breakfast, and pour myself a huge cup of coffee. I'm feeling a bit low on *chikara* today. It will take a major caffeine hit to give me the strength to tell Jerry, my boss, I'm quitting at the end of the week.

Three girls come in, their flip-flops flapping. "Hey, isn't that one of the Manga-loids?" one of them says, just loud enough so I can hear. Giggling ensues.

Through the curved security mirror, I see them in more detail. There's a beach club on Lake Washington that the rich kids belong to. That's probably where they are heading, since it's a rare Seattle day of milky sunlight. I see Kelly Morgan and Emily Woodside loading up on celebrity rags while the third girl makes a beeline for the candy aisle. Guess they're planning some intellectual stimulation while they rot their teeth and get skin cancer. Good times.

And who's the girl in the candy aisle? She turns. It's Mardi freaking Cooper.

If I'm with my friends at school, lost in our fantasy worlds of comics and anime and role-playing games, we don't have to deal with these idiots. But if I'm not with my friends, I'm visible. Someone to laugh at.

"I don't know." Mardi sighs. "Starbursts or Kit Kats?"

"Are you in a chocolatey mood or a fruity mood?" Emily asks.

"Do they make a candy that's fruity in the middle and chocolatey on the outside?"

Through the security mirror, I steal another look at Mardi. Would Edge *like* her? She's pretty, with emerald eyes and long, red hair, both of which I once envied. But she's not Edge's type. She's in honors classes with us, but smart in a memorize-the-textbook way. In junior high, she turned into one of those people who is endlessly painting and hanging signs in the halls promoting School Spirit Day, or Alcohol Awareness Day, or Pajama Day, or the Homecoming Dance. It's like her dedication to school spirit sucked away her soul.

I know there used to be more to Mardi, and I know this because we used to be friends. Years ago, when she, too, lived with a single mom in the Hunters Run condos. In grade school, we rode our bikes together in the parking lot and made fairy wings out of crepe paper. We walked to and from school together. We swapped books and *Sailor Moon* anime DVDs. We memorized *Kiki's Delivery Service* and pretended that we, too, were witches in training. We shared our deepest secrets and our wildest dreams.

Then her mom got remarried. Mardi and her mom moved into the guy's fancy house near Sheridan Beach. That's where her shape-shifting began. She tossed all her *Sailor Moon*s and declared herself too old for Kiki. She got herself some trendy clothes, followed by rich, snobby friends. She joined a bunch of sports teams and got too busy to hang out. One day in seventh grade, she just stopped talking to me. She erased our whole friendship with one blank stare.

These days, she still ignores me, except when her friends call me Manga-loid, and she laughs along with them. And this month, the yearbook came out with a caption by my only extracurricular picture. VIOLET ROSSI, NATIONAL FART HONOR SOCIETY. I found out that Mardi, a yearbook staffer, was responsible for proofreading the National Art Honor Society page. She'd let the joke slide all the way to the printer.

Edge knows all this. So why would he hang with her now? Maybe he can see glimmers of the Mardi I once knew. Or maybe Mardi in her new form has bewitched him.

I hurry to the register and throw ten dollars down on the counter.

"So Mardi, what happened with you and Steven Spielberg last night?" Emily asks.

I can't hear her whole answer. The cashier loudly counts back my change.

". . . was really, really good. And then, after that, just totally crashed," Mardi finishes.

Crashed? He *crashed* at her house? And he was *good.* At what?

"You know, he hangs out with the Manga-loids," Kelly says.

"Yeah, but he's not really one of them. He's a serious film buff, not just into cartoons."

Cartoons! I grip my coffee cup. How can she lump anime in with Scooby-Doo?

"And he could be soooo much better," Mardi goes on. "Some new clothes, the right hairstyle, maybe ten minutes of crunches a day to tone up. I see a lot of potential. He's my special summer project. Come September, people are not going to recognize Edgerton Downey."

I can't listen to this. I bolt from the 7-Eleven, spilled coffee burning my hand.

7

As soon as I burst into Jet City Comics, Jerry approaches with a Big Gulp in one hand, a box cutter in the other. "Well, look who's here. Thanks for showing up."

"Sorry." I toss my backpack on the floor behind the counter. "I'm staying at my dad's in Fremont, and I have to take two buses to get here."

"Lots to do today. The Yoops came in." Jerry nods at a massive stack of UPS boxes, then hands me the box cutter. "I need these babies on the racks, and subscriptions pulled, pronto."

I cringe as he picks up a notepad by the cash register. It's filled with characters I copied from the *Death Note* manga series yesterday. I forgot to throw them away. "I found your doodles. Obviously, you have way too much time on your hands," Jerry says. "Now get busy." He flings the notepad down and retreats to his office, belching loudly.

Doodles! Ugh! Jerry is such a *baka*! And I guess this isn't the best time to give notice.

I restock the small box of manga first, setting aside *Vampire Sleuths* 43 for myself. I'm just starting in on the Marvel and

DC boxes and stealing a sip of coffee, when the door opens.

In walks Edge. Smiling, flashing his adorable dimples, he hands me a Venti Starbucks. "I figured you had a long commute this morning. Thought you might need fuel."

"Thanks. I did. And I do." I take the coffee from him, and our fingers brush for one split second. My eyes turn into hearts like in a romance manga.

Edge is not movie-star cute. Maybe the space between his front teeth and his slightly chubby waistline have kept him from being a total girl magnet. But those are two things I happen to love about him. And the way his hair falls into his eyes. Oh, and his clothes. Today he wears a crisp white button-down shirt with the sleeves rolled up to his elbows. A 1940s waistcoat, brown twill pants, and spectator shoes. How could Mardi even think of trying to change him? "Did you walk all the way here with this coffee?" I ask, suddenly conscious of staring at him.

"My mom dropped me off. We hit a drive-through Starbucks on the way. I mean, we didn't hit it, literally, but we drove through. Through the drive-through part. Where the cars go." He looks down. Guess he's pretty nervous about revealing his rendezvous with Mardi. "Oh. It looks like you're already fueling up," he adds, noticing the 7-Eleven cup in my other hand.

"It's okay. I'll drink them both. I had a really long night."

"Yeah? Me too."

"Oh?" I take a sip from each cup and set them both down. Then I continue my *X-Men* restock. "I left you some messages," I say cautiously.

"I know. I'm sorry I didn't call you back. I was at, um, at Mardi Cooper's."

I shove a stack of *X-Men* into a rack so hard I crease a cover. Jerry will kill me.

"Turns out she's going to the same film camp. She has a music video she made for some friends. That's the demo she's bringing to camp. But she's having trouble with her editing software. We had to reinstall everything and start over. I didn't get home till midnight. I figured it was too late to call you back."

Now I feel stupid for assuming the worst. Edge was just being his helpful self.

"She shot her video at Sheridan Beach," he goes on. "She's got the band out on a dock. Dry ice. Superimposed ghosts on waverunners. Pretty spiffy stuff. She's got some talent."

"Ghosts on waverunners. Wow." Frowning, I grab a stack of *Superman*s.

"You okay?" Edge asks.

"It's nothing. I just . . . hate . . . Superman," I mutter.

"How can you hate Superman? He can leap tall buildings in a single bound."

"Because. Look at this. Superman, and all his spinoff titles, take up three whole rows on this rack. All these male superheroes, actually, take up three-quarters of the racks in the stores. Now look at the manga. Just that one small bookshelf over there. I keep telling Jerry we should order more titles. But he's clueless. He thinks manga's just for girls, and that we won't sell enough here." I'm babbling, but I can't stop. I can talk about comics on and on, but I just can't talk about the one thing that really matters.

"Once *Kimono Girl* is published," Edge says, "your boss will realize the error of his ways. And he'll have to stock it."

"Yeah. Right. Like I'm going to publish it and fill a shelf in this store."

"Who said anything about a shelf? I'm talking *wall*, Violet. Picture it." Edge makes a sweeping gesture. "A wall of shelves full of *Kimono Girl* episodes. Floor to ceiling."

For a moment, I can picture it. I manage a smile. "I guess then Jerry would be on his hands and knees, begging me to do signings." And Edge would be standing there, his arm slung around me, staving off the reporters and throngs of fans.

"You seem kind of far away today," Edge says. "What's up?"

"I'm just tired."

"You're not mad at me?"

"Why would I be mad at you?"

"I know you're not the president of the Mardi Cooper fan club."

"Oh. That." I shrug. "Ancient history. Anyway, it's nice of you to help her out."

"That's a relief to hear. Because, um, I'm sort of taking her to the Hitchcock film festival." He scrapes at a piece of tape stuck to the glass countertop.

"What?" A thought bubble explodes above my head. Asterisks, number signs, ampersands, and exclamation points shoot off in every direction.

"Yeah, at the Egyptian. Tomorrow night. Can you believe she's never seen a single Hitchcock movie? She's going to get laughed out of film camp." *Scrape, scrape, scrape.*

"That's a shocker." I practically dive into the nearest box and take my time rummaging for a stack of *Spawn* so Edge won't see my face.

What would it take to get noticed by Edge? By my dad? By anyone? Everyone but me has a Special Thing they can do. Edge has his films. Mardi has her school spirit, and now, apparently, killer music videos with waverunning ghosts. Reika rocks the school literary rag with her poetry. My parents have careers that are taking off. What do I do? Doodle in a sketchbook, knowing I'll never be brave enough to share *Kimono Girl* with the world.

I need a Big Thing, to make my dad and Edge and everyone else finally notice me. Suddenly, it's not enough to find a lead or two on the van Gogh case. I want to find that art.

And Edge and I could solve this mystery together, just like Kyo and Mika.

"I thought the band's song was kind of depressing, you know?" Edge is saying. "But Mardi convinced me it's actually atmospheric, kind of mysterious."

"Speaking of mysterious, here's a mystery. A real one." I set down the comics, and I tell him everything that went down last night.

"Zounds!" he exclaims when I'm done. "And you're really going to Japan next week?"

"No joke." I take out my sketchbook and show Edge the characters I was working on last night—the Scarf, Sockeye, the Cormorant. I explain how their real-life counterparts might be suspects. "But Skye Connolly is the prime suspect in my mind."

Edge studies my pictures. "Yeah, maybe she used your dad to get a job with the Yamadas and get access to their private collection. Now she has the art. She doesn't need your dad. So she ditches him and plans her getaway. Which she'll finance with her 'cash windfall.'"

"Exactly!" I smile. I love how talking to Edge always feels like building something.

Edge is looking at my sketches. "These are really good, by the way."

"Thanks." I smile wider. "So. Where do we start looking for clues?"

"We?" Edge puts down my sketchbook. "You said the FBI was on the case."

"They are. But does that mean we can't look for the draw-ings or tail a suspect?"

"We don't have police badges. We can't get search war-rants. We can't wiretap phones. We can't analyze forensic evidence. Hell's bells, we can't even drive!"

"That's all TV and movie stuff. There are other ways to look for stolen art. Plus, it's not against the law to look for lost objects if you're a concerned citizen."

"I guess not." Edge looks doubtful.

"Did I mention the Yamadas are offering a one hundred thousand–dollar reward?"

"Crikey. That's a lot of dough."

"It is." Edge's family, like mine, does not exactly have a lot of extra money lying around; he's going to camp on scholar-ship. "Think of the film equipment you could buy."

He tips his head. He seems to be thinking.

"And if we recovered the van Gogh drawings, drawings that most of the world hasn't seen, it would be a really big deal for the art world. It's important."

Edge is looking at me intently now. "Okay. I'm in. You have to get to that meeting at the Yamadas' house this Sunday, with your dad. View the crime scene. Ask questions. And we need to get on Skye's trail. See if she's up to anything suspi-cious. Where did you say she worked?"

"Some art conservation firm in Belltown. I'll look it up."

On the computer, only one link comes up for *art conser-*

vation in this small downtown neighborhood. Moore and Leavey Fine Art Conservation, on First Avenue and Virginia.

Edge jots the address on a sticky note.

Jerry opens his office door with a bang. He stands in the doorway, Big Gulp in hand. "This guy again?" He glares at Edge. "Violet, didn't I talk to you just last week about your friends hanging out here? If they're not buying, they have to go." He waves at Edge. "Bye-bye."

"There aren't any customers here. I'm getting the restock done."

"Are you working or are you wasting time gabbing?" Jerry demands.

I look past him, at the racks. At Superman. At all the other heroes flying on covers, punching through barriers, slashing at bad guys with swords or ray guns, with waves of energy. With webs. I think of Kimono Girl, and how I want her to be really tough.

"Actually, neither." I set down the box cutter. "I'm quitting."

8

I'm not sure how much we accomplished by following Skye around downtown Seattle all afternoon, but least Edge didn't talk about Mardi. And it was *fun*.

As Edge sits down at his computer later that same day and uploads the video from his camera, I sit in a chair beside him and reluctantly slide the blonde wig off my head. I'm almost sorry our stakeout is over. I loved feeling like somebody else.

While Edge connects the video camera to the computer and starts the upload, I comb out the tangled wig with my fingers and mentally replay our day.

After I walked out of Jet City Comics, Edge and I hopped a bus downtown. We camped out at a Tully's Coffee across the street from Moore and Leavey Conservation. Near lunchtime, Skye came into the Tully's and ordered a drink. She was carrying a large black portfolio case tucked under one arm, with a brown portfolio peeking out from the top. "Mitsue said the drawings were in a portfolio!" I whispered. "And that brown one in there looks old, doesn't it?"

Edge whipped out his camcorder, and we were on her tail fast. We followed Skye down Pine Street and into Pike Place

Market, pretending we were tourists in case she happened to turn and notice us with a camera.

She stopped in a seating area to eat a sandwich wrap and to call someone on her cell. Then we followed her several blocks to First and University, and into the Seattle Art Museum. We pooled our money and bought two student-rate tickets. We checked all the galleries and exhibit halls, but we'd lost her. Then Edge spotted her going down the escalator to the lobby . . . *without the big black portfolio case.* Then she hurried back to her office.

"I burned you a DVD." Edge hands me a jewel case. "Let's see if we got anything."

Clip by clip, we go through the footage on his computer and relive our stakeout. We grin at each other when we discover the audio feed picked up her phone conversation.

"Do you think they'll offer that much?" Skye says with a mouthful of sandwich. "Anything less, it's just not worth all the work that I . . . Okay, then, wish me luck!"

In the next scene, Skye passes the magazine stand on First and Pike. I lean forward. I notice two Japanese men in blue raincoats. One man is thin, the other stocky. They duck behind a magazine rack when she passes, then emerge and follow her down First Avenue.

"Edge, these guys were near Margo's gallery last night. For two hours."

"At your dad's show?"

"No. They just stood in the rain by their car. A green Prius. I saw them during the reception, near an alley, and I saw them across from the gallery when my dad and I were leaving. I don't think it's a coincidence we got them on film today. Let's go back to the beginning."

We review all the footage. This time, I keep an eye out for the men. Sure enough, a green Prius drives down Pine Street as Skye heads to the Market. It passes Skye slowly, then parks on Pine. Two men in blue raincoats get out. In the Market, I glimpse the men again as Skye goes to buy her sandwich; they're at a booth of Native American tribal art, inspecting a mask of a raven. Then we forward to the museum. The men show up again in the museum lobby. There we can see them more clearly as they linger by the escalator. The tall, stocky man has ears that stick out, and it looks like his nose has been broken. The short, thin guy has an angry rash on his cheeks, either a flaming case of acne or scars from God knows what.

"You think they were following us?" Edge asks.

"No. I think they were following Skye. Hey, what's weird about the short guy's hand?"

Edge hits some buttons on the keyboard and zooms in close. I clap my hands to my mouth. Now we can see that the shorter man, holding a coffee cup, is missing most of his pinky finger on his left hand. Only a stub remains. I get chills.

As Skye heads out of the museum, the men follow. But outside the door they go left when she goes right, veering toward the *Hammering Man* sculpture and disappearing by the sculpture's enormous iron foot. They do not appear again.

Edge drums his fingers on the desk. "This is big, V. Really big."

"Seriously, right? We have evidence on film that these guys were following Skye. Oh my God. Remember I said someone broke a window at my dad's house yesterday?"

"Yeah. You think those guys did it?"

"No. I think Skye did."

"How could she get to Fremont so fast and break a window?"

"We stopped to get gas. She might have had just enough time."

"But why would she try to break into his house? Why not just walk in?"

"Because my dad never gave her a key. He has commitment issues. Edge." I clutch his arm. "Listen. I think that Skye had hidden the stolen van Gogh drawings in my dad's house. For safekeeping. Then, when they broke up, she hurried over there to retrieve them."

"Wait, you really think your dad could have unknowingly had van Goghs in his house?"

"The place looks like an art supply store exploded. I bet he doesn't know what he has. It's the perfect hiding place for art."

Edge nods. "So maybe these guys in the Prius are undercover policemen, trying to get enough evidence to arrest Skye."

"They don't look like policemen to me. Especially the guy with the missing finger."

"What kind of villains wear REI gear and drive an eco-friendly hybrid car?"

"I don't know. But I think they knew Skye had cleaned Kenji's van Gogh drawings. I bet they knew or suspected that she stole the art, and now they want to steal it from her. That's why they were hanging around outside the art reception last night: because they were tailing her."

"If they had their suspicions, why wouldn't they intercept her and grab the portfolio when she was walking around with it today?"

"Broad daylight. Too obvious."

Edge nods. "Okay. But last night, if they followed Skye to your dad's reception, why didn't they just demand the drawings then? Or later, when she broke into your dad's house?"

"Maybe she was never alone long enough. And that big fight with my dad could have thrown them. Maybe she went over there so fast they couldn't catch up."

Edge replays the final image of the two men on the screen as they turn toward *Hammering Man*, leaving the frame. "Why would they follow her all the way to the museum and then stop?"

"Because she left the portfolio there," I say. "Maybe she

met someone and handed it over, either in an exhibit some-where or in an office."

"We have to find out who Skye left them with."

"How? Just knock on some office doors and ask for them? 'Excuse me, did a woman with a cormorant tattoo give you anything to sell anything on the black market recently?'"

"You're right. That's ridiculous." Edge sighs. "Museums have good security. It'd be much harder for those guys to break into SAM and steal the drawings from there. Besides, if Skye took the drawings to a museum, and everyone in the city knows about this art theft, she probably wanted the art to get returned."

I sit up straighter. "Yeah, maybe her 'cash windfall' had something to do with getting that reward money! Maybe she pulled off this whole stunt as a scam, and she's having some-one else return the drawings for her. Maybe they'll split the reward."

Edge snaps his fingers. "An inside job. With someone working at SAM."

I think for a moment. "But why are we assuming Skye's going to turn in the art? What if her connection at the museum is really someone who will sell it to the black market and split the money with her?"

"That's a great theory, Violet. You know what? I think you're a natural sleuth."

"Really?" Am I imagining it, or is he now leaning a mil-limeter closer to me?

My heart is beating so fast, I'm sure he can hear it. He has a funny, soft look on his face, like he might be about to zoom in. To me. His lips part. His breath feels warm.

I lean closer to Edge. The case of the missing art fades away. For a moment, there is only Edge's face, tilting toward mine, and the cool green of his eyes.

Taps at the door. We jerk away from each other.

"Edge? I need a word with you."

Chikuso! When did Mrs. Downey get home from work?

"Okay, Mom. Just a sec."

"Now. It's important."

Edge sighs and pushes his chair back. "Fine."

I pop the DVD Edge burned for me into a jewel case while he and his mom talk in the hall.

"Edge, I don't want you two in there with the door closed. It's inappropriate."

"But Mom—"

"And frankly, I don't feel comfortable with you entertaining her here when nobody's home. You and Mardi have been spending lots of time in there these past few days."

"*Mom.* Give it a rest, okay? Mardi's not here. It's Violet."

"Oh!" Mrs. Downey's tone completely changes. I mean, *completely.* You'd think the sun had just burst through the clouds and unicorns were dancing over rainbows. "Hello, Violet!"

"Hi." I can barely manage to croak that one word. Edge's tone of voice said it all. I'm not the kind of girl his mom has to worry about. I'm not a temptation. I'm safe.

Worse, yesterday evening's little tutorial session with Mardi was not the first. She and Edge have hung out before. At his house. In his room.

When Edge comes back in, I'm standing up, slinging my backpack over one shoulder.

"Whoa. Rewind. I missed something."

The words fly out. "How long have you been hanging out with Mardi? It wasn't just last night. Why didn't you tell me?"

"See, you *are* mad. I knew it. Why did you tell me you were fine with it, if you're not?"

"I didn't think you guys would actually be friends."

"She's not that bad, Violet. You two just had some misunderstanding. You should talk."

"*You're* the one with the misunderstanding. She's getting you to do all this stuff for her to make her look good at film camp. She's using you. And then she's going to ditch you." I hear my next words as if I'm floating up by the ceiling, but I can't stop myself. "Her friends think it's this big joke, that she's hanging with Spielberg. They're all cracking up over it."

Edge steps back as if I've slapped him. His face flushes.

This is the worst thing I've ever said to him. To anyone. But now my nasty, hideous words sit there between us, like an ugly rock hurled through a window.

He gives me a long look. "I get it. You just don't want me to make new friends."

"What?"

"It's easier for you, isn't it, if I'm always available. Good old reliable Edge. He'll show up at a moment's notice. He'll be a sounding board for all your ideas. He'll bring you coffee. He'll film your suspect."

"Look, if you don't want to help me solve this mystery, then don't. Nobody's forcing you to do anything."

"So you don't want my help?"

"I don't. I can do this on my own."

"That's what you want?"

"That's what I want. Go to film camp with Mardi. Have a nice summer."

"Fine. I will."

"Fine."

"Great."

I run out the door, out of the house, past Mrs. Downey, whose mouth drops in astonishment. I run all the way to the bus stop, imagining I'm Kimono Girl, running so fast she becomes airborne, surrounded by radial speed lines and sparks.

9

Sunday morning, the brakes complain as my dad coaxes the Volvo down a steep private drive. I should be excited as my dad pulls up beside an iron gate. Soon I'll be viewing a real crime scene. But mostly I feel nauseated. I can't stop replaying my fight with Edge.

I haven't even wanted to think about the van Gogh mystery since then. After I got back to my dad's on Friday evening, I cried for a couple of hours, trying to figure out how a great day with Edge turned so ugly so fast. I don't know how we'll ever erase the mean things we both said and start over.

Eventually, I escaped into *Kimono Girl*, a story I could control. I picked up on page eleven. I managed to storyboard four more pages. In my story, a van Gogh painting called *Sunrise Bridge* is swiped off the wall of the Seattle Art Museum. The suspected thief is a notorious Seattle art criminal, the Cormorant, so called because she always leaves a sketch of a cormorant behind, the curved neck shaped like a question mark.

Kimono Girl resolves to catch her. She hides in the museum paintings, studying the people who work there, thinking this might be an inside job. She gradually begins to suspect a free-lance conservator named Kara Mirant, who comes and goes at odd times, always lingering in the gallery of nineteenth-century European paintings. One day, KG follows Kara to her studio in Belltown to look for clues. She watches Kara work at a drafting table late into the night, then leave, walking briskly down to Alaskan Way and the piers. She follows the art conservator onto Pier 43, then gasps as she morphs into the Cormorant and flies out over Elliott Bay. Now KG *knows* she has to find that painting. And she's dying to see what Kara was working on at that drafting table.

Well, KG wouldn't sit in a car gaping at a fancy house. Neither would Kyo and Mika in *Vampire Sleuths*. They'd all get inside to view the crime scene and start asking questions. Just because Edge is off the case doesn't mean I should quit, too. I don't have much time left. My mom gave her permission for me to go to Japan, and we're leaving in just four days.

Holding our bouquet of obviously-last-minute flowers, I get out of the car. As I follow my dad to the Yamadas' front door, I frantically pick the red sticker off the plastic, wishing we had gotten something nicer than discount pink carnations from the nearby Mobil station.

The Yamadas' house is flat and low, tucked into the hill-side, with a wide deck facing the lake. Deep blue tiles shimmer on the roof. The yard resembles a real Japanese garden with pruned shrubs, red maples, winding white-stone pathways, and a miniature stone pagoda. A fountain bubbles up from a pond, where orange *koi* glide among lily pads.

Kenji greets us at the door. "Please, if you don't mind." He gestures to a basket of slippers by the door. "It is a Japanese custom."

We exchange our shoes for beautiful silk slippers. I choose green ones with a pattern of white cranes. My dad chooses black with red dragons. Then we follow Kenji into a living room. One whole wall is windows, displaying the gray-blue lake. As Mitsue comes forward, it's like she's walking out of a painting.

Mitsue greets us warmly, then excuses herself to fix our tea.

Both Kenji and Mitsue act gracious, the perfect hosts. But they look exhausted. I can tell the investigation is taking its toll.

I sit on a long, white leather couch, at the far end from my dad and Kenji. I inspect a collection of framed photos on a table behind the couch: snapshots of Mitsue and Kenji on exotic vacations. One way to hide in the open is to look absorbed in something; my friends and I do this all the time at school. If I'm looking at pictures, I'll vanish, and my dad and Kenji will talk.

I pick up an old black-and-white picture of two Japanese boys. It's a formal picture, taken in a studio, with the boys dressed in identical outfits: crisp button-down shirts and pleated pants. The older, bespectacled boy, around twelve years old, smiles with his mouth closed. He faces the camera squarely, but his eyes rest on the younger boy. He looks protective. The little guy, with tousled hair, looks right at the camera with an impish, gap-toothed grin. I'm guessing this is young Kenji and his little brother Tomonori. I stare at Tomonori, trying to find hints of the sadness that would lead him to jump off a subway platform as an adult. I can't see the shadows. He's radiant.

"Yeah, so, tomorrow's my summonsing," my dad says to Kenji.

I clutch the photo frame.

"Yes. I feel terrible, Glenn, putting you in this awkward position. It is but a formality. You know Mitsue and I have no suspicions about you. Clearly, you were teaching that night, and besides, you are an artist. Artists are not art thieves. The idea of it is absurd."

"Well, thanks, I appreciate that. Have the detectives talked to anyone else yet?"

"Margo and Julian. They've been cleared. The gallery's security tape proved they were at the gallery at the time, planning the show. And UPS documents proved that Julian signed for a delivery there that evening."

I know Skye was questioned on Friday, too. It's all I can do not to speak up and ask what came of that. But my dad beats me to it. "And Skye? They talked to her, I guess?"

"Yes. She is considered a person of interest."

My dad frowns. "She didn't do it."

"This is a sensitive subject. I should not have mentioned it."

"No, no. I want to know. What are they saying about her?"

"Apparently, there was an incident, three years ago. Skye was questioned about missing art. She was rehousing a client's collection. A Matisse sketch vanished. It was never recovered."

My dad chews his lip. "And now they think she's taken the van Goghs? It's pure coincidence, Kenji. Skye takes her job very seriously. Besides, she wasn't anywhere near here on Wednesday evening. She runs at Green Lake every Wednesday, rain or shine."

Kenji smiles sympathetically. "Yes. I'm sure. But a hazard of running alone is that there is no one to prove you were doing that."

"She has nothing to do with this. Nothing at all!"

I'm surprised at how passionately my dad is defending Skye, a person he just broke up with.

Kenji strokes his chin. "Her conservation studio has an excellent legal team. I am sure she is well represented and her name will be cleared. And then we'll be happy to work with her again. I am sorry. I am aware it must be difficult to hear such things about your fiancée."

"What—what did you say?" my dad asks, echoing my own thought. *Fiancée?*

"Skye told me your news. Last Monday, when she was here working."

"But I'm not—we're not—I never—oh, shoot." My dad looks really unhappy now. "Look, Skye and I decided to part ways after my show on Thursday. And we weren't engaged."

"Oh. So the ring—it wasn't from you?"

"Ring? What ring?"

"Matcha!" Mitsue sings out as she comes in with a black-and-red tray.

1
0

I want to hear more about the supposed engagement between my dad and Skye. I want to understand why Skye would lie about something like that. But the topic doesn't come up again. Instead, we sip dark green *matcha* served in elegant cups with no handles. The tea smells both fresh and earthy and tastes way better than my mom's bags of Lipton. We eat *wagashi*, Japanese confections, and Mitsue points out the two layers of gelatin in the small, fish-shaped cakes. Between bites, my dad and Kenji talk about some Seattle construction project, and Mitsue asks me about my work at Jet City Comics.

After tea and *wagashi*, Mitsue takes me downstairs to see their print collection while my dad and Kenji talk about the mural project. Most people's basements are pretty junky. Boxes, dusty exercise equipment, the occasional artificial Christmas tree. Not this place. It looks like a real museum archive. The ceiling has recessed lights, and there's a climate control switch on the wall. Two huge metal tables stacked with flat boxes take up the center of the room. Flat-drawer cabinets line the walls. Horizontal windows, high up by the ceiling, are covered with gray screens to filter out daylight, except for a window at the end. That one's boarded up.

"That's where the thief entered and escaped," Mituse says, following my gaze.

"The thief must be pretty skinny," I remark. The windows are less than two feet tall.

I step closer to the wall, observing two angry black streaks halfway up.

"And those marks came from hard-soled shoes," Mitsue explains. "Climbing up."

The sill doesn't have a big overhang. "You'd sure need a lot of upper-arm strength to hang on." I picture Skye's wiry bicep with the cormorant tattoo. "So did an alarm go off?"

"Yes. The police responded to it, but when they arrived, the thief was already gone."

"Any witnesses?"

She shakes her head. "Our neighbors did not see or hear a thing. I regret that we lined our garden paths and walkways with all those white stones. No footprints were left behind."

"What did the thief use to break the glass?"

"A large rock. From our Zen garden out back. Ironically."

I think of that ugly rock at my dad's house. He seemed certain there was no connection, but two rocks shattering two windows seems like some kind of link to me.

"Forgive me. I do not wish to frighten you with these details," Mitsue apologizes. "Let me show you some prints."

From one of the flat boxes, she removes a stack of portfolios.

Brown portfolios! Just like the one I saw peeking out of Skye's bag!

"We have acquired a great number of Japanese prints from estate sales and print fairs," Mitsue says, slipping on white gloves. "Eventually, we will transport all of them to Tokyo. These boxes contain *ukiyo-e* prints, from the 1600s through early 1800s. The other boxes contain *shin hanga*, or 'new' prints, from the early twentieth century. We are going to display some of each in our exhibit next month."

"Wow. My dad's paintings are going to be shown in the same room with these?"

"Yes. The exhibit will focus on the influences of Japanese woodblock prints on contemporary artists. Your father has studied some techniques and used them in his paintings."

"You mean like van Gogh did?"

Mitsue smiles. "Yes, there are similarities. Van Gogh was a great collector and student of *ukiyo-e*. Japanese prints influenced his perspective, his composition, his color choices, even his brushstrokes. He copied three prints and turned them into paintings. They're in the Van Gogh Museum in the Netherlands. In fact, we think the drawings for the *Moon Crossing Bridge*, and the painting that accompanied them, were intended to be his fourth major work inspired by a Japanese print."

"Do you have the Hiroshige print that van Gogh studied?"

"We do. Though ours is only in fair condition."

"I'd love to see it."

"Of course." Mitsue goes to a flat-file cabinet, turns a combination lock, and pulls out a drawer. She carries a portfolio to the table, opens it, and reveals the most amazing print.

The bottom third of the long paper shows a narrow bridge. Long canoes, poled by people in pointed hats, drift down a wide river of brilliant blue. Tiny figures wearing kimonos cross the bridge on foot or lean against the railing. In the background, the whole middle section of the print, are lush trees bursting with cherry blossoms. Green rolling hills and blue mountains rise up in the distance. The top third of the print shows a milky-white sky with a band of bright blue. The details blow me away. I learned about printmaking in Studio Art. This all had to be drawn, then cut into wood, then the blocks inked, then the image transferred to paper one color at a time.

While I'm gaping at it, Mitsue opens a cardboard tube and gently shakes out three large, rolled-up papers. "And these are high-quality photocopies of van Gogh's drawings. We had all three copied for insurance purposes. Sadly, they are all we have now."

At first, van Gogh's drawings look less vibrant, compared to the Hiroshige print. They are rough sketches in brown ink on yellowing paper. But as I stare at them, they come to life. The composition is similar to Hiroshige's: the bridge, the boats, the hills, and the mountains. Yet the pictures are also distinctly van Gogh's. The lines are heavier, resembling the brushstrokes in his famous paintings. He exaggerated certain details from the Hiroshige print. And all three images show elements of Hiroshige's print from different angles, as if van Gogh had been working out the best perspective. As if he had been playing the Frame Game.

"That's amazing," I say. "They're copies—but they're not."

"That is right," Mitsue says. "It's not plagiarism. It's inspiration. Van Gogh made Hiroshige's image his own. And he drew these studies to prepare for a painting."

"My dad draws a lot before he paints, too. Hey, isn't it weird that the thief didn't take the Hiroshige print, too?"

"The print is rare but not one of a kind. Multiple copies were made at a time. So I suppose he could find another Hiroshige without too much work."

I scan the room, taking in all the boxes, portfolios, and flat-file cabinets. "And you're sure the thief only took the van Gogh drawings?"

"Quite sure. We've inventoried everything. He could have helped himself to any number of valuable works—we have drawings by Cézanne and Renoir here, too. But it's as if he had a need for only the van Gogh drawings. He was very focused."

So the thief had to be strong enough to hurl a big rock. Small enough to fit through the window. Fearless enough to drop to the floor. Knowledgeable enough about the Yamadas' collection to go straight for the van Goghs. Strong enough to pull him or herself up the windowsill and outside again. Fast enough to run away while alarms wailed. Smart enough to make a clean getaway.

The face that comes to mind is Skye's. She's been associated with a client's missing art. She knows the Yamadas' collection. She talked about a cash windfall and some kind of financial deal. She's strong and agile enough to have pulled off this heist. The picture is coming together. She has to be the thief. And those Japanese guys must have figured out, somehow, that she did it. They're following her around trying to steal the drawings for themselves. But why?

The only thing clear to me now is that I have to get back to the Seattle Art Museum. I have to find out who Skye talked to there and if she left the portfolio. I'm sure she didn't hand it in for reward money, or the art would have been returned to the Yamadas by now. She must have an inside connection, her own personal Sockeye, to ferry the stolen art away.

But Monday morning brings a setback. After our breakfast of champions—cold, stale cereal and microwaved instant coffee—I tell my dad I'm off to the Seattle Art Museum.

He shakes his head. "The museum's closed on Mondays," he says as if I should have known that. "All the art museums are. Well, I'm off to my interrogation. Wish me luck." His voice sounds cheerful, but his face is tight as he walks out the door.

I feel powerless. I know his alibi is sound. But I hate how close he is to all this. I can't forget about the broken window.

I pick up the phone. Maybe I should call the police now and tell them about my DVD, about the Japanese guys following Skye. That would shine the spotlight on her, and the detectives, with a search warrant, could scour the art museum and interview employees. Then they'd focus on her, not my dad.

I start to dial 911. Then I stop and set the phone down. That call could also cause trouble. Skye looked almost maniacal when we drove away from the art reception the other night. If she was desperate enough to break my dad's window, who knows how she might react if I ratted her out? Also, all the video shows is a suspicious-sounding phone call, men tailing her, and a portfolio. Not the actual drawings. I need stronger evidence before I make that call.

To calm myself, and to blot out the image of my dad sitting under a dangling bulb in an interrogation room, I focus on *Kimono Girl*. First, I research cormorants online, copying them into my sketchbook and morphing them into my villain. I learn that they are diving birds who swim deep underwater to fish. Asian cormorants love *ayu*, a little river fish. My research sparks a story idea, which I storyboard in a two-page spread.

The Cormorant uses Sockeye to help sell stolen art. In thought bubbles, we see her plan gradually taking shape. In bird form, using her beak, she will place the stolen *Sunrise Bridge* painting in a kayak near the museum she stole it from. Pushing the kayak from beneath, Sockeye will deliver it to her client's home, a houseboat in Portage Bay. The client will retrieve what looks like a lost kayak, drifting, and take the package into his home. No footprints, no fingerprints, no evidence to capture on security cameras.

The doorbell chimes. My pencil skitters across the page, the strayed mark ruining the panel I was working on. Annoyed, I get up and answer the door.

It's Skye. Holding a flat box. She narrows her eyes. "Oh. Violet. Hello."

"Hey." My mouth is dry.

"Is your dad around?"

I shake my head, then instantly regret it. Now she knows I'm alone.

"I came by to drop off these re-matted prints for the Yamadas. I thought he could give them to Kenji or Mitsue. I'll just run them up to his studio."

"I can take them." Knowing he was going in for questioning today, she might plant incriminating evidence to connect my dad to the heist. As revenge! I position my body to block the doorway.

She brushes right past me and heads upstairs.

I stand at the foot of the stairs, listening as she slides things around in the studio. It sounds like she's opening and closing drawers.

Five minutes later, she comes downstairs.

"I'll tell him you were here," I say, moving toward the door to lead her out.

She folds her arms. She's wearing a striped T-shirt today, and I can see her wiry muscles. "Tell me something. Why were you and your friend following me last Friday?"

I freeze.

"Let's take a walk," she says.

"No, that's okay. I'm busy, and my dad will be—"

"We're walking. Come on."

I follow her outside. "Where are we going?"

"Away from the house. For all I know there are video cameras wired up somewhere. I don't trust you. I don't trust anyone." She leads me up North 36th Street, all the way to the Aurora Bridge, and the famous Fremont Troll sculpture beneath the bridge. A massive concrete ogre with hubcap eyes, insane hair, and a maniacal smile, crushing a concrete VW bug.

Often, tourists gather there to snap pictures, or kids climb on it, or homeless guys camp out beside it. Right now, mid-morning, the giant troll is alone. Tires hum on the bridge over-head. The Fremont drawbridge clangs as it raises to let boats through the ship canal. Everything sounds precise, almost painful. Are these the last sounds I will hear before I am killed?

Skye crosses her arms and glares at me. "You followed me. You filmed me."

"I didn't."

"You wore a wig. But I remembered your face. I have an eye for details. Who are you?"

"What do you mean?"

"You're older than you look. Are you a spy? Did some cheapskate private investigator hire you? I mean, how weird is this?" Skye starts pacing. "I go to Glenn's reception, and you're there. I run an errand on my lunch break on Friday, and you're there. I show up at Glenn's house to return this stuff today, and *you're there*. At his house!"

"Where else would I be? I'm supposed to stay there this

summer. My mom's in Italy." I glance at the Fremont Troll, as if for help. He just leers at me, his hubcap eye winking in the lone beam of sunlight that finds its way under the bridge. "I'm just a high school kid. I swear."

"Glenn's daughter." She sniffs. "Right. Where was Glenn Marklund born?"

"North Bend, Washington."

My ready answer startles her. "High school?"

"North Bend High, one year. Then he moved to Seattle. Graduated from Garfield."

She sucks her teeth. "Smile."

Smiling is about the last thing I feel like doing. But her hands are in her jeans pockets; what if she pulls a knife? So I smile like my life depends on it, which it very well might.

"Huh. You have his dimples. I guess you really are his kid. It's just odd he never mentioned you to me. Not once in ten months of going out."

"If it's any consolation, he never mentioned you to me, either."

"He didn't?" She blinks a few times. "Oh." She sighs. "Still, you were following me. You know, it's illegal, filming someone without permission. I could turn you in."

My heart pounds. I hadn't thought of what we were doing as illegal. I can't tell her we suspect her of stealing van Goghs. Maybe she'll buy some watered-down variation of the truth. So I tell her Edge and I were working on a student film, set in

Belltown, when I happened to spot her on our coffee break. "You were being followed, but it's not what you think." I tell her about the two guys in the Prius. "We followed, too, to try to catch them on film."

"You're serious? What did they look like?"

I describe them in precise detail and add that I noticed them outside Margo's gallery, too.

"My God. Who else knows about this?"

"Just my friend—I mean, just this guy from school." I can't even say his name. "I didn't want my dad to worry. Who do you think they are?"

"I can't be sure, but they sound an awful lot like *yakuza* to me."

"Japanese gangsters?" The *yakuza* is Japan's version of the mafia. In detective manga, they often show up as thugs, with black suits and elaborate tattoos. I've never thought of them as real and definitely not here in Seattle.

"That missing pinky," Skye says. "Sometimes *yakuza* get their fingers cut off for missions they've failed to accomplish or errors they've made. It's like an apology to their boss."

"You think *yakuza* would be driving a Prius? In the manga I read, they drive flashy cars."

"Well, that's manga. That's not real life. These days they try to blend in more. Most of them look and act like real businessmen. If people in Seattle like hybrid cars, that's what they'd probably use."

"How do you know about all this?"

"I spent my junior year in college in Japan."

"And you took Yakuza 101?"

"Very funny. No, I studied near Osaka, which is a *yakuza* hotbed, and I kept my eyes open. I asked my friends questions, and I learned pretty fast."

"So why would Japanese gangsters be following you in Seattle?"

She thinks for a moment. "Here's a theory. Let's say some mob boss heard about Kenji's discovery of the drawings back in February. He wanted those van Gogh drawings. He sent a couple guys here to nab them and maybe to sniff out that lost painting, too."

"Yeah, I read some articles about the van Goghs. I know Kenji's brother bought the drawings along with a painting. But I thought the Yamadas didn't know where it was."

"Right. But maybe the yakuza *think* the Yamadas know. Maybe they even think I'm doing restoration work on it! Violet, you'd better tell Kenji and your dad about these guys."

She starts walking back toward my dad's house, and I follow. I can see glimmers of niceness in her, like sun leaking through gray sky. But I need to know a little more before I rule her out as a suspect. Is she a liar? "I'm sorry about you and my dad, by the way. I noticed you're not wearing your ring." I point to her naked left hand.

"What?"

"Kenji said you announced your engagement."

"Oh! I had to say that, to get the guy away from me. It sort of flew out, and then I put on my grandmother's old wedding ring to back it up. See, Kenji hit on me a few weeks ago. He came downstairs while I was working. We were looking at the Hiroshige and discussing some cleaning I might do on it. He took my hand and said he'd love to take me to a place like the one in Hiroshige's picture. Said all this junk about being a romantic at heart."

I feel like I've been punched. Kenji and Mitsue seem so happy.

"I meant to tell Glenn before the reception the other night," Skye goes on. "I just didn't get a chance. So your dad heard about the ring? He must think I'm completely crazy."

"I'll explain it to him." I'm starting to feel sorry for Skye. She sure has problems.

"No. The Yamadas are his most important clients. I don't want to mess anything up."

One last test. I need to know what she dropped off at SAM on Friday. "I noticed you brought a portfolio to the art museum." We turn up my dad's street. "What if the *yakuza* thought you were bringing the drawings to the Seattle Art Museum to sell to someone?"

She laughs. "If they want that portfolio, they can have it. I already got the job."

"Job?"

"I had an interview at SAM Friday. I brought examples of my restoration work."

"Oh. Um, congratulations, I guess."

We're back in front of my dad's house. Skye gets into her car. Before she closes the door, she looks at me. "How's he doing anyway?"

"My dad? He's working. Like, a lot."

"Yeah, what else is new?" She smirks. "You seem like a nice kid. It's good for your dad that you're with him. Make sure he eats something once in a while. He forgets when he stresses over a show. And, seriously. These *yakuza*, they're dangerous. Tell your dad and Kenji. Now."

I watch Skye drive off. My emotions swirl like a dropped palette of paints. Relief: she didn't kill me. Confusion: if she didn't steal the drawings, then who did?

Almost twenty-four hours later, Skye's parting words still give me chills. But it's impossible to tell my dad about the *yakuza*. Other than spending yesterday morning at his questioning, which he said went quickly and mostly involved questions about Skye, he's been locked up in his studio. He stumbles into the kitchen now and then to grab a slice of cold pizza. "Not now," he mumbled, the one time I tried to bring it up. "I'm in a conceptualizing phase. I am carrying this entire mural around in my head, and I don't have room for one more thing."

I pictured him walking around with a big rectangular head, bashing into walls.

"Sounds painful," I muttered.

"What?"

"Never mind."

As for calling Kenji or Mitsue, I can't bring myself to do it. They might be annoyed that I got this involved in the case. They might think I'm some nosy kid and un-invite me from the trip. Worse, my dad's connection to Skye might make the Yamadas worry the *yakuza* will follow him, too. They could postpone the Japan trip or call off the whole mural commission. Bottom line: if I blow this opportunity for my dad, he'll never forgive me.

I wish I could tell Edge about my run-in with Skye. He leaves for film camp tomorrow. There's still time. I could call and apologize, then fill him in on the mystery. But a part of me knows it would be like painting a dark canvas white. The ugly underpainting would seep through. My dad may have disguised his damaged living room wall by turning it into artwork, but it doesn't mean the damage is gone. Inspecting the wall now, I see the stains are oozing beneath his paint, the cracks in the plaster still spreading.

We just have to get through two more days, and then we're out of here, and maybe time and distance will ease some of the pain I have about Edge. I decide to spend the morning packing for Japan, thinking of the future instead of the past.

In her last email, after a paragraph of exclamation points in response to my upcoming trip, Reika advised me to load up on gifts for people I meet in Japan. "Baseball cards, key chains, Seattle knickknacks. Small gifts will open doors here." So after lunch, I venture out and hit the Fremont shops to buy some *omiyage*. As I head back to my dad's house, I pass Deluxe Junk. I pause in the doorway, but the smell of musty old things is an overpowering reminder of Edge, and the day we danced together. My eyes fill with tears. I hurry back to my dad's house.

And I stop cold when I see a plain white van parked out-side. I approach slowly. No driver. The *yakuza* might have changed their vehicle. They might have come looking for my dad because of his connection to Skye. Oh my God. Could they be *in the house*?

I mount the steps and take out my key, but the front door is already cracked open. I grab a stick of driftwood, though I have no idea what to do with it. Men's voices mumble upstairs.

"Dad?" I call into the house.

"In the studio, Violet," my dad calls back. "Come on up."

He doesn't sound like he's in mortal danger or talking through layers of duct tape. I run upstairs, still holding the stick.

I set it down when I see it's just Julian Fleury and my dad in the studio, flipping through stacks of canvases. Everything looks normal, except the studio is messier than ever. It's like a windstorm has scattered art supplies, drop cloths, unframed canvases, books, and bits of nature in cryptically labeled boxes. "*Reflections on Wind.*" "*Moss, etc.*" "*Random Sticks.*" "*Shifting Sands.*" "*Detritus.*"

"Violet, you remember Julian Fleury, Margo's assistant? He's here to pick up some work for the Tokyo show."

Julian nods curtly at me and hefts four unframed paint-ings onto a table. "I'll just get these crated and load up the van." He opens a toolbox. Then he glances at the boxes and portfolio that Skye brought over the day before. "These are the Japanese prints we're taking for the Yamadas? Did Skye finish the re-matting?"

"I haven't looked at them yet, but yeah, I'd assume they're all set."

"Oh, really? I wouldn't assume anything about that woman," Julian mutters.

"What is with everyone suspecting her?"

"What's with your defending her honor?" Julian snaps. "It doesn't exactly make you look good, being associated with her. It doesn't make Margo or me look good, either. Everything you do casts a shadow on us. We had detectives taking pictures outside the gallery today."

"Look. Can't we put this whole Skye thing behind us?"

They're circling the table, glaring at each other, as if they might draw swords.

I back up and try to become one with a file cabinet.

"What you did, Glenn, was unacceptable. Just because you're some hotshot artist, you think you can swoop in and steal any woman."

"Whoa! I did not 'steal' your woman!"

"That is a fiction. You most certainly did."

"Skye said you were never going out. That it was all in your head. That you had an ambiguous brunch, a little non-date, and you got the crazy idea that—"

"It's not crazy. She was my girlfriend." He takes a swing at my dad.

I retreat to a corner and look for something I might use to distract them. "Hey, guys? Hello? Kid in the room here." I wave a white paint rag, but they don't notice me. They circle the table faster now, their eyes locked on each other.

"You make Skye sound like some brainless moron," my dad snarls. "She has a mind of her own. She obviously chose the better man."

"You arrogant son of a bitch." Julian swipes at my dad again. This time his punch lands right on my dad's nose.

My dad recoils, holding his hands to his face and moaning.

"Hey! Stop it, you guys! Cut it out!" I yell, but they still ignore me, so I bolt for the door just as my dad swings back at Julian. Then they're on each other, scuffling and wrestling.

My dad is bigger than Julian, but Julian shows a surprising burst of strength. He shoves my dad into the file cabinet I was standing by moments before. My dad pushes back. Julian falls into a stack of blank canvases. Jars of paint fall off a shelf and crash to the floor, splattering all over Julian's clothes. He gets up and lunges at my dad, clutching a paintbrush in his fist.

"Stop!" I scream. I shove a tabouret of art supplies in Julian's direction.

Julian trips and falls on top of the tabouret. It slides all the way across the studio floor, carrying him until he crashes against a wall. Two drawers fall out, scattering pencils.

"Just stop it!" I yell again. "You guys are acting like complete idiots."

My dad, breathing heavily, lowers his head. "She's right, man," he says. "Just finish doing what you have to do and get out. You're messing with my headspace."

My dad retreats to the bathroom.

Not wanting to hang out with Julian by myself, I escape to my room. Julian Fleury's just rocketed to the top of my suspect list. He's stronger than he looks; he could have pulled off the heist. And he has motives galore. He wants to be an art dealer, but Margo treats him like dirt. He holds a grudge against Skye. Maybe he stole the art to make a name for himself as a black-market art dealer—or to make money from the sale and go do his own thing. And maybe he wanted to make it look like Skye did it. To get back at her by framing her.

Kenji said that, according to a UPS guy, Julian signed for a package on the evening of the crime. That, plus the security camera, was proof he was at the gallery and not stealing art. But is that strong enough proof? Maybe Julian paid one of the art handlers to sign his name. Or maybe he paid off the UPS guy. And if he had some technical savvy, maybe he changed the time stamps on the security video. Something like that happened in *Vampire Sleuths* 17.

My mind drifts to Edge. I stare at my cell phone. When I think of him going off to camp with Mardi, and of my going overseas in just two days, I get this pulsing ache in my chest.

But the phone remains silent. All I hear is the sound of the front door slamming and Julian's van starting up. Driving off.

At the drafting table, I lose myself in *Kimono Girl*, inking panels. Hours later, hunger forces me to stop. In the kitchen, I find my dad, his nose swollen and ugly.

"Hey, what do you say to dinner at Blue C Sushi?" he says. "I better learn about sushi before I embarrass myself in Japan. You can teach me what to order."

"Yeah, definitely! I love Blue C Sushi." My mood lifts a little. I'm glad he sees me as an expert on something, even if it is raw fish. "But your nose. Are you okay?"

"Better now. I should have ducked. I haven't been in a fist-fight since eighth grade." He grabs his car keys and we head out to the street together. At the bottom of the steps, he slaps his forehead. "My wallet. I don't have any idea where it is."

"I saw it in your studio. On the little table by the window."

"Oh, yeah. Right next to my brain. Wow, you're really good at finding stuff!"

"Thanks!" Two compliments in two minutes? "I'll just run up and get it."

The studio still shows signs of the fight: a sea of papers on the floor, an overturned chair, a puddle of spilled paints, bleeding together. Just as I grab the wallet, something catches my eye.

Near the tabouret of art supplies lies a brown portfolio.

Time stops. Even the dust motes stop dancing. What if that portfolio holds the van Gogh sketches? What if *Julian* stole them from the Yamadas' house and then planted the stolen drawings today to frame my dad, not Skye? He seemed upset about my dad "stealing" Skye. He can call the police, say he saw something suspicious in my dad's studio, and the police will be all over it. If they can nab my dad and recover the drawings, Julian's one hundred thousand dollars richer from the Yamadas' reward money.

I pick up the portfolio and shake some papers onto the table. Drawings. They're beautiful, but they're not van Goghs.

They're charcoal sketches of Skye. In one, she's in a canoe, trailing her hands in the water and staring into the distance with a dreamy expression. In another, she's picking flowers. In another, she's sitting on a porch swing, holding a cup in two hands. In the next three, she's nude, and I quickly shuffle those to the bottom of the pile.

In all of these pictures, she looks softer than she does in real life. And happy.

A photograph falls out of the pile. It's a picture of her and my dad at a holiday party at some funky warehouse-style art gallery. They stand arm in arm by an aluminum Christmas tree decorated with old car parts, gazing into each other's eyes.

There's more to their story than the fight they had. My dad looks really happy, too.

Not like now. I look outside. My dad's talking on his cell phone and pacing.

He's been through a lot today, with Julian. He's nervous about the trip, too; whenever he's not locked in his studio, he's on the phone with Margo or his friends, muttering about trying to please Hideki Yamada. I put the sketches back and head downstairs.

Outside, my dad's just hung up the phone. He looks shaken as I hand him the wallet. "I can't go out to dinner," he says, his voice cracking. "Julian's been attacked."

1
3

"**W**hat? When? Who attacked him?" My breath comes fast.

"Margo called. A couple of guys jumped him. Messed him up pretty bad. Lacerations. Concussion. He's in the hospital. And my paintings." He grimaces. "Slashed."

"No way!"

"Margo's on her way over to Virginia Mason Hospital right now. She wants me to come. Guess I'll have to talk to the police again since Julian had come from my house." He hands me a twenty from his wallet. "I'm sorry about dinner. Get yourself some takeout. I'll have leftovers later."

I have the uneasy suspicion that the two *yakuza* had their hands in all this, minus one missing pinky. If I'd come forward with my information sooner, maybe this assault wouldn't have happened. "I'm coming with you. I need to tell you something. Wait one second." I dash into the house and throw the jewel case with the DVD and my laptop into my backpack.

On the way to the hospital, I tell my dad everything.

He's quiet. Then he explodes. "Jesus, Violet. Why did you

keep this to yourself? The police could have been looking for these creeps."

"I tried! You were really, really busy! I can't talk to you!"

"And what on earth possessed you and your friend to stalk Skye? You really crossed a line, Violet. Not to mention, you're acting on pure speculation."

"I just wanted to help. Besides, if I hadn't heard Skye was a suspect, I never would have followed her, and then I never would have caught those guys on film. Plus, you said you didn't want to talk to the police."

"When did I say such a ridiculous thing?"

"When we came back from the party the other night. The broken window?"

"Oh. Right." My dad sighs. "Look. I probably gave you the wrong idea about not reporting stuff. If you noticed someone casing a place of business or a house, or following a person— even though you shouldn't have gotten involved in the first place—you should have brought it to my attention. What happened to my house was just petty vandalism, remember?"

I look at him. "You see no possible connection to the Yamadas' break-in?"

"None whatsoever."

I don't understand the connection yet. I'm just certain these two events are linked.

AT VIRGINIA MASON, we rush down cold, white corridors and find Julian's room. Margo is pacing outside the door. She throws her arms around my dad. "Glenn! The nurse is checking his vitals, but then we should be able to go in and see Julian—oh my, what happened to you?"

"I ran into a wall." My dad extracts himself from Margo's claws. "Where are my paintings?" He looks around as if they might have been given hospital beds.

"I'm afraid there's no hope for the paintings, Glenn." She notices me. "Oh. You. Hello."

"Violet has some information that might be helpful. Turns out there may be a connection between this incident, the Yamadas' case, and some things she's noticed recently."

"Is that so? I'm intrigued." She looks down her long nose at me.

But now a nurse is ushering us into the room, pushing an equipment cart aside so we can all squeeze in. "Mr. Fleury is groggy from the painkillers, but he can talk," the nurse says.

With his two black eyes, cut lip, scratched face, and splinted arm, Julian looks like a wreck. Not at all like a prime suspect in an art heist.

Margo pats Julian's foot through the sheet. "You poor, poor thing. How are you feeling?"

"Unnnnghhh."

"Can you tell us what happened?"

"Arggngush." He motions to a pitcher. Margo pours him

water and brings the glass to his lips. At last he speaks in a raspy voice. We all lean close to hear.

"After I left Glenn's house, I ran a few errands, then drove to the gallery. I parked in the alley by the service door. I unlocked the door and went back for the paintings in the van. That's when two Asian guys jumped me. One guy pulled out a knife. He was holding it funny. I noticed he was missing part of his little finger. They shouted at me, 'Where is it?' I didn't know what they were talking about. One guy held the knife to my neck while the other guy ransacked the back of the van. Then they both started screaming at me in some other language. Japanese, I think. They threw some punches, kicked me around. Then I passed out."

He pauses to sip his water. "When I came to," he goes on, his voice fainter, "the police were there, EMTs, and I was being loaded onto a stretcher. Guess some wino found me and got someone to call 911. I told the EMTs to close the van, protect the paintings. They looked at me like I was crazy. Said the van was empty. But just as they wheeled me into the ambulance, a policeman said four paintings were found in a Dumpster. Canvases slashed. Then I passed out again. Woke up here. Sorry about the paintings," he mutters to my dad after he drinks again. "And sorry, Margo. Looks like I won't make it to Tokyo after all. I'm in no shape to travel."

"That's okay, dear. Your job right now is to recover." Margo turns to me. "Well, Violet, I'm on pins and needles."

I tell them what I know about the two Japanese men with the Prius lurking outside her gallery and following Skye.

"But the *yakuza* are in Japan, not Seattle," Margo says.

Julian shakes his head. "Not true," he croaks. "The *yakuza* have penetrated the art world. Internationally."

"Whatever for?" Margo asks.

"They're selling art on the black market to buy weapons, drugs, things like that. Or they use it for collateral to secure loans from other gangsters."

"Do you guys want to see them? I have a video." I reach into my pack for the DVD.

Margo gives me a withering smile. "Oh, sweetie. Your video is not valid evidence. It was not shot under controlled circumstances. It would never hold up in a court of law."

For a moment, I feel deflated. But I've worked too hard to let this all be for nothing. I pop the DVD into my laptop and point out the two men.

"Julian, are those the men who attacked you?" Margo asks him when I'm done.

"Yeah, yeah. Without a doubt. I got a good look at their faces."

Margo taps her lacquered nails on the bed frame. "Maybe these hoodlums were after your paintings, Glenn. But why would they destroy them? Now they have no resale value."

"Maybe to send some kind of message?" I offer. "*Yakuza*

sometimes mess people up like this in the manga I read. To threaten them and stuff."

My dad frowns. "This isn't a comic book, Violet. Get a grip."

"Could these men have mistaken Julian for somebody else?" Margo asks. "Doing something else?"

"I'm sure that's it," my dad says, though his eyebrows are knitting together.

"Of course that's it," Margo snaps. "Julian would never get mixed up in illicit business."

We all look at Julian. His eyelids flutter, then close.

I watch the rise and fall of his skinny chest under the white sheets. He looks almost peaceful now, like an innocent victim. I no longer think he stole the drawings himself. But I can't shake the feeling that he's not as innocent as he looks.

1
4

Later that evening, my dad and I follow Margo to her gallery, where a policewoman stops us at the door to check our IDs. "You can go into the gallery, but you can't access the alley," a policewoman says. "The investigator is still taking pictures."

"And the damaged paintings?" my dad asks in a small voice. "Where are they?"

"No one is permitted to view the evidence, sir."

"But I'm the artist."

"No one is permitted to view the evidence," she repeats.

My dad lets out a long breath. He looks like somebody died. I try to imagine how I'd feel if I lost my *Kimono Girl* storyboards, all those hours of work down the drain. I reach out a hand to pat his arm, but Margo opens the door and he brushes past me and walks inside.

Inside the gallery, Margo immediately lowers the blinds, shutting out the gathering crowd of curious onlookers. Surrounded by the tree paintings, it feels like we're in a safer place, an enchanted grove. But moments later, the outside world leaks in. Flashing red and blue lights from police cruisers slice through the blinds and stain the walls.

Margo and my dad lift the lone madrona painting off the wall and set it on the floor. They're about to choose three others to use as substitutes in the Tokyo show when the front door buzzes.

Margo answers it. In walk Kenji and Mitsue, followed by two people I've never seen. One is an Asian American woman, maybe in her late thirties, wearing a black pantsuit. The other is an African American man, a bit younger, in khaki slacks and a striped polo shirt.

"FBI," says the woman, flashing a badge. "I'm Special Agent Jessica Chang. This is Special Agent Thomas Denny, my assistant. We're with the FBI Art Crime Team."

"The FBI!" Margo exclaims.

"We have some reason to believe there's a connection between the assault on Mr. Fleury tonight and the missing van Gogh drawings," Agent Chang goes on. "We also suspect the involvement of an international organized crime group."

"Which one of you is Violet Marklund?" asks the man, Agent Denny.

"Me." My voice comes out like a squeak. I clear my throat. "Violet Rossi, actually. Not Marklund." Then it hits. This is no game. Serious law enforcement officials—more intimidating than the policeman who took my statement at the hospital—want to talk to me.

"We spoke with the Seattle police. We understand you

have a video," says Agent Chang. My hand shakes as I give her the DVD, which she pops into a tiny laptop. I point out the gangsters. When it's over, Agent Chang rewinds to a scene and writes down some numbers. "Nice shot of the license plate. Now Violet, tell us where you first noticed these men."

I tell my story for the third time, starting with the night of the art reception.

"Do you think these men ever saw you and Edge?" Agent Denny asks. "Think carefully."

"I'm sure they didn't see us filming. Even if they did, I was in disguise. Plus, we got them on video accidentally. It's not like we were *trying* to film them. They were just in the frames."

"That's good," says Agent Denny. "You don't want to be on the *yakuza*'s radar."

"So why would these gangsters lurk around my gallery, follow Glenn's girlfriend, and attack my employee?" Margo demands. "Do you have a theory? Because frankly, I'm stumped."

"Actually, we do have a theory," says Agent Chang. "Violet's information has led us to suspect that members of a *yakuza* gang stole the drawings. We think these two men, perhaps acting on orders of their boss, broke into the Yamadas' home and made off with the van Goghs."

I wrap my feet around the legs of my chair. I'm so dizzy I feel like I might fall off. I knew those guys in the Prius were creepy. I'm glad I gave the FBI useful information, like their car license plate, even if it was accidental. But I can't believe I went so far down the wrong track with my thoughts. First, I thought Skye stole the drawings. Then I suspected Julian. But I never imagined these Japanese guys could have stolen the drawings themselves. I guess it makes sense. But if those men had already stolen the drawings, why were they following Skye?

An idea comes to me. "Could these guys be looking for the van Gogh painting? The one that goes with the *Moon Crossing Bridge* drawings?"

Agent Chang nods. "That's a possibility we're exploring now."

Agent Denny turns to Kenji. "Mr. Yamada, would you please share your news?"

Kenji looks sober as he opens his briefcase. "A letter arrived today from Japan. It is in Japanese. I will translate." He unfolds it, clears his throat, and reads from the *kanji* characters typed on thick white paper. "'The drawings of the *Moon Crossing Bridge* are now in my possession. My sources tell me that you possess the corresponding painting. I am also told that you removed the painting from Japan some time ago and transported it to Seattle. As I have indicated in previous correspondence, both the drawings and paintings are rightfully mine. Your brother, Tomonori Yamada, purchased them on my behalf. My associates will expect a personal delivery of the *Moon Crossing Bridge* painting on Monday, July 7, at 7:00 P.M. They will meet you in front of the *Hammering Man* sculpture outside the Seattle Art Museum. As an added incentive for your cooperation, I will return the drawings in exchange for the painting. They are less valuable to me financially, due to their condition, and I understand from my source that they hold sentimental value for you. I am a family man myself, and I can sympathize. You see, Yamada-san, you will find I am quite a reasonable man to do business with. However, if you do not deliver the painting, I will be forced to employ drastic measures. Hiroshi Fujikawa.'"

Kenji takes a photo out of the envelope and passes it around. It's the three van Gogh drawings, spread out on a table. "He enclosed this picture of the drawings as proof that his associates have them."

"Monday? That's six days from now!" my dad explodes. "You're going to find a painting that's been lost for decades and what, hand it over in six days?"

"And who is this fellow?" Margo asks.

Kenji folds the letter and replaces it in the red-and-yellow international courier envelope. "Hiroshi Fujikawa is chairman of the Fujikawa-gumi."

"One of the *yakuza*'s most notorious gangs," Agent Chang elaborates for us. "And we believe the two men who assaulted

Julian Fleury—and who presumably took the van Gogh drawings—are working for Fujikawa himself."

"You mean your brother bought art for a mob boss?" my dad asks.

Kenji emphatically shakes his head. "My brother loved to attend art auctions, and he occasionally bought art for me, or for friends, on his travels. He had a great talent for finding treasures. But I believe Fujikawa is lying. He just wants the painting for himself."

"What does he mean by 'drastic measures'?" I ask.

Kenji pauses a moment before he speaks. "I can guess. Fujikawa has extorted money from our business from time to time over the years. He left us alone for a while. But after I found the drawings in my Tokyo office four months ago, he began contacting me about the drawings. When I ignored his requests for them, we began to experience some difficulties at our construction sites. Accidents. We suspect sabotage. So it is possible he is planning a more drastic action at a site or a building if I do not come up with the painting."

I have serious chills. I think back to the articles I read last week—the explosions, the broken scaffolding, the collapsed bridge. If those accidents weren't really accidents, who knows what this guy is capable of? Maybe Tomonori's suicide in 1987 wasn't really a suicide. Maybe someone *pushed* him off that subway platform! I wonder if this Fujikawa guy knew that the drawings and painting were real van Goghs long before they were authenticated.

"And you really don't know where that painting is?" Agent Chang persists.

"I wish I did," Kenji says. "As I have already explained to you, my brother died before he could tell me where he put it. Over the years, I have searched our office building and my brother's house. I interrogated his late wife, his friends, and his connections at various museums. Eventually, I had to give up."

"He didn't leave a single clue?" Margo asked. "Not even a note or something?"

"No note. Not even a suicide note," Kenji says. "Well, not a proper note. On the subway platform were his shoes and socks, which is why we knew it was suicide."

"No autopsy?" Agent Denny asks, pausing from taking notes.

"They were seldom performed in Japan back in the 1980s," Kenji says. "Especially when all signs pointed to suicide. Well, beside his shoes was his briefcase. And inside the briefcase was a drawing of two *ayu*. No business papers. Just this pen-and-ink drawing."

"*Ayu?*" my dad asks. "What's that?"

Ayu. It sounds familiar, but I'm not sure why.

"It's a kind of fish. A river trout. It's very popular in Japan," Mitsue explains.

Maybe I saw *ayu* on a sushi menu or something. "Who did the drawing?" I ask him.

"My brother, I am sure. It was his characteristic style, intricate line drawings. It was——" Kenji's voice breaks. He looks down at his hands in his lap and falls silent.

Mitsue pats his arm. "Tomo was a talented artist, but the Yamada family was unsupportive of his dream. They pressured him to go into the family business. It is why he consoled himself with collecting art. We interpreted the *ayu* as a symbolic message, his way of explaining his decision. It was all we had to comprehend his mind-set. Such a happy person, with everything going for him—a thriving business, a healthy young son. I suppose there are disturbances in some people, beneath the surface, that are too deep to create even a ripple. Things you never know until it is too late."

"So he was basically a misunderstood artist," my dad says.

Kenji nods. "And since he left no message about the whereabouts of his most recent art purchases, we were looking for needles in haystacks. Which is why finding the painting and handing it over six days from now is, well, problematic."

"Wait, why would your brother have hidden the painting separately from the drawings?" I ask Kenji. "Especially if an appraiser said these weren't even van Goghs?"

"He planned to seek a second opinion on the appraisal at some point," Kenji explains. "He had an instinctive feeling that the drawings and the paintings were authentic. He wished to keep the art safe until it could be proven. And since the painting was potentially so much more valuable than the drawings, he thought it best to hide them in separate locations."

"He wanted to keep the art safe from whom?" Agent Denny demands.

"Fumiko. His wife. He feared she would dispose of it. He was having marital problems. He had recently altered his will to leave his collection to Mitsue and me."

"He didn't want his *wife* to inherit his art? That's harsh," I remark.

"Violet," my dad murmurs. "Please."

"I'm just saying."

"Violet is correct," Kenji says. "It was harsh. But theirs was an unfortunate match. Fumiko and Tomo did not see eye to eye about art. She felt it distracted him from his focus on the company. 'Gambling,' she called it. She was always threatening to sell off his collection."

"And where is Fumiko Yamada now?" Agent Denny asks.

"Deceased. She succumbed to pancreatic cancer nine years ago," Kenji replies.

"When Kenji and I cleaned and closed up her house, we searched, but there was no sign of the painting. We do not believe it was hidden in their home," Mitsue adds.

Would Kenji lie about the painting? To the FBI? To my dad and to Margo? He seems so sincere. Yet there's a piece that doesn't fit with him, too. Skye said he hit on her. That means he betrayed his wife in some way. He's capable of deception.

While the adults keep talking, I take my sketchbook out of my backpack and draw some of the information I've picked up, adding it to other bits I've sketched out since Friday.

"Mr. and Mrs. Yamada, do the two of you have children or relatives who might have an interest in the art?" Agent Chang asks. "Or who might have some insight into the painting?"

"Mitsue and I were not blessed with children. My only heir is my nephew, Hideki. He was a child when his father hid the painting, though, and has no idea of its whereabouts now."

"Fascinating history," says Margo, "but I still fail to understand what any of it has to do with Julian being attacked and Glenn's paintings being destroyed."

I notice she's looking at my sketchbook. I turn it to shield my work from her view. Then I look at the panels I've just drawn along a timeline, and suddenly a few things jump off the page. Things I never noticed before. It's like playing the Frame Game, looking for that new angle on something you've looked at a million times. A pattern emerges, a sequence or story that almost makes sense. The image I keep staring at is the broken window at my dad's house. I'd been assuming Skye dashed over there after their fight, but that window could have been broken any time between four, when my dad left for the art show, and nine, when we returned. I stand up so fast I knock my chair over. "I think I know what might have happened!"

"Violet," my dad warns.

"It's all right. Go ahead, Violet," says Agent Chang, watching me with interest.

"Okay. Let's say Fujikawa sent the two gangsters to find the painting. They broke into the Yamadas' basement and took the drawings. But they couldn't find the painting." All eyes are on me. I look back at my sketched panels to steady myself. "So they followed Skye around. They thought she had some connection to the painting, since she did restoration work on the drawings. Maybe they followed her to my dad's house one day, thinking she hid the painting there for safekeeping."

"In my house? That's absurd," my dad says.

"I'm not saying Skye actually put a van Gogh painting there. I'm saying the *yakuza thought* she might have. So when your window got broken the other night, after the art show—"

"Your window got broken?" Margo turns to my dad. "You didn't tell me that."

"Just petty vandalism."

"Sorry, Dad, but I don't think so. I think the *yakuza* came that evening or maybe even before the art show. I think they broke in to look for a painting hidden in your house."

Agent Chang stares at me. Agent Denny types furious notes.

I take a deep breath and wrap up my theory. "They were probably nearby today, watching the house. Maybe they thought Julian was crating the van Gogh painting along with your stuff. They followed him all the way to this gallery and saw their chance to get the van Gogh. When it wasn't there, they got mad and took it out on Julian. And on your paintings."

Everyone is quiet. I close my eyes. I feel kind of sick.

"But that is preposterous. Who would have led the *yakuza* to think Glenn, of all people, was harboring a stolen van Gogh?" Margo asks.

Agent Chang shuts her laptop. "That's exactly what we need to find out. And we need to get these *yakuza* into custody and investigate their possible connection to the Yamadas' break-in. But Violet's theory gives us some fresh avenues of exploration. Good thinking, Violet. And with the license plate number, we can start making inquiries at car rental agencies right away."

"Thanks." I steal a glance at my dad, but he's picking a hangnail instead of beaming at me with fatherly pride. I sink back into my folding chair.

The phone rings. Margo retreats to her office to take the call, apologizing to us for leaving. "It's Julian's mother," she says. "She's quite distressed about her son, as you can imagine. I'll rejoin you all in a moment."

The FBI agents confer in low voices, and then Agent

Chang faces the rest of us. "Here's how we're going to handle this letter. We'll stage a sting operation." She explains: Kenji will write a response letter, promising to show up with the painting. In six days, an FBI agent will pose as Kenji and go to the *Hammering Man*, carrying a blank canvas wrapped in paper. At the handover, a team of undercover FBI agents, posing as tourists, will nab the two thieves and get the drawings.

"It would be helpful if you could all get out of town for a bit, while we take care of the situation," Agent Denny says. "Might be a good time for you folks to take a little vacation."

"Actually, we are all scheduled to travel to Japan on Thursday," Kenji says.

"Hold on," my dad says. "Isn't Tokyo crawling with *yakuza*? I don't think we should go."

I chew my lip. After how close I've come, is he really going to call off our trip?

"Actually, I see no reason why you can't keep your travel plans," Agent Chang says. "*Yakuza* generally do not bother foreigners. They don't want the interference of foreign governments investigating, or the media sniffing around."

"I, too, see no great cause for alarm, Glenn," says Kenji. "The museum and the mural site are both in our office building, which has security. Your hotel has excellent security as well. But if it would put your mind more at ease, I can arrange for Violet to have personal protection."

"Wow! You mean like a bodyguard?" I exclaim.

"Precisely. We've worked with a personal security agency for years."

"Oh, wow. That'd be so cool." Reika will freak when she hears this.

My dad scratches his neck. "I don't know. I'm uneasy about it."

"Why don't the two of you talk it over?" Agent Chang says. "Agent Denny and I have a few more questions for Mr. and Mrs. Yamada."

Margo emerges from her office, and the FBI agents take the Yamadas in there to talk.

My dad doesn't mention the sting to Margo, but he confesses he's having second thoughts about taking me to Japan while the FBI sorts things out here in Seattle.

"Oh, take the child, Glenn," Margo says. "Nobody's going to trouble the two of you there. And it might do you good to have her along. You're a lot more fun to be around ever since Violet showed up. You're not quite as intense. And the Yamadas *like* her," she adds. "They like that you're a family man. Remember what I told you." She waggles a ring-encrusted finger. "Keep the clients happy, they'll come back for more."

"I see your point. Keep the clients happy. I guess we'll stick with the plan."

While my dad and Margo continue selecting substitute paintings for the Tokyo show, I go look at the lone madrona painting. *Keep the clients happy.* Scowling, I shove my hands in my jeans pockets. It's not like my dad actually wants me to come on this trip. I'm just part of a plan.

I should be happy, right? I'm still going to Japan in two days. The case is in the hands of professionals. My information was helpful. The *yakuza* almost certainly took the drawings. And there's a good chance of getting the drawings back, assuming the sting works.

And if it doesn't work? I look at the clouded glass windows of Margo's office. The agents and the Yamadas are silhouettes now. Silhouette Kenji rubs his forehead. Silhouette Mitsue pulls her wrap around her shoulders and sits hunched over, shaking her head.

I will be forced to employ drastic measures. That might mean more sabotage on construction sites, more lives lost on the Kobe bridge project. Who could stop something like that from happening? That's a job for Superman. Not for Kimono Girl. Not for me.

But as I pick up my sketchbook to put it away, it falls open to those copies I did of cormorants the other day. And suddenly I know why *ayu* sounded familiar. That's what these diving birds eat in Asia. Or carry, I should say. They dive for the *ayu,* hold it in their throats, and deliver it to fishermen who hold them by a leash. One picture I copied shows a cormorant with a collar around its neck. The collar keeps the birds from swallowing. They can't keep the rewards of their work. Maybe Tomonori Yamada was like a cormorant, and the art was like the *ayu*. Maybe that drawing he left in his briefcase the day he died is a clue to the painting.

PART 2 TOKYO

With two metal paint boxes banging against my legs, I hurry after my dad. We're walking from the Grand Prince Hotel to the Yamadas' West Shinjuku office, through a canyon of silver skyscrapers. "Hey, wait up!" I call. But he doesn't slow down.

If my life were a painting right now, it would be by Salvador Dalí, with everyday objects warped and weird. It's my fourth day in Japan, but I'm still in a jet-lagged daze, my days and nights upside down. I'm hungry at the wrong times. And I'm dripping like a Dalí clock. It's a billion degrees in Tokyo. Walking in the humid air feels like pushing through heavy curtains. I smell different scents with every step: rice, teriyaki sauce, fish, and perfume. They intrigue me until they all mix together, and then it's like breathing a thick, weird soup.

The asphalt everywhere traps the heat. I envy the Japanese girls in their gauzy skirts and camisole tops. They carry lacy parasols to ward off the sun. They slice the thick air with paddle fans. It's like I'm in a dream, dressed in all the wrong things—jeans and T-shirts. I bump into people and trip over my feet. I thought I'd fit right in here, but I'm constantly aware of my difference.

On top of jet lag and heat exhaustion, I'm freaking out about the FBI sting. It's scheduled for seven Monday evening, Seattle time, which is eleven tomorrow morning, Tokyo time. And this undercover operation has to work. Now we know exactly what kind of people the Yamadas are dealing with.

We found out on Saturday. On our first full day in Tokyo, Kenji and Mitsue showed up at our hotel, in a car with a personal driver, to take us sightseeing. At Sensō-ji Temple, they seemed to feel relaxed enough on sacred ground to bring us up to speed. Outside the towering red-and-gold pagoda, with incense swirling around us, they told us about their most recent phone conversation with Agent Chang.

"The FBI tracked down the Avis rental car to a Mr. Uchida and Mr. Nishio, both of Osaka, Japan," Mitsue said. "Agent Chang turned the names over to her associates in the CIB, the Criminal Investigation Bureau, as well as the Organized Crime Bureau. Criminal record databases in Japan are not kept and available the same way they are in your country. However, Uchida and Nishio both turned up in Tokyo Metropolitan Police Department files."

"They are no strangers to law enforcement," Kenji added as temple pilgrims dressed in white filed past us, holding candles. "They've served jail time in Japan for assault and robbery. They have ties to Fujikawa's gang."

"But if Agent Chang traced the guys back to Avis, couldn't the FBI just nab them that way? I mean, the car rental agency would know where they're staying." I couldn't resist asking this, even as my dad frowned at me. Before we left Seattle, I had promised my dad that I wouldn't get involved in the case in any way or pester the Yamadas with questions.

"I wish it were so simple," Kenji said. "The men returned the car the same day that Julian Fleury was assaulted, and checked out of their hotel. Agent Chang presumes that they've now rented a car with a different agency, under different names, and changed their accommodations. She has people checking on that. Meanwhile, we must hope they follow their boss's instructions and appear at the appointed time at *Hammering Man*."

My dad sighed and shook his head. "I sure I hope the Feds know what they're doing."

"Let us turn to happier topics," Mitsue said quickly. "Violet, would you like to purchase a fortune?" She steered me over to a wall of wooden drawers by the shrine to the bodhisattva Kannon, the Buddhist goddess of mercy. She showed me how to insert coins into a box, get a numbered bamboo stick, and find the matching number on a wooden drawer. My fortune came out of that drawer. "If it is a bad fortune, you can tie it to a tree outside, and the wind will take it away," Mitsue told me as I unwrapped it. "Oh, it's good," she said, reading over my shoulder.

The fortune was in many languages. Mitsue was right; in the English section, it did say NO. 83. EXCELLENT FORTUNE. Beneath that, it said: TROUBLE AND DISASTER ARE GETTING OFF AS TIME PASSES BY, SIGN OF THE FORTUNE IS OPENING UP TO US. GETTING SUCCESS IN LIFE, YOU ARE REAL BUSY. THE LOST ARTICLE WILL BE FOUND. YOU ARE SOON TO CROSS DARK WATERS, BUT PERSON WITH OPEN HEART AWAIT ON OTHER SIDE.

I wasn't sure how excellent this fortune was. *Trouble and disaster are getting off*—did that mean I'd have to experience those things first before they went away? *The lost article will be found*—maybe that was the van Gogh portfolio. But the fortune shed no light on who might find it or where. A *person with open heart* waiting sounded pretty good. But *soon to cross dark waters*? Not so much.

Around us, the Buddhist pilgrims began to chant prayers. I hoped some energy from those prayers to the bodhisattva might drift in our direction. I folded the fortune up neatly and placed it in an outer of pocket of my pack. Given the news about those *yakuza*, I figured it would be a good thing to have Kannon watching our backs.

Now, as we walk to the Yamadas' office building, I catch up with my dad at a crosswalk, panting. "Hey, slow down. These boxes are heavy."

"Sorry. Hideki is checking in first thing, and I don't want to be late," my dad says.

I raise an eyebrow. My dad has never met me on time for anything in his life.

I turn to see if Yoshi's keeping up, too. Sure enough, he's there, watching my back in case Kannon, the goddess of mercy, gets lazy. My personal bodyguard has been consistently five feet behind me ever since we arrived at Narita Airport. The moment I leave my hotel room, he pops out of his room across the hall. I don't even think he takes bathroom breaks. The guy has a bladder of steel. Maybe that's his superpower.

Other than that, I know almost nothing about Yoshi. He speaks "no Engrish," as he's always reminding me, wringing his hands and stepping backward, when I try to strike up conversation. He seems to be in his late twenties. Originally from Hokkaido, in northern Japan. Heavyset, broad-shouldered. Dressed in a suit, hair neatly combed. Pleasant enough to look at. If I drew him as a shape-shifter character, he'd be a man that turns into an ox. Strong and loyal.

His one distinctive quality is that he's a huge fan of *besuboru*. On our sightseeing excursions this weekend, he stopped a lot to check ticker signs and newspapers for the latest scores on the baseball teams he follows, both Japanese and American. And he looked thrilled when I presented him with his *omiyage*: a Seattle Mariners cap and a pack of Mariners trading cards. ("Ichiro!" he said with a grin, donning the cap and swinging an imaginary bat.)

Maybe I can teach him some English and draw him out in conversation. As someone in the Yamadas' inner circle, maybe he knows something about the investigation.

"Hey, Yoshi," I say, as we cross the street, "what are all these buildings here?"

"Ah, sorry?" He smiles, embarrassed, and waves his hands. "No Engrish."

I point to a skyscraper across the street. "This. Building. Name?"

He nods. "*Hai.* Tokyo Metropolitan Government Office." With growing confidence, Yoshi goes on to name other buildings we pass. "Sumitomo Building, very famous. Sompo Japan Building, very famous." He pauses before a tall building with a dome on top. The glass windows gleam brilliant blue, as if the building had been lifted from the sea and plunked down in West Shinjuku. "Yamada Building."

"Let me guess. Very famous?"

"*Hai!*" Looking pleased, he motions for us to go in.

The revolving door sucks us in, whirls us around, and spits us out again. Suddenly, we're standing on a white marble floor studded with marble pillars, in a paradise of air-conditioning. Security guards and receptionists in navy blue suits bow as Yoshi leads us through the lobby, which still smells of recent construction from the building renovation. A tall, white wall rises before us. Two bright lamps hang from each end, like spotlights. A stepladder leans against it.

My dad studies the wall as if it's a mural that was already painted. Then he presses his hands on the wall. Then his cheek. He closes his eyes.

"Uh, Dad, what are you doing?" A small crowd of office workers forms around us.

"Reading the wall," he replies, eyes still closed. He moves down the length of it, caressing the surface. Then he opens his eyes. "Someone did a crap job on the primer."

I am suddenly aware of another silent presence behind me. I turn to find a handsome man in a crisp gray suit standing with arms folded and a trace of a smile. He's like a younger Kenji—maybe not much younger than my dad. A tall, trim man, with just a couple of silver threads in his styled hair. I clear my throat to alert my dad, who thankfully stops becoming One with the wall.

"Marklund-san?"

"What?" My dad looks startled and stares at the Japanese man. "Oh. Right. That's me."

"Welcome. I am Hideki Yamada. It is a great pleasure to meet you."

So this is Kenji's nephew, the guy who's caused my dad so much stress this past week. Hideki's such a handsome man, it's actually painful to look directly at him. It's kind of like looking at the sun. Which is embarrassing to admit, since he's obviously way too old for me. But he's the first guy I've looked at twice since Edge.

"It is an honor to have you here, Glenn-san," Hideki says to my dad. His accent is heavier than Kenji's, but his English just as precise. I think of a beautiful dragon emblazoned on silk, his words curling outward like swirls of smoke. "I am an admirer of your work. I feel confident that your mural will impress our visitors."

"Right," says my dad. "Please, call me Glenn. I'm not that big on formality."

"Certainly. Glenn. As you know, Japan has experienced difficulties in recent times," Hideki goes on. "The earthquake and tsunami. The economic situation. But Japan is building. Japan will hold a strong position in the world again. The bridge is a powerful symbol of this endeavor."

"That's all great. But, about that bridge idea. I was thinking, it's kind of difficult, design-wise, to—"

"And, excuse me, there is one more thing I must mention. My father, Tomonori Yamada, would have been delighted to know that your painting would transform our lobby. He loved art and greatly admired artists, both high-ranking ones and emerging ones, such as yourself."

"Right." My dad smiles back. "Emerging. Well, thank you, I guess."

I try to figure out how I'd draw Hideki. Frame Game. I zoom in while he and my dad talk art. Hideki's arms are folded tight. The fingers on his left hand twitch. Twice he glances at his Rolex. Unlike Kenji, he's impatient. Tense and intense.

My dad looks at the gathering crowd. "Just one thing. I can't work with an audience."

Hideki blinks rapidly, though does not break his smile. "Oh? What do you mean?"

"Yeah. It makes me nervous. All these people. And distractions can impair my process. Do you think we could get a curtain or a screen or something to put up while I work?"

Hideki nods, still smiling. "Yes, I understand. This can be arranged." He acts polite, but I get a sense of a cool breeze surrounding him. Or maybe it's the air-conditioning.

"And the air-conditioning—do you think it could be turned down, or, I don't know, off?"

Hideki makes a sucking sound through his teeth. "The air-conditioning affects many people, in many offices," he says. "Actually, I think changing the air may be kind of impossible."

"Right. But, see, the paints won't really cooperate in this air. Acrylics can be temperamental."

I try mental telepathy on my dad. *Stop! You're blowing it!* I know from all the manga I've read how important hierarchy is in Japan. My dad is violating a social code, asking the second-most powerful man in the company for these personal accommodations.

"I see," Hideki says through a tightening smile. "I apologize for the space not matching your specifications. I will remedy the situation immediately."

But now Hideki's gaze has drifted, past my dad, past me,

to something by the door. His face softens. A corner of his mouth turns up.

I turn to follow his gaze. A girl with long, dark brown hair saunters toward us. She wears platform sandals, a tight skirt with black leggings, a green bolero jacket, a plaid newsboy cap, and dangling gold hoop earrings. She swings a yellow patent leather tote bag and chomps a wad of gum. She's a jarring contrast to the office ladies who are now watching her in wonder.

And she's the best thing I've seen in Japan.

She waves and comes running, a huge grin on her face. "Violet!"

"Reika!" I brush past my dad and an astonished-looking Hideki and throw my arms around the one person in this country who knows me. I'm scared she'll dissolve like a dream.

I was going to call you today," I tell her. "I don't have to start work till tomorrow. How'd you find me here?"

"You said you were working for the Yamadas, so I Googled their building and found the address. Am I good detective or what?" She flashes a sly grin.

"Not bad."

"Good, because I cut Japanese school today to track you down. What's up with the mystery? I haven't had an update in days."

"Shh." I lead her a few yards away to a cluster of black Eames chairs, aware of Hideki's eyes on us. On Reika, I mean. Even as he's talking to my dad, his eyes flick toward her. I sigh. This always happens when I'm out with Reika, and a guy comes into the picture. Guys notice her. I fade away. "The FBI said I shouldn't talk about the case in public or even email anyone about it," I whisper. "They don't want us to do anything that might compromise the investigation."

"You talked to the FBI? No way!"

"Shh! I'll fill you in as soon as we're alone, I promise."

Except I'm never alone now, I remember, as Yoshi slowly circles.

"Hey, who's your dad talking to over there?"

"That's Hideki Yamada. Kenji's nephew. Soon to be CEO of the Yamada Corporation. I mentioned him in one of my emails to you."

"You never mentioned he's like a movie star. He's totally *kakkoii*!"

I roll my eyes, even though I have to agree he is hot. "I know you have a thing for older guys, but he's ancient, Reika. I'm sure he's over thirty."

"So? Talking to him isn't a crime, is it? You have to introduce me! We can go over there and ask your dad if you can go to Harajuku with me. Then I can meet him." She straightens her skirt and swings her purse. "Do I look okay? Do you like the lipstick? It's new. I'm not sure."

"You look great. As always." I sigh. Whenever there's a cute guy around, Reika gets this gleam in her eyes. She starts calling the shots, changing our plans, and trying to reel him in. Whenever she's going out with someone, she disappears on me and my friends, and returns to us only after it's over a few days or weeks later. My mom calls it Hormones. I call it Annoying.

I guess Reika's already made up her mind. She's walking toward Hideki.

Dragging my feet, I introduce her.

"Otsuki-Silver?" says Hideki. "What an interesting name. You are Japanese and . . . ?"

"American. My mom's from Tokyo. My dad was born in Seattle, and so was I."

"Do you speak Japanese?"

"A little." She tips her head and smiles.

Hideki and Reika chatter away in Japanese for a few minutes. I knew she spoke some Japanese, but I had no idea she was this good.

Hideki seems impressed, too. "Your Japanese is excellent," he says in English.

"I'm just a student. I hope I can improve." She nudges me and looks at my dad. She mouths the word *Harajuku* at me.

"Hey, can I go shopping in the Harajuku district with Reika?" I ask my dad.

"Not today."

I'm already turning to go when it hits me that he's actually said *no*. "Why not?"

"Best to stick close to the building."

"But it's just blocks away. I need something lighter to wear. I'm dying in these clothes."

My dad presses his lips together and considers this. "All right." Then he takes me aside and adds in a low voice, "But stay close to Yoshi. If you see anyone remotely suspicious, don't follow them. And please don't tell your friend anything about the investigation. If you do, you will be spending the remainder of this trip in your hotel room. Oh, and take my cell phone." He hands me the rental phone the Yamadas arranged for him. "Kenji and Mitsue are one and two on speed dial. If for any reason you and Yoshi get separated, call them."

I pocket the phone, wondering why he's chosen now of all times to lay down the law. Strangely, I'm almost happy about it. He sounds like a Real Dad.

"After all, I can't concentrate on my work if I'm wondering where you are and if you're safe," my dad adds. "I have to focus on the mural."

I scowl. Same old story. Just as I think he's enjoying my company, I find out it's all about his work. Keeping his precious headspace clear. "Got it," I snap. "I'll keep it on the downlow. You focus on the mural." I turn on my heel and leave.

"START TALKING!" SAYS Reika when we're outside. "What's up with the van Goghs?" She glances behind us. "And who's your wingman? That guy was following you in the lobby."

"Oh, him? Yoshi Tanaka. Personal security." I try to sound like it's no big deal to have a bodyguard. But it's hard not to gloat. Though Reika doesn't flaunt her wealth like Mardi does, I'm always aware that Reika's family has money. Nice cars. Regular housecleaners. The ability to wear a different outfit every day of the month without repeating. Annual summer trips to Japan. This is the first time I've had something that really seems to impress her.

"A *bodyguard*?" Her eyes dance. "What's going on?"

Now I can't suppress my grin. "Tell you later," I say. "Not in front of him." Yoshi might catch some key words, like *van Gogh*. That might get back to Kenji, then to my dad.

"Okay. Safe topic for now. Edgerton Downey. How's film camp going?"

His name feels like pins on my skin. "Um. No idea."

"Aren't you guys in constant communication? Like through your brain waves or something?"

"Actually, his camp is really strict about using email." I don't want to talk about our fight. Reika's so experienced with boys. She always knows what to do or say around them. I'm embarrassed to tell her how I blew a possible relationship with Edge right out of the starting gate. We might have been about to kiss, and I exploded on him. Then again, it's not all my fault. He said I didn't want him to make other friends, that I wanted him always around for me. That is completely warped and wrong.

I'm also trying to convince myself that the camp email policy really might be why he hasn't written me. I've checked my email at the hotel business center six times, but there's been no word from Edge. I keep hoping he'll break the silence first.

That fierce hope makes me feel worse. Maybe there's truth in what he said to me that day. Maybe I do sometimes take him for granted. *Good old Edge. He'll come around and apologize first.*

"But you're emailing him, right?" Reika's giving me this strange look.

"Sure. Of course." Actually, I am, but not in the way she thinks. At each email check, I've been drafting a long note to him, listing things I wish I could tell him. I've written about how everyone slurps their noodles loudly in restaurants. I've described taxis with lace doilies on the headrests and white-gloved drivers. I've explained what it's like to hear Japanese all the time, the soft staccato like the patter of rain. I've mentioned the birdsong noises piped into the hotel hallway in the mornings, and the fake cricket sounds every night. The wedding parties that come through the hotel lobby at least once a day: flocks of women swishing slowly in their full kimonos patterned with cranes. The *swoosh* of *zori*—fancy flipflops—on the marble floors. And the toilet in my room that plays five different songs, including "Jingle Bells," to cover up the sound of bodily functions and flushing. But I can't finish this epic email, or bring myself to hit SEND. I'm not going to cave in first. I'm the lone madrona tree in my dad's painting, with really thick bark.

Reika's still staring, clearly dying to know more. I change the topic. "Hey, aren't you going to fall behind if you miss a day of Japanese school?"

"I'll live. God, I'm really happy to see you, and to speak some freaking *English*."

"What's wrong with Japanese?"

"I like Japanese, but being *forced* to speak it is so not fair. You know how my mom likes me to do the whole connect-with-my-Japanese-roots thing? My aunt and uncle are under strict orders to prevent me from speaking English. So they have this ceramic pot in the kitchen, and I have to put in two hundred yen every time they catch me talking in English."

"That sucks," I agree. "But don't your friends here want to practice English with you?"

Reika slides on a pair of aviator sunglasses and tosses her hair.

"What friends? My relatives live in the most boring suburb, and I don't fit in with the other kids. Tokyo equals Dullsville most of the time."

Dullsville? How can she say that? I've spent most of my time so far just running from window to window in my hotel room, gawking at the city that sprawls in all directions. And Tokyo has this quiet but pulsing current of energy, like the buzz and thrum from the electric signs everywhere. "Why don't you fit in?"

She shrugs. "I'm a *haafu* here. Half Japanese. Half *gaijin*, foreigner. I confuse people."

Suddenly, Reika doesn't seem as sure of herself as she usually does. I want to ask her more about how she doesn't fit in here.

But I'm distracted. We've come to a wide, tree-lined street full of shops and sidewalk cafés. Music spills out of some of them, even at ten in the morning. The tourists and businesspeople I saw in Shinjuku have been replaced by Japanese teens sporting wild outfits—colors and styles I've never seen together, like magenta and turquoise, or chartreuse and orange. I see all shades of dyed hair, from brown to purple to blue. There are even some hard-core manga fans, dressed up head to toe in Loilta goth attire or other cosplay outfits. Schoolgirl skirts with froufrou petticoats. Glittery makeup. Even a guy dressed up in a furry, blue, alien-rabbit costume, totally *kawaii*, walking by himself and sipping an iced coffee.

I don't even know where to look. There's so much. "This is like Sakura-Con gone wild," I say just before I trip over a bicycle rack. "Is there a convention going on?"

Reika laughs. "Isn't it great? My aunt and uncle's house is so freaking repressed, I come here for a breath of fresh air. Here, people are actually trying not to be clones of each other."

I try to imagine what would happen if I could walk around my school so confidently, sharing my interests openly instead of retreating to manga or hiding my ideas in my sketchbook. I wonder if people outside my small circle of friends would eventually come to accept me.

Reika spins around. "We're in the heart of Harajuku! Omotesando-dori. The main drag. There's Issey Miyake and

Comme des Garçons. Over to our left, Hanae Mori. The flagship store! So." She flashes a mischevious grin. "Retail therapy?"

"There's nothing I can wear in these stores, Reika." I pause to stare at a boutique shop window. Mannequins strike contorted poses—as if they all suffer from severe cramps—and sport tube tops and miniskirts in metallic fabrics. One wears thigh-high pink leather boots with a twisting pattern of peacock feathers. "They're not going to have a thing my size." In four days, I haven't seen a lot of five foot nine, curvy women walking around these streets. And I've already tried looking for sandals at some shoe stores near our hotel. I had no luck finding anything for my monstrous size-nine feet. Salesclerks just shook their heads.

"You're not working in that, are you?" Reika looks at my jeans and Sakura-Con T-shirt.

I'm too embarrassed to admit how little spending money my dad gave me. "I'm working in archives. It doesn't matter. Anyway, all these shops have are club clothes."

"They have normal clothes, too. Come on. This store has a good fitting room. Nice thick doors. Private." She glances back at Yoshi, then looks hard at me. "*Very* private."

Oh. Got it. I let her drag me by the arm into the crampy mannequin shop.

Reika grabs an armload of outfits off the racks and beckons me to a hallway.

Yoshi follows us, but a clucking saleswoman shoos him away.

The fitting-room door clicks behind us. "Mystery time!" says Reika. "Spill it!"

I bring her up to date, ending with the FBI sting, now just twenty-four hours away.

"That's intense," Reika breathes when I'm done. "Oh, FYI? You shouldn't say the Y word in public. People kind of freak out if they hear *yakuza*. Gangs have a lot of power in Japan, and everyone's afraid of them. Let's call them 'yahoos.' Here, try this shirt."

"We're seriously trying on clothes?" I look doubtfully at the clingy fabric of a red blouse.

"Yes! You don't want Yoshi to think we were in here dishing about the case, right?"

"True." I slip the sleeveless blouse over my head while wriggling out of my T-shirt. An old locker room move I perfected for those dreaded PE classes.

"So now you're just waiting to hear news from Agent Chang tomorrow morning?"

"Pretty much. What else can I do? I mean, it's not like I'm going to track down some gang boss on my own and get the drawings back." All the determination I felt back in Seattle faded when I got to Tokyo and saw how vast it was. I realized this mystery was way bigger than me, covering two countries, more than two decades, and a key player who'd died long ago. It was like trying to look at an enormous mural and never being able to take it all in.

"But you worked so hard. How can you just stop thinking about the case?" Reika persists.

"I do think about it. All the time. I think about how if the sting operation fails, something bad might happen to Kenji and Mitsue and the people who work for them. There've been all these bad accidents on their company's construction sites ever since Kenji found the drawings in his office." I swallow hard. "Reika, what if this Fujikawa guy does something to the Yamada Building? While my dad and I are in it?"

"That's exactly why we have to get to the bottom of this."

"By finding Fujikawa?"

"No! By finding the painting."

I stare at her.

"Fujikawa's probably not too hard to find," Reika goes on. "Gang bosses and gangsters here live in houses with addresses, like regular people. They have real offices, too. They're so powerful, most regular people just leave them alone. Unfortunately, so do the police, most of the time. Finding a gang boss isn't impossible, but it isn't the greatest idea, either. They're kind of known for seeking revenge, violently, when people try to nab them."

I nod slowly, thinking of the polite-yet-menacing letter that Fujikawa wrote to Kenji.

"So we'll look for the painting," says Reika. "Then Kenji

can give Fujikawa what he wants and get this guy off his back."

She's so cheerful, I have to laugh. "You act like we could really find the painting."

She frowns. "Why not? Don't you think it could be here in Japan? Maybe even in the Yamada Building, right under Kenji's nose, just like the drawings were."

"Yeah, but wouldn't the painting have turned up during the renovations, like the drawings did? Especially since a painting would be a lot bigger than the portfolio of drawings."

"It's a huge building. Maybe not every nook and cranny was explored."

"I don't know, Reika. Kenji's been looking for over two decades. He would have found it by now. At the meeting with the FBI people last week, no one even mentioned find- ing the painting as a remote possibility."

"Why are you so freaking cautious?"

"Cautious!" I glare at her. "After all I did, following Skye around downtown Seattle? Coming up with scenarios to explain stuff? Which, FYI, actually helped out the FBI."

"That's all great. But no offense, sometimes you hold back, you know?" says Reika. "I feel like you need to jump in and really *look*. The painting's still out there. Don't you see, Violet? You're getting a second chance at solving this mystery!" She pumps a fist in the air. "*Ganbatte!* Let's find that painting!"

Something stirs inside me. I've been going down the

wrong path, looking for the person or people who took the drawings. It's the *painting* I need to look for, not the *criminal*. "I guess I could talk to Kenji and find out where he's already looked for the painting."

"Now you're talking. Are there any clues we could start with?"

Suddenly, more than anything, I want to find that canvas. Having a great victory would be the only way to make my dad notice me. If it's success he appreciates, I'll give him success.

"There might be a clue," I say. "Kenji mentioned something about a picture of *ayu*. That's a river trout, I think."

"Right." Reika nods. "A freshwater delicacy. They're popular to eat in the summer."

"Okay, so Tomonori Yamada was an amateur artist, and when they found his body on the tracks, the only thing in his briefcase was a drawing he did, showing two *ayu*. They thought it was a clue as to why he killed himself, like he couldn't live because he couldn't be an artist. But you know what? I don't think he really killed himself. Someone could have pushed him off that platform, and taken his shoes and socks off to make it look like a suicide."

Reika nods. "I'd buy that. I read somewhere that there are tons of suicides in Japan, but lots of them are probably murders that were never investigated."

"And I think the *ayu* could be some kind of clue related to the painting," I go on, thinking out loud. "Maybe Tomonori knew his life was in danger and wanted his brother to find the art."

"Yeah! So here's the deal. When you start work tomorrow, you have to look around the Yamada Building for anything related to *ayu*."

"Maybe the fish are in some office art. Or a symbol on a door. Or woven into a rug."

"Or a maybe someone named Ayu works there and knows something about the painting. I can check the company directory online, and call a receptionist, too."

"Great idea!"

"Oh, and maybe I can come to the office again and talk to Hideki." Reika twirls a lock of hair around her finger and inspects her dark eye makeup in the mirror. "I bet I could get him to open up about his memories of his dad, and find out what *ayu* might have meant to him."

"No way."

"Why not? He could have key information about Tomonori and the painting!"

"My dad's working for Hideki. There's a lot of money riding on this mural. If my dad finds out we're asking questions, especially to someone as important as Hideki, I'm grounded."

"All right, don't bite my head off. By the way, you are rocking that shirt. It's so *sugoi!*"

"Nice recovery. But you're still not talking to Hideki. No matter how *kakkoi* he is."

We walk out of the fitting room a few minutes later with our new plan and a few *sugoi*, or awesome, outfits from the store's sale rack. At the end of the fitting-room hallway, we find Yoshi. He creases his newspaper and pockets it, then escorts us to the cash register.

With Yoshi shadowing, Reika and I stroll down the street to find a *kissaten*, or manga café. For a blissful couple of hours, I don't worry about the van Gogh case. We swing our shopping bags and laugh at the funny English phrases on them. Mine says IT'S DURABLE, AND IT WILL STAY IN FASHION. Reika has two bags. One says BE SATISFINED WITH PURE BEAUTY. The other is decorated with black cats floating serenely in bubbles. The words FRIENDSHIP WORMS THE HEART weave around the bubbles.

While lunching at a noodle shop, Reika and I use our cell phones to check the Yamada Building's vast online employee directory. I read the English page; she reads the Japanese one. The only person we find with *ayu* in the name is a Mayumi Ozawa. But when Reika calls to speak with her, she finds out she's only twenty-two, a brand-new office girl at the company. She wasn't even alive when Tomonori hid that painting. There's nothing we can do until I start work.

After lunch, we hit another *kissaten*, browsing shelves bursting with manga titles, playing a few video games, drinking way too much bubble tea, laughing uncontrollably over nothing at all. Reika flirts with two guys playing video games. While they drool over her and completely ignore me, I buy the latest two issues of *Vampire Sleuths*. They're untranslated, but out a full year before the English versions will hit the shelves. My consolation prize for being invisible.

When Reika finally tears herself away from the guys, she promises to help me read them if I can't understand them from the pictures alone. Her offer is so sincere that I forgive her a little for ignoring me while she flirted.

In the afternoon, I walk Reika to a subway station. She gives me a sad little wave from the steps. "Oh, hey, Violet!" she calls back to me.

"Yeah?" I turn.

And then she says as crowds of people swarm by, "Don't worry. The sting operation is totally going to work. The FBI does this kind of thing all the time. But still, as soon as you find out, email me, okay?"

Chikuso. I thought Reika was more careful than that. Anyone nearby could have heard!

Even though Reika has just broadcast the secret sting operation loud enough for everyone on the street to hear, it seems, fortunately, like no one is paying attention. The only people not swarming toward the subway entrance are a flock of uniformed schoolgirls eating sticks of chocolate Pocky.

And Yoshi, of course. But he's transfixed by a big flat-screen TV on the side of a building. A baseball game. Yomiuri Giants versus Hiroshima Carp. A player is scoring a home run. The camera pans to the stadium crowd going wild with applause but no cheering, and an electronic sign above the playing field proclaiming, in English: "We can be shinin' stars." There's a sentimental smile on Yoshi's face. He looks on the verge of weeping.

I manage to tear him away from the screen. We walk back toward the Yamada Building.

Crossing Omotesando-dori to leave Harajuku, I forget that Japanese drivers use the other side of the road. A passing taxi nearly takes me out. Yoshi grabs my arm and yanks me back onto the sidewalk just in time. Minutes later, when a group of schoolchildren run up to practice English phrases, Yoshi shoos them away. "I am a pencil!" one boy shouts at me inexplicably. Yoshi takes him by the collar and hauls him off to his teacher. When I trip over a curb and fall, Yoshi steers me over to a bench and buys me a cold, sugary drink called Pocari Sweat from a vending machine. "Hey, uh, thanks for saving me today," I tell him. "Like, over and over again."

"*Douzo*," he murmurs shyly, looking down.

I smile. I think I officially have a second friend in Japan.

BACK IN THE Yamada Building, the temperature has risen a few more degrees, thanks to my dad's selfish request. Businessmen are loosening ties, receptionists fanning themselves. Another change: my dad is now protected from curious onlookers by an assortment of screens. Some are folding Japanese screens, gold with patterns of *koi*. Some are office cubicle partitions, or bulletin boards on metal stands. For a guy who says he hates drama, he's sure got quite the stage.

I poke my head in. The smell of paint makes me choke. "Knock, knock," I say.

"Who's there?" my dad asks. He has white flecks of paint all over his hair. He sits cross-legged at the foot of the wall, a pencil and a pad of paper on his lap. A few feet away, on a stool, is a bento lunch box with rice and teriyaki chicken. Eight small glass Coke bottles are strewn around the floor.

He's drunk all the Coke, but barely picked at his food. I remember Skye told me to make sure he eats.

"Violet," I reply.

"Violet who?"

I could have hiked up Mount Fuji and never returned, and he wouldn't have even noticed.

He actually smiles. "Remember you used to do those knock-knock jokes all the time?"

"Huh? Oh. Sure. About a hundred years ago."

"What happened to those? Some of them were pretty clever."

"Thanks. But I'm in high school now? We don't really do knock-knock jokes anymore."

What happened to playing the Frame Game? I want to ask him. *And what happened to all the school photos I gave you, and why aren't they in your house?*

"Well? Violet who?" he prompts.

"Violet a good meal go to waste?" I point to the bento box.

He chuckles. "See, you haven't lost your touch."

"You should really eat something. Lunch was a long time ago."

"I know. I'll get to it."

"I ate lunch," I volunteer, since he didn't bother to ask. "Reika took me to this awesome noodle shop. The only sign for it was a piece of blue fabric with some *kanji* characters on it. People wiped their hands on the cloth when they left. It's how they thank the chef."

"Cool." He's staring at that wall again, so intensely you'd think he was trying to bore a hole through it with his eyes. I don't think he heard a word.

"Can I watch you work?"

"Well, that'd be as exciting as watching paint dry. In fact, that's exactly what it would be. I spent my day re-priming, and I can't do anything else till it settles, so I'm working out some ideas on paper." Frowning, he studies the pencil sketch on the paper, the outline of a bridge.

"You're doing a bridge painting? Like van Gogh did?"

"Hideki wants to use a bridge as a metaphor to connect Eastern and Western cultures, and as a symbol of their company. But the design I proposed isn't going to work after all."

"Do you have to paint a bridge? It's your art."

"There's a lot of money in a commission like this. And everyone's got an opinion. Especially Hideki. Even though the guy didn't inherit one shred of his dad's or his uncle's vision for art. He should stick to closing deals and stop looking over my shoulder."

"My art teacher says if you try to please everyone, you just end up with a mess."

"She's right. Then again, if someone wants to pay you a hundred grand for some feel-good corporate crap, and to match the colors in the carpet samples, you tend to forget that advice. But somewhere the integrity of the artist has to count for something. I have to find a way to sign my name to something I believe in."

I watch as he crumples that paper and starts again. "Maybe there's some other way to show a bridge," I suggest. "Sometimes people are kind of like bridges, stretched between two things. Like Reika, with two cultures—oh, it's stupid. Forget it," I mumble as he crumples another page. He's clearly not in the mood for advice. "Hey, can I lay out some paints or brushes for you for tomorrow?" Maybe if he remembers the knock-knock jokes, he'll remember that I used to do little jobs for him. That we used to hang out and have fun.

But he's sketching now, "in the zone," I guess, as my art teacher likes to say.

I retreat, shifting the screens to close him off completely from the rest of the lobby. Maybe the best way to help him is just to let him have his space. An art he's perfected over the years.

The next morning, I say good-bye to my dad in the lobby and head upstairs with Yoshi for my first day of work. I'm wearing one of my new Harajuku outfits: the silky red top with a swishy black-and-red floral skirt. Only my black Converse sneakers ruin the look. I've still had no luck finding sandals my size. My feet are already sweating. The temperature in the building is up another ten degrees from yesterday.

A smiling receptionist comes up and to me and explains, in English, that Mitsue wanted me to tour their museum before reporting for work. I expect to be taken to some other building and am surprised when Yoshi leads me into the elevator. When we step out of the elevator on the third floor, we're in a corridor facing a set of sliding wooden screens lined with white paper. Yoshi removes his shoes and exchanges them for slippers on a rack and motions for me to do the same. Then Yoshi slides back the *shōji* screen and leads me into another world.

We're in a street in old Japan. We stand on a simulated cobblestone street before a wooden building façade with heavy beams and a low, shingled roof. The building within the building is lined with straw mats—*tatami*, I ? manga and from Japanese restaurants. They sm/ grass. I follow a winding route from room to room. The a/ sculptures, and artifacts on display proceed chronologically through centuries of Japanese history. I take in the silk kimonos on the walls, emblazoned with dragons, flowers, birds. I move on and see scrolls, decorative screens, pottery, jewelry, hair combs, porcelain dishes, lacquered bowls, dolls, and musical instruments—stringed instruments called *kotos* and *samisens*. Heavy, barrel-shaped *taiko* drums. Delicate wooden *fue*, or flutes. There's even a whole room devoted to ancient swords with elaborately decorated scabbards. I want to draw everything I see.

Room after room, the museum unfolds like a fan, until finally we end up in a brightly lit modern gallery space that reminds me of Margo's gallery. A sign in Japanese, French, and English reads SPECIAL EXHIBIT: THE INFLUENCE OF JAPANESE PRINTS ON CONTEMPORARY ARTISTS. Velvet ropes mark off the area, which is bustling with art handlers unpacking crates, hanging pictures, drilling holes in walls. The crate with my dad's four paintings takes up much of the middle of the room. Near it, Mitsue is talking to some handlers. She immediately comes over to greet me.

"Violet-chan! *Ohayou gozaimasu.* Good morning."

"*Ohayou gozaimasu*," I repeat. I've been listening carefully to the hotel staff at breakfast every morning, trying to copy their pronunciation. "Your museum is amazing," I add. "I didn't expect it to take up a whole floor of an office building. Wow."

"Yes, many private galleries and museums in Japan are inside office buildings," Mitsue explains. "We do not have districts dedicated to art galleries, like your Pioneer Square in Seattle. I am glad to hear you enjoyed your tour. The museum has been open for only a few months, since the renovation, so it is still a work in progress. The storeroom and archives, where you will work, are just down this hall." She gestures to a doorway. "Yoshi will take some time off while you work, and he'll return to take you to lunch. Are you ready to begin?"

"Sure. Any news from Agent Chang?" I can't resist asking as I follow her down the hall.

"Not yet. The sting takes place in two hours."

"Are you worried about it?"

"There is no reason to be. The FBI is quite confident these men will walk into the trap. Once they do, the drawings will be returned, and these bad men will be in police custody."

But now I notice a slight tremor in her voice. Her appearance betrays her state of mind, too. I notice shadows under her eyes that makeup fails to conceal. She's dressed in a smart, blue sheath dress, but the belt at her waist has missed two loops, and her scarf is tied sloppily.

Just outside the storeroom door, I notice a row of six

framed *ukiyo-e* prints. I pause to look at them while Mitsue searches her purse for a key. "Fish," I whisper.

They all seem to show carp, but the print closest to the door shows two slender, gray fish that seem different. "What kind of fish are these?" I ask Mitsue.

"These are *ayu*," she replies.

I think back to the last "note" Tomonori had left his family, the drawing in his briefcase. "Are they the ones Tomonori drew?"

"Oh, no," says Mitsue. "This is a print by Hiroshige Ando, who did the original *Moon Crossing Bridge*. These are all prints from his Small Fish series."

I can't stop looking at it. It seems significant, because of the fish and the Hiroshige connection. "How long has it been on this wall?" I ask.

"At least as long as I've known Kenji. And far too long. See the fading from the overhead lights? We usually rotate woodblock prints monthly, but these are so light-damaged that we don't bother. Ah, here is my key."

The storeroom feels like a fortress, which calms my nerves a little. Like the Yamadas' basement in Seattle, long metal tables march down the center. The walls are lined with flat-file cabinets. I can see two doors in the back that lead to adjacent halls, and more rooms with storage cabinets and shelves.

It's hard to believe that in this same building, on the thirty-third floor, Kenji and Hideki are working at desks, and down in the lobby, my dad is putting his pencil to the wall and beginning to outline his mural. I imagine every window of this building as a manga panel, showing a scene. Except the panels don't seem to belong to the same story.

Kind of like what I know about the van Gogh mystery so far. Skye. Julian. The destroyed paintings. The *yakuza*. A ransom-note writer who feels the van Goghs are rightfully his. A businessman-slash-art lover who died soon after he hid the van Goghs. A construction company plagued with problems. A soon-to-be CEO who is clueless about art, determined to have a painting of a bridge in his lobby. Shuffle all these elements any way you like. They make interesting shapes and patterns, but they do not tell a story.

Mitsue leads me to a table with portfolios and solander cases neatly stacked. She hands me a pair of white cotton gloves, then slides on an identical pair. She opens a flat box on the table and takes out a portfolio with a green cover. "The prints are very sensitive to oils, so you must take care," she says. "The slightest drop of water, even saliva, can cause ink to bleed."

The portfolio contains about ten unbound papers. Mitsue slides off a thin sheet of cloudy white paper. "Glassine," she explains. "We place it between prints to protect the images. When you look through a portfolio, turn back the glassine first. Then pick up the print by opposite corners of the paper. Like so." She demonstrates. If you didn't see the paper, you might look at her hands and arms and think she was dancing. The glassine slides away with a whisper.

This print is in excellent condition, the colors so vibrant the ink almost looks wet. It shows a woman in a green kimono, holding a parasol that hides most of her face. She walks through snow toward an orange temple. Pine tree branches laden with snow seem to bow before her. I imagine I'm Kimono Girl, diving in, hearing the crunch of snow underfoot.

"These are more prints by Hiroshige, as well as some of his contemporaries," Mitsue explains. She turns over page after page.

Temples, tea gardens, and country roads flash before my eyes. Some landscapes have people in them, but the faces are never clear; they are dwarfed by the landscapes. Some prints show houses or restaurants with colorful hanging lanterns and warm yellow lights in the windows. Some show boating parties on rivers, with courtesans lounging on pillows.

"No wonder van Gogh loved this stuff," I say.

"Yes. When I look at *ukiyo-e,* I like to imagine escaping to a happier, simpler place," Mitsue says. She gazes at a boat on a river, a lady in a kimono who trails her fingers in the water. "In fact, *ukiyo-e* means 'pictures of the floating world' because the prints show scenes of transient pleasures. Beautiful things to enjoy in the moment because they cannot last."

"Maybe van Gogh thought the same thing," I suggest.

"He was mentally ill, right? Maybe this is how he escaped his problems." Maybe he escaped into prints like I escape into manga. I go on my biggest manga-reading binges when I'm frustrated by my personal life. I like going into a world where stories are laid out in neat panels.

Mitsue opens a second box, and this time she lets me move the pages. I imitate her movements, slow and deliberate, as if I'm moving underwater. She clasps her hands together and looks genuinely happy for the first time all morning. "Very good! You have steady and gentle hands. You are ready to measure. We need dimensions of the images printed on every page. We will enter these measurements into a database."

Measuring takes all my concentration. Mitsue teaches me how to use a cloth tape measure to determine the exact height and width of each image. I have to measure through the glassine, to protect the print. Sometimes the glassine slips, so I have to start over. Each piece of paper is the same—9½ by 14½ inches. But every image has slightly different dimensions. Every millimeter matters for describing and valuing the prints.

But I make my way through six portfolios. Close to noon, I have a crick in my neck and my stomach is rumbling. A phone extension on the wall jangles, startling me.

Mitsue speaks in hushed tones, in Japanese. Her voice rises

in pitch. When she hangs up, she stands still, one hand on the receiver, one hand at her throat, head bowed.

"Everything okay?" I ask. My stomach is an elevator, dropping down fast.

"That was Kenji. He has heard from Agent Chang. The sting was not a success."

I stare at her. "Oh my God. What went wrong?"

"The two men, Nishio and Uchida, approached the meeting area. However, at the University Street Hillclimb, they turned and fled. Federal agents pursued them, but the men escaped in a car parked on Alaskan Way. They must have become suspicious of a setup."

"You think someone told them about it?"

"That is possible. They could have received a last-minute tip from some informant."

"Does Agent Chang think those guys are still in Seattle?"

"That is uncertain. Forgive me, but I must attend this conference call. I will send Yoshi."

The door clicks closed. I shiver, despite the stifling air. The *yakuza* are still on the loose. Fujikawa must be furious about being set up and not getting his painting. It's only a matter of time before he seeks revenge or sends his henchmen to harass the Yamadas.

I wish I really were Kimono Girl. I'd wrap the Yamadas in my magic robe and whisk them away, into the print. And my dad, too. If that rock through his window was an attempted break-in, and if his paintings were destroyed because someone expected to find something among them, he must be on their radar.

Somewhere along the way, the *yakuza* got bad information. Why else would they think my dad or Skye or Julian had any idea where the lost van Gogh painting would be? Now the Japanese mob is barreling down the wrong path. Full throttle. And we can't get out of the road.

19

As soon as Mitsue leaves the room, I take out my dad's rental cell phone, which I purposely forgot to return yesterday after I discovered I could get my email on it. I fire off a text message to Reika: OMG STING FAILED!!! WAITING FOR MORE INFO!!!

I circle the storeroom, feeling caged and helpless. Reika was right. Finding the painting would put an end to all of this. I no longer have thoughts of glory, of changing the face of the art world by handing over a previously unknown van Gogh. So what if a van Gogh painting would remain lost to the art world? It's already been lost for decades. I just want it to resurface so it can immediately sink into the underworld of organized crime. Then Fujikawa will call off his henchmen, and we will all be safe.

His henchman. The *yakuza* in Seattle. Who tipped them off to the sting? Where are they now? I wonder if they noticed Edge and me filming Skye that day. Maybe that's why they suddenly vanished at the Seattle Art Museum. If they thought we were deliberately filming them, they might think our video footage of them had something to do with the sting.

They might come looking for Edge and me, demanding the camera—or seeking revenge.

Could they find us? They might have followed us back to the bus stop that day, back to North Seattle. They might know where Edge lives. They might ask the neighbors questions and track him down in Port Townsend.

Now my heart is pounding. I have no proof they know who Edge and I are, but I also have no proof that they don't. Edge could be in serious danger. I have to warn him, even though it means breaking our silence.

I open up my ongoing draft email to Edge and delete it, sentence by sentence. He's not going to be interested in Japanese toilets. (*Japanese toilets!* What was I thinking?) I'm still mad at him, but that doesn't matter now. He's in danger. His life is more important. I type a simple warning note and avoid any emotional language. All I want to do is help save his life. It's just business.

> FBI CALLED. THE YAKUZA WE FILMED ARE
> STILL ON THE LOOSE IN WASHINGTON STATE.
> IF THERE'S ANY CHANCE THEY CAUGHT US
> FILMING AND FIGURED OUT WHERE WE LIVE,
> YOU COULD BE IN DANGER. THOUGHT YOU
> SHOULD KNOW. BE EXTRA CAREFUL. —V.

As soon as I hit SEND, my phone rings. Margo Wise shows up on caller ID. I stare at her name. Why would

Margo call me? Then I remember this is my dad's phone.

I let the phone ring, then listen to the voice mail. Margo sounds breathy, agitated. "Glenn. How are you? How's Japan? Call me as soon as you can. Julian got out of the hospital yesterday. And he left me a message. He's quitting! How could he leave me scrambling like this before the regional show? If you know anyone, *anyone* who might be a candidate for the job, call me. . . ."

This news seems really big. Maybe Julian got scared, thinking the *yakuza* might come back for more. I remember when I heard him talking to his mother on the phone, the night of my dad's reception. He sounded so proud about his art gallery job. And my dad said Margo had done a lot for Julian. Quitting so abruptly and leaving Margo in the lurch for a show seems drastic. It has to mean something. Maybe the FBI should be keeping their eye on Julian, too.

I have to tell my dad about the sting failing. And about Julian quitting. I know he warned me not to get involved, but this news is too important to hold back. Maybe Julian found out about the sting and tipped somebody off! I dash to the elevator. In the lobby, I run to the big wall and slip between the screens.

Using a Japanese *sumi* brush, my dad is painting the outline of a bridge in black ink. He's concentrating so hard he looks as a fierce as a *samurai* warrior.

"Hey, can I talk to you for a sec?"

My dad jerks his arm. Black ink splatters on the wall, on the floor, à la Jackson Pollack.

"Oh, sorry!" I exclaim. "I didn't mean to startle you. I just have to tell you about—"

"Can it not wait?" he growls. Seeing the ink splatters, he flings down his palette and grabs a drop cloth. He rubs at the black spots on the wall but they only get larger. "Oh, Violet."

I back away. "Sorry," I whisper, fighting tears. "I'm sorry." I run back to the elevators.

The conference call. I have to get in on that and tell Agent Chang about Julian.

I get off the elevator on the thirty-third floor. I run down one corridor after another, past startled receptionists who call out, *"Sumimasen?"*

Near the end of a corridor, I come to a closed door with Kenji's name on it in both Japanese and English. I tap softly. Then I push it open. No one is there. The room is still. I enter the office and softly close the door behind me.

A small, framed picture above Kenji's desk catches my eye. I walk up to it.

It's a pen-and-ink drawing of two *ayu*. They seem to be circling each other in a whirlpool, almost forming a yin-yang symbol. I quickly snap a photo of it with my dad's cell phone.

I scan Kenji's desk area in case anything else related to his brother might be there. A more recent photo or something. I feel like I want to understand the man who hid this art, and maybe a look at his face would help.

I don't see any photos, other than one of Mitsue on the Spanish Steps in Rome. But underneath the desk, I see an old-looking cardboard file box. I kneel and lift the lid. It's filled with files of architectural plans. Blueprints. I can't read anything on them or the label on the box. I snap a picture of the label, in case it might be significant. I email it to Reika to translate. Then I stand up and head to the door.

As I reach for the doorknob, it turns on its own. Suddenly Hideki Yamada is there. Startled, I drop the cell phone.

He blinks at me. "Violet?"

I fumble to pick up the phone, hoping Hideki doesn't notice my shaking hand. "I heard there was a conference call with the FBI here. I just got an important voicemail, and I wanted to tell you guys."

He gives me a long look. "This is a private family matter. The call is confidential."

"I just heard news from Seattle about someone who might be connected to this case. The guy the *yakuza* beat up last week. It's really, really important!"

His eyes rest on me. A muscle twitches near his temple. I now see that this whole art heist business is as hard as him as it is on Kenji and Mitsue. After all, it concerns something his dad was closely involved in. "All right," he says at last. "Then you had better come. The call is about to take place in my office. Follow me."

He gestures for me to walk in front of him. Through the glass window on the office door, I catch his reflection behind me. He snatches a large yellow-and-red mailing envelope off Kenji's desk, rolls it into a tube, and slips it into his jacket pocket. It's kind of a funny way to pick up someone's mail.

But I forget all about it as we approach Hideki's office. I can hear Kenji's voice. "No, I am proposing a financial settlement instead."

Agent Chang's voice crackles through the speaker phone. "Well, I think that's a terrible idea. If you pay him off, he walks, and so do the van Goghs."

"I am afraid you do not grasp the severity of the situation. Fujikawa is furious about the way we tried to trap him. A courier has just hand-delivered a letter from him. In this letter, he has given me one last chance to comply. He says if I attempt to deceive him again, or if I do not deliver the painting by July eighteenth, he will erase the *gaijin* artist."

Erase the gaijin *artist.*

My dad! He's going to kill my dad!

"For that reason," Kenji continues, "and because under-cover operations are illegal here in Japan, Hideki and I are gathering the necessary funds. We will pay whatever it takes to appease Fujikawa. Lives are more important than art."

My legs stay rooted to the deep plush rug. I look at my hands, and they're shaking. But Hideki beckons me into the office, where Kenji and Mitsue are sitting at a round table with a phone. They look up, startled.

"Violet! Didn't Yoshi appear? I called him to take you to lunch," Mitsue says.

"I didn't see him. I just got a voicemail from back home, and I have some news about Julian Fleury. I wanted to tell you while you had Agent Chang on the phone. But my dad, is he—is he—"

Kenji and Mitsue exchange a worried look. Kenji pulls back a chair for me. "Please. Join us. And be sure to speak loudly," he adds, gesturing to the speakers on the phone.

"Hi, Violet," says Agent Chang. "What do you have for us?"

I try to block out everyone in the room and just talk to Agent Chang. I tell her about the message that Margo left for my dad. "I don't know if Julian might have tipped them off about the sting," I conclude, "or if he's so freaked out about the *yakuza* assault that he didn't even want to go back to work at the gallery. I just thought it seemed like a weird coincidence, and I thought you guys should know."

"I am very glad you brought this to our attention, Violet," says Agent Chang. "Every lead helps. We definitely want to get in touch with Julian Fleury."

"Thank you, Violet," says Kenji. "Personally, I find it unlikely that Julian knew of the sting, since he was in the hospital when the plan was discussed and he did not return to work. But we should let Agent Chang and her team explore this possibility."

"Yes, thank you for your information, Violet," Hideki says, standing up, indicating that I should do the same. "I will escort you to reception, where you may wait for Yoshi."

We walk down the hall. Hideki has removed his jacket. I don't know what he did with that yellow-and-red envelope, but I didn't see him give it to Kenji.

But we're near the elevator, and I'm running out of time to ask Hideki about that threat. "I didn't mean to eavesdrop, but I heard Kenji say something about my dad. Is he in danger?"

"Oh, I am afraid you misheard," Hideki says in a gentle and reassuring voice. He smiles, and his eyes crinkle at the corners. He's movie-star handsome again, and a little part of my heart melts. For a moment, without Reika around, I have his full attention. It feels nice.

"This is just the way that Fujikawa talks," Hideki goes on. "He is seeking money, which we will provide once we agree on a sum. It is a business negotiation. Your father is perfectly safe. Please do not worry yourself about this. Ah, here is Yoshi now. Thank you for your information and your time."

I want to believe Hideki that Fujikyaya is just making empty threats. But all I can think of as I follow Yoshi to a noodle shop is that this does not sound like business as usual. I'm sure my dad's in danger.

At the end of the day, back at the Grand Prince Hotel, I flop on my hotel bed, exhausted. My eyes burn from staring at Mitsue's prints all afternoon, as well as at my cell phone photo of the *ayu* drawing in Kenji's office. It has to be Tomonori's. When I enlarged it, I saw a series of small *kanji* characters running vertically down the lower left side. I emailed the picture to Reika for a translation, as well as my photo of the old file box, but hours have passed with no reply, so I call her cell.

"*Moshi moshi?*" says a breathy, high-pitched voice.

"Oh, sorry," I mumble. "I mean, *sumimasen*." I have no clue how to say "wrong number."

"Wait—Violet? Is that you?"

"Reika! You sounded so different. I didn't even recognize you."

"I was just about to call you. My aunt and uncle found out I skipped Japanese school yesterday. They took away my daytime cell-phone privileges. Oh, and now my 'responsible older cousin' has to take me to and from school personally!"

"That sucks!"

"I know! Anyway, I just got your news, and that picture you sent me. Good work, finding Tomonori's *ayu* drawing. That's his signature in the corner."

"What about that file-box label? I'm wondering if that's the box of old blueprints where Kenji first found the portfolio of van Gogh drawings."

"There is a year on the label. 1987."

"That's when Tomonori bought the van Goghs!"

"I know, right? And the label on the box translates to something like 'Fine Ayu Food Products.' It sounds like the name of a company."

"So Tomonori probably didn't hide the van Gogh drawings in some random file box."

"He was very deliberate. The *ayu* on the picture he left in his briefcase must have been a clue to the drawings hidden in that file box. I bet wherever he hid the painting connects back to the *ayu* clue, too."

Next, I tell Reika about the conference call. "It's kind of weird that Hideki hosted this conference call and not Kenji. I mean, it's Kenji's art that got lost," I say.

"Well, Tomonori was Hideki's dad," Reika reminds me. "Even if the art is Kenji's now, he's probably next in line for it, after Mitsue. It makes sense he'd want to be involved. Though it must be painful for him, all this talk of his dad, who, like, *died* when he was a kid."

"Yeah, I can see that. But here's what's really freaking

me out." I tell her what I overheard Kenji saying about my dad. "Reika, I don't know if Fujikawa's going to accept cash instead of a painting on July eighteenth. I'm really worried something is going to happen to my dad! He said the *gaijin* artist would be 'erased.' That can only mean one thing."

Reika is silent for a moment. She lets out a long breath. "July eighteenth. That gives us ten days to find the painting. I'm going to search online, right now, for Tokyo businesses that have *ayu* in the name. First thing tomorrow, you start searching that art storeroom for anything, uh, fishy."

Fishy! I think of the Hiroshige *ayu* print by the storeroom door. Mitsue said the print has been there for a long time. Decades. Maybe the Hiroshige *ayu* print is a clue! Woudn't it be amazing if the painting was hidden in the very storeroom where I'm working for eight hours every day?

"Should I warn my dad? Even though he said not to get involved in the case again?"

"How can you even ask that, Violet? If someone wanted to kidnap or kill me, I would want to know. Absolutely. Tell your dad."

I DECIDE TO tell him at dinner, since we'd made plans to meet up at the hotel restaurant. I get a table and wait. A half hour passes.

I pull up my email on my dad's cell phone and scroll down

my inbox. I skip updates from manga and anime forums and a message from my mom that I can't even bear to read right now because I miss her so much. There's no message from Edge, no grateful response to my warning. Either he didn't get the message yet or he's still really mad at me.

The only other new message is from Jerry at Jet City Comics.

> HEY, VIOLET. I NEED YOUR MAILING ADDRESS
> SO I CAN SEND YOUR FINAL PAYCHECK. I
> ASSUME, FROM YOUR ABRUPT DEPARTURE, YOU
> WILL NOT BE PICKING IT UP IN PERSON. I'M
> SORRY YOU QUIT. I DIDN'T SEE THAT ONE
> COMING. YOU COULD HAVE AT LEAST GIVEN
> NOTICE. I GUESS YOU HAVE YOUR REASONS.
>
> I WAS THINKING ABOUT THOSE DOODLES OF
> YOURS. NOT THAT YOU SHOULD HAVE BEEN
> DRAWING WHEN YOU'RE ON THE CLOCK. BUT
> YOUR STUFF'S PRETTY GOOD. THE SEATTLE
> ASIAN ART MUSEUM IS SPONSORING A MANGA
> ART CONTEST THIS SUMMER FOR TEENS. I'M
> ATTACHING A FLYER. I GUESS MAYBE YOU
> ALREADY KNOW ABOUT IT. BUT IN CASE YOU
> DON'T, HERE IT IS.

WELL, I GUESS THAT'S IT. SAYONARA, AS YOU
ALWAYS SAY, AND GOOD LUCK AND ALL THAT.
JERRY.

A manga art contest. That would be an amazing opportunity, if I weren't totally consumed with trying to find lost van Goghs and save my dad's life. I glance at the flyer, wondering if I could ever have enough *chikara* to finish an episode of *Kimono Girl* and enter it in the contest. Then I check the time.

Nearly an hour has gone by. Still no dad. I can't call him; I have his phone. Thinking he's been hurt or worse, I dial the Yamada office's main number. After a confusing exchange with a receptionist who can't understand a word I'm saying, someone puts my dad on the phone.

"Violet? Is that you?"

"You're still at the office!"

"I got a second wind and lost track of time. I'm on a roll, I think. How about you order some room service? I'm going to stay on a bit later."

"But I have to—"

"I'll catch you at breakfast, okay, Violet? We'll get some omelets in the hotel."

"Omelets. Awesome." I punch the END button. Here I am trying to save him from *becoming* an omelet at the hands of a greedy gang boss, and he can't even make time for a meal with me. Remind me, why am I doing all this for him? I'm so depressed, I can't stand the thought of staying in this hotel restaurant alone.

I think of my fortune from Sensō-ji Temple. *The lost article will be found.* Could that mean the painting? But when? Where? By whom? *You are soon to cross dark waters.* Yikes. That sounds like death. But maybe it's travel. Maybe I already crossed, flying over the Pacific Ocean. *Person with open heart await.* It'd be good if that person showed up soon.

"Anytime now," I say aloud.

But except for Yoshi at the hotel bar a few yards away, drinking a beer and watching a ball game, I'm totally alone. Not even my bodyguard cares to dine with me.

I check email again. Still no word from Edge. He's either so busy with camp or with Mardi that he hasn't checked his email, or he hates me so much he deleted my urgent message. Or he's beat up and lying in a ditch. Or worse.

I go back to my room, order a sushi boat from room service, and eat the whole thing while watching J-pop videos on TV. I can't understand one word of the songs. I've never felt so alone.

THE NEXT DAY, Yoshi takes a break from his bodyguard-slash-babysitting gig while I'm on the clock with the print-measuring project. Mitsue starts me off with a portfolio of *kabuki* actor prints. They're playing *samurai* warriors, facing off, brandishing swords. Their faces convey intense concentration and smoldering rage. Their taut bodies are coiled springs, poised for action.

Satisfied by my measuring skills and progress, Mitsue eventually leaves the storeroom to work on setting up the gallery show.

Alone at last, I look around the storeroom. And now I remember how in *Vampire Sleuths* 29, Kyo and Mika found somebody's will in the false bottom of a drawer in an antique cabinet. I gaze at the cabinet-lined walls. Could any of them have a secret panel concealing van Gogh's lost painting?

There are twenty cabinets in all, a mix of modern metal and antique-looking wood. They're all filled with large files and solander cases of prints, watercolors, and calligraphy scrolls. I flip through the files and then inspect the bottom of every drawer and the back of each cabinet, feeling around for false panels. This is not glamorous work. I'm no action hero. I sneeze a lot and get paper cuts. I feel as far from Kimono Girl as I can get. I figure at the rate I'm searching, I'll probably find the painting about ten years from now. And I don't have ten years. I have ten days before something really bad happens to my dad, and possibly the rest of us.

I need more information. Mitsue said van Gogh's other three Japanese paintings now hang in the Van Gogh Museum in Amsterdam. I go to their virtual gallery and check the dimensions of van Gogh's other *Japonisme* paintings. Roughly two feet wide by three feet tall. *Moon Crossing Bridge* should be of similar size if he meant it to be in the same series.

Then I measure all the cabinets, noting which could conceal a canvas that size. I'll only search those, to save time. I keep my eyes peeled for *ayu*. Maybe Tomonori cut a fish pattern into the wood of a cabinet or etched fish into the metal.

I glimpse Kenji and Hideki only once, when I leave for lunch with Yoshi. They're walking briskly through Mitsue's museum, conferring in low voices. I jog after them, hoping to ask if they've heard from the letter writer yet, if he's accepted their offer of cash. But Hideki, noticing me nearby, shoots me a dark look that makes all my courage drain away.

"Violet-chan, I am sorry," Hideki murmurs when Yoshi and I run into them again at the elevator. "I am so distracted today. I thought you were one of our office girls wanting something, and I could not be interrupted at that moment."

"That's okay." In the elevator, I'm aware of him standing behind me, and aware of how Reika would kill to be in my shoes right now, standing so close to this handsome guy. I breathe in the subtle scent of Hideki's cologne and decide that maybe it's not so weird that Hideki would mistake me—with my pale skin and frizzy hair—for a Japanese office girl.

Yoshi and I have lunch at the nearby noodle shop. I wolf down my *udon* and still have twenty minutes left of my lunch break. Yoshi's absorbed in some game on his cell phone. In my sketchbook, I start drawing Kimono Girl, but for some reason I end up sketching a dragon. One side is beautiful, shiny scales and elegant features. The other side is scarred. Studying the drawing, I realize Hideki's not so different from me. He, too, didn't know his dad well. He, too, looks for his dad in art.

I turn to a new page and sketch myself presenting Hideki with the painting. "Thank you! This means the world to me!" he says while Reika, in the background, looks on.

I slam the sketchbook closed, feeling silly for drawing such a crazy thing. "Ready?" I say to Yoshi, nodding to the door. I have to get back to work. My real work. Searching for van Gogh.

"ANYTHING?" REIKA ASKS when she calls me that evening on my dad's phone.

"Just a handful of paper cuts from portfolio edges. You?"

"I couldn't get much done. I had a big exam at Japanese school. But I did spend my breaks on the student lounge computer, looking for Tokyo businesses related to *ayu*. It's taken me a while to go through the links. I speak Japanese way better than I can read. I'm pretty slow, and I have to use a dictionary all the time. But so far I've found six restaurants, two English language schools, a massage parlor, and the Ayu Beauty Salon.

"Anyway, when I called all these places, I found out none of them even existed back in 1987. I'll keep looking. I did find out something interesting in a link to an old newspaper article, though. A short one, so I could get through it at lunch. The Yamada Corporation got contracted years ago to build a fish-processing plant. It was called—get this—*Fine Ayu Food Products.*"

"The name on the box in Kenji's office! Tomonori hid the van Gogh drawings in that box!"

"Right. The investors pulled out, and the Yamada Corporation lost the contract before construction could begin, though I guess they already had the labels for the file boxes printed. I thought it was interesting that this big contract fell through in 1987. Same year that Tomonori bought that art. Same year that he killed himself. Maybe the *ayu* drawing was a cryptic suicide note. Maybe he did something to mess up that deal, and he couldn't recover from the loss."

"You think he'd kill himself over a fish-processing plant? That is completely sad."

"It's possible," says Reika. "Japanese salarymen have a lot of pressure to support their families and save face and all that. It could have been a major blow. But I do think it's a clue to the drawings as well. Which means the *ayu* drawing has got to be a clue to the painting. I'll keep doing *ayu* Internet searches and calling businesses with that word in the name."

"We should find out where the fish plant was supposed to be built. Maybe the painting's hidden in a building on that site."

"I'll look for that, too. By the way, did you tell your dad he's in mortal danger?"

"Yep," I lie. "We've got a ton of extra security in the lobby now." I'm too embarrassed to tell her I didn't see my dad at breakfast today, either. He worked so late last night he overslept.

It's seven when I get off the phone with Reika, and I figure my dad's pulling another late night. I call the main number, and once again he apologizes and makes excuses and promises we'll have breakfast, for real. "Whatever," I sigh. I decide not to tell him about the threat hanging over his head. He already sounds like a nervous wreck and is losing sleep over this mural. Telling him he's in danger is only going to make things worse.

I scan the room service menu and order a forty-dollar hamburger. I don't know why I'm craving American foods. I'm actually getting sick of sushi and rice.

While I wait, I take out my sketchbook. A piece of paper flutters out from the back. A block of gray pencil rubbing with white letters showing through.

PICK UP SUIT!
CALL MOM

KAZOO 6:30
2535554612

It's like finding an artifact from an ancient civilization. This is the notepad rubbing I did from Julian Fleury's pad, back when I had no idea real live bad guys were after Kenji. Bad guys so creepy they would beat up Julian and cause him to quit his job. I use the note as a bookmark now, to separate my sketch notes on the case from my unfolding *Kimono Girl* story.

I read over *Kimono Girl* so far, surprised that the story and art aren't so bad. And even Jerry said my stuff was really good. Good enough to enter a contest? I'm not sure.

But if I entered the contest, I might at least finish my story. My brain clicks into gear. Within minutes, I'm drawing fresh panels and continuing KG's adventure.

WE LAST SAW Kara Mirant, in her human form, in her Belltown conservation studio.

Kimono Girl was hiding outside, watching her every move through the window. She's been observing the Cormorant's daily routines for a week now, waiting for a good chance to get into that office. She's seen enough suspicious behavior—like the Cormorant moving a wrapped canvas around from time to time while talking on the phone—that she is convinced the stolen van Gogh painting, *Sunrise Bridge*, must be inside. Today she's come to liberate it. Concealed in the folds of her kimono is a sword in a sheath. An antique *samurai* sword that she's "borrowed" from a woodblock print she slipped into at the Seattle Art Museum. A handsome warrior in the print loaned it to her and gave her some lessons on using it.

A woman enters Kara Mirant's office. She opens a portfolio with a stack of Japanese prints. When she goes outside to her car for another portfolio, a breeze stirs the prints and they scatter. Flustered, the woman gathers them up. KG seizes the opportunity. She folds the right side of her kimono over the left and jumps into the nearest print.

Concealed in the print carried in by the woman, KG enters the Cormorant's office.

The print KG hides in shows two women walking through snow, toward an orange pagoda in the woods. KG appears as a third woman, walking a few feet behind them. She strikes a pose similar to theirs. She watches. She listens. Back in the office, the Cormorant and the client discuss levels of damage and costs of repair.

After a while, KG's legs start to cramp from holding an awkward pose. She lurks there, waiting for the Cormorant to finish her meeting and for the client to leave. Then she can come out of the print and look around the studio for that painting. But the longer she waits, the more the studio seems to blur and fade, as if layers of glassine—now resembling sheets of ice—are piling up, screening her off from the real world. She panics. This is the longest time she's stayed hidden in art. What if the enchantment of the robe wears off? What if she can't get back? She grips the handsome warrior's sword, hoping its energy will give her strength.

KG summons all her strength to stay focused on the world outside the print. She fears if she blinks she will lose the connection to the outside world. Already she can hear the conversations of the two women in the print more clearly than those in the world outside. A crow caws, and it's not in the Cormorant's office. It's up in a tree in the print.

A face looms through the misty layers. The Cormorant. "Hmm. I don't remember a third woman in this print," she says to the client. "This must be quite rare. I'll have to look into it." Her gaze lingers on KG but finally passes over.

The client leaves the office.

Soon after, there is a knock at the door. In comes Sockeye, in his human form.

KG's eyes are burning from trying to keep her focus on the outside world. She can just make out the outlines of the Cormorant and Sockeye as they look at something on a drying rack across the room. She strains to hear.

"What do you mean your buyer fell through?" snarls the Cormorant. "After all the work I've done to keep this painting concealed?"

"Concealed? What do you mean? You've destroyed it!" says Sockeye.

"I have not. I painted over it in acrylics. They won't bond to the oils. And I have a special solvent that will remove them without a trace. But that solvent has to be applied within two weeks. And I don't want this thing hanging around here, with or without the over-painting. The police have already come by once to sniff around."

"I'll find you another buyer. I can swing a more lucrative deal. Just give me a little more time. I won't let you down. Look, can I buy you brunch? Tell you what I have in mind?"

"Brunch? I guess," says the Cormorant. "I'm hungry. But understand, this is *not* a date."

Thought bubble rising up from Sockeye's head: *Just give me one chance. . . .*

The two of them leave. KG crosses the left side of her kimono over the right, telling it to take her out of the art. She lands in the studio. At last she is alone, free to look around. She runs over to that drying rack to see what the Cormorant and Sockeye were arguing about.

AFTER AN HOUR, I stare out the window, trying to bring the real world back into focus. There is the orange-and-white Tokyo Tower, Japan's version of the Eiffel Tower or the Space Needle. There, thirty-five floors down, are the landscaped gardens of the hotel, the turquoise swimming pools pressed in like jewels. And there, in the corner of my room, is where my dinner is not. When I call Room Service, I get a string of apologies and a promise that it's on its way.

I leaf through my fresh pages while I wait. I've drawn landscapes and other backgrounds with more detail than usual. Characters' facial expressions are stronger and more varied, the emotions clearer. Staring at *ukiyo-e* prints for two days has affected my work. In a good way.

But what's more surprising is how many panels and pages filled up. It felt like the story was writing and drawing itself. I must have been "in the flow." Maybe that's how my dad lives 90 percent of the time, flowing down the river of his imagination, oblivious to all who shout and wave from the shores. Maybe that river's not such a bad place to be.

The door buzzes. I check the door peephole. It's Room Service Dude. I let him in.

I watch him fuss with the cart, pushing it toward the window, smoothing the white tablecloth on all sides. He's not too much older than me. And totally *kakkoii* in his blue uniform. This makes two guys I've noticed since Edge. Maybe there *are* other fish in the sea.

And maybe these room service deliveries aren't a great idea. It'd be easy enough to get a hotel uniform and wheel a cart into anyone's room, especially in a hotel like the Grand Prince.

Room Service Dude bows several times, backing out of the room and, I swear, looking all around the room as he does so. As if he's checking for something.

Gingerly, as if moving a woodblock print, I pull up a corner of the tablecloth and peer under the delivery cart tablecloth. All I find is a small stack of extra napkins, neatly folded.

I'm losing my mind. I don't know what I expected to find under there. An electronic surveillance device? Explosives? Ridiculous.

Still, I lock the door. I shove a nightstand in front of it. And an armchair.

When I'm done, my forty-dollar hamburger, a disk of gray meat atop a miniature bun, with a dollop of bloodred ketchup on the side, has completely lost its appeal.

2
1

It's my third day on the job, and Mitsue's so busy with the exhibit that I'm left alone most of the time. By afternoon, though I've made little progress on measuring, I've searched every cabinet big enough to hold a van Gogh canvas, and nothing has turned up.

Just because the pencil-rubbing trick from *Vampire Sleuths* worked in real life doesn't mean the hidden panel business is going to work, too. Mr. Fujikawa is expecting a van Gogh in eight days. I wrangled it out of Mitsue that the financial offer was declined last night. He will only accept the painting. I've wasted three days on a crazy theory.

And Reika's wasted time, too. She turned up a dead end on the fish-processing-plant venue. She went to a library and read some old newspaper articles on microfiche about the project. The plant was to be built outside of Kyoto. But after the investors pulled out, the building site sat empty for three years. In 1990, an entirely different company built a factory that packaged ramen noodles. And Fine Ayu Food Products no longer exists; that company went bankrupt in 1991 when Japan's economy began to decline. "It took me eight freaking hours to make it through that newspaper article with a dictionary and with the help of a librarian. And for nothing," Reika grumbled.

I had to agree with Reika that the painting is not likely to be in a noodle factory.

In my last hour of the workday, I return to measuring prints. I hope Mitsue won't notice how little I got done, and I hope Reika's having better luck doing Internet searches on businesses with *ayu* in their name. I look at my cell phone photo of Tomonori's *ayu* until my eyes burn.

Then, almost mechanically, I go to the oldest-looking file cabinet, which I haven't searched yet because it would be too small to conceal a painting. Its five drawers contain smaller flat files with more of the same—prints and scrolls and drawings. I look through each file carefully for anything with a fish symbol that might match Tomonori's *ayu*.

As I'm closing the bottom drawer, about to give up, I notice, toward the back of the drawer, a stack of international art auction catalogues. They're from the 1980s. The top one, from Christie's auction house, says 1987. I pick them up, and beneath is a box with a smudge on the lid. I look closer. Not a smudge. A fingerprint.

No. Not a fingerprint. A stamp.

A faint stamp, showing two *ayu* circling around in a pool. Shaking, I grab my phone and compare it to the photo. It's the same image as Tomonori's drawing!

I lift the box lid. Inside is a faded brown eight-by-eleven-inch mailing envelope. When I pick it up, something shifts inside. I turn over the envelope. There's no name or address.

The envelope is so old that the flap practically springs open in my hand. I tip the envelope toward the table. A slender leatherbound notebook slides out.

It's a sketchbook. About sixteen pages are filled with finely inked sketches, so detailed, so meticulous, they take my breath away. The rest of the pages are blank.

I see landscapes that remind me of *shin hanga* prints. Statues on pedestals. Buildings and sculptures that look more like Europe than Japan. Here and there I find notes in *kanji* characters, running vertically on the page.

The door opens as I'm turning the fourth page, and I look up with a start. Kenji is standing in the doorway, watching me with a quizzical expression. "Hi," I squeak, sliding the sketchbook under a portfolio of *kabuki* actor prints. "Mitsue's in the gallery."

"Thank you, I will look for her there," Keniji says. "How are you doing with the prints?"

"Pretty good. I'm learning a lot." I look closely at him. He's trying to appear cheerful. But like Mitsue, he looks tired and drained, with dark circles under his eyes.

"Good, good." He comes over to the table and studies the prints scattered about. "Which of these do you like best?"

"The *kabuki* actor portraits are so cool. They remind me of manga."

"Ah, yes, I couldn't agree more!"

"You read manga?"

He laughs. "Nearly every person in Japan reads some form of manga. Even frighteningly old people like myself." He pulls up a stool. "Which series do you follow?"

I list some of my favorites. To my amazement, he recognizes them. And it turns out we both love *Akira*, as well as the anime film. Then he mentions older manga artists like Rumiko Takahashi and Osamu Tezuka. I confess that I've heard of them, but I haven't read their titles.

"What?" Kenji pretends to look shocked, or maybe he really is. "Why, Tezuka is the god of manga! I will loan you the *Astro Boy* series. It is from the 1950s, but you will be astonished at how modern it feels. But you made a connection between *ukiyo-e* and manga. This interests me greatly. What is the resemblance you see?"

"I guess the way emotion is conveyed. Especially in the *kabuki* prints, you get this feeling of movement and energy. But also the simple composition mixed with elaborate details."

"You are very observant. Manga does have its roots in *ukiyo-e*. And just as manga is popular today, so was *ukiyo-e*. The prints were once inexpensive and circulated widely."

"Maybe Mitsue should put some manga in her art show.

You know, since it's all about the influences of Japanese prints."

"What an excellent idea! I will mention it to her. Just this morning she was lamenting an empty display case. A sample of manga pages juxtaposed with prints might be just the thing."

As I bask in Kenji's praise, it occurs to me we're hanging out and talking art—exactly the kind of thing I wish I could do with my dad. I wish my dad really were more like Kenji. Kenji is busy, but he seems to make time for his family. He loves art, but it doesn't take over his life.

As much as I'd like to go on talking, we're running out of time. I can't believe we're discussing *Astro Boy* when we're inches away from a possible clue. I lift up the *kabuki* portfolio and slide the book across the table to him, along with the box and the envelope. "Here. I found this."

He stares at the *ayu* on the box, then picks up the book and leafs through it. When he looks at me, his eyes are moist. "This book." His voice falters. "It belonged to my brother."

"**I**t is a sketch journal," he says softly after he's looked at all sixteen pages. "Tomonori kept these his entire life, starting when he was around seven years old. When our parents, and later his wife, did not support his passion for making art, sketching and collecting were his only artistic outlets. This must have been his last journal. I see it is not complete. And these sketches show buildings in Paris. He took only one trip to Paris, in 1987."

"The year he bought the van Goghs!"

"That is correct. I believe you have found something that could greatly aid us in recovering the lost van Gogh painting." He taps the book cover. "I also believe my brother meant me to find this. You see, when we were children, he used to draw pictures as codes for me to decipher. He was never particularly good with words. He lacked diplomacy and tact. He occasionally made impulsive or rash decisions. This held him back in business. But through his art, he could be quite thoughtful—and playful." Kenji smiles, a faraway look on his face. "He used to make little boxes filled with candies or comics or small treasures, and lead me to them with his art. I'd have to figure out clues in the pictures or understand hidden messages in a story he was telling, in order to get the treasure. He was exceedingly clever that way. His games were maddening but strangely compelling."

"So you think these pictures might have clues to where he hid the painting?"

"That is exactly what I think. And so I am going to study this sketch journal."

My heart is pounding. This journal is the biggest clue I've found yet, and it might just lead us to the painting. "Let me help you." The words fly out. "I mean, please, can I help?"

"That is a kind offer, but I'm not sure how you could help. The journal is in Japanese."

"I could still look at the pictures. I'm good at understanding pictures. And since I never knew your brother, maybe I'll see something you don't."

"Yes, I see how a fresh perspective could be useful. But your father said he doesn't want you to be involved in any way."

"I know, I know. But all I'd be doing is looking at pieces of paper. I'm not talking to anyone. There's no danger in looking at pictures. And he doesn't even have to know, right?"

Kenji considers this. "All right. This is reasonable. I will make you a photocopy of this sketchbook. But in exchange for your absolute discretion, I must ask for yours."

"What do you mean?"

"I won't tell your dad you're helping. And you must not share this copy with anyone. We would not want this to fall into the wrong hands."

"Of course."

As he turns to go copy the journal, I can't resist asking one question, to get some insight into Tomonori and why he might have hidden this art so carefully. "Kenji. Did you see the van Gogh drawings and painting before your brother hid them?"

He pauses, his hand on the doorknob. "Why, yes. I did."

"And back then, did you think the drawings and painting were really van Goghs?"

"I had doubts when I heard of this purchase. There was no clear, documented history for the painting and the drawings, they were unsigned, and he paid a relatively small sum for the collection. When I saw them for myself, however, I had a strong feeling about them. I knew I was in the presence of something extraordinary. I supported my brother's decision to put the art away for safekeeping until we could find another appraiser."

"You must have been really excited to find those drawings."

"It was like having a link to my brother. But I would trade them in an instant to have my brother back. Lives are more important than art."

That's the second time I've heard Kenji say those words. They have an ominous ring.

"LET'S DIVIDE IT in half. You do pictures, I'll do words. Then we'll switch sets."

Reika leafs through the pages Kenji copied for me at the office an hour ago. We're in a huge electronics store in the Akihabara district, huddled in a photo booth, where Yoshi can't follow us. Throbbing music from the store's stereo section masks our voices. I figure we're good for a few minutes, as long as we keep feeding coins into the machine and taking pictures.

Reika hands me a set of eight papers. "You take the first half, with Paris. The rest look like sketches from Japan. Museum exhibits and country landscapes and some drawings of a woman in a kimono. I'll look at those."

I take my set of pages and get to work, looking closely at the drawings. When the machine spits out our first set of photos, mine look like mug shots. You can see the guilt. I'm betraying Kenji, sharing this journal copy with Reika. But the journal pictures have captions and notes; I needed a translator. Reika called to say her "responsible older cousin" was meeting her boyfriend, an appliance salesman at a store in Akihabara, instead of escorting her directly home, so we could meet up in the electronics district.

"A lot of these sketches show art exhibits. Maybe Tomonori hid the painting in a museum," Reika says. "We could search all the museums in Tokyo."

"That would take forever. Plus, I think Tomonori was more creative than that. Switch?"

I pore over the sketches with renewed energy as a pulsing techno song kicks in. The most interesting images to me are two pages with about ten pictures of a beautiful, young woman wearing a floral kimono. Tomonori's wife, Fumiko, I guess. She's smiling and posing. Not some art-hating nag.

I wish I had KG's magic kimono to take me deeper into Tomonori's images. I stare at them so hard my eyes water. Nothing comes to the surface.

After thirty minutes in the photo booth, we're out of coins and ideas. We're also the owners of twenty-five strips of wallet-size photos, mostly showing the tops of our heads.

As I return to the Yamada Building, I'm thinking so deeply about the journal that I don't even hear Yoshi call out a warning. I collide with a delivery guy coming out the revolving door. We both murmur apologies. I can't help noticing he's dressed in red and yellow, and his shirt has a familiar logo on it. As he gets on a bicycle, I realize he's a courier. That red-and-yellow envelope I saw Hideki take from Kenji's office must have been delivered by this service. It must be an international courier service, because the envelope Kenji pulled out with the FBI, in Margo's gallery, looked the same.

But I'm zooming in on needless details. As my dad would say, if he were looking at the picture in my frame right now: this image does not tell a story.

The image that greets me behind my dad's screens does. I'm in some kind of trouble. My dad stands there with his arms folded, glaring. "Where have you been?"

"Akihabara. Reika needed a new phone charger. It's okay. Yoshi was there," I add quickly.

"It's almost seven."

"I didn't realize I had a curfew. Anyway, the subway took

forever." It was scary, actually, taking the Yamanote line at rush hour. Platform workers pushed us into the trains. I could barely breathe in the crush of people. I was grateful to have Yoshi by my side. He helped me find a safe place to stand and found me a hanging strap to hold on to.

"Mitsue's seeing her sister tonight, and Hideiki's on an international conference call. So Kenji's taking us to dinner," my dad says. "He wanted us to leave an hour ago."

"Guess your mind-meld failed. I didn't get the message." How nice of him to keep a dinner date for business, while he abandons his daughter to room service.

"There's no need for sarcasm. Look, here's the deal. Except for any planned excursions with the Yamadas, you are not leaving the hotel grounds for the rest of our time in Tokyo."

"What? I'm being grounded? For going to Asakusa? I didn't do anything wrong!"

"Not grounded. Confined. I simply can't concentrate on my work if I'm worrying about where you are, with those jerks on the loose. I just learned from Hideki that the sting failed."

"Yeah, I know." I suddenly feel really tired. Does he have any idea how hard it is for me to concentrate on *my* work knowing *he's* in real danger?

"You knew about the sting? And you didn't tell me?"

"I tried. Yesterday. I startled you. I made you splatter paint."

"Right." He sighs. "I suppose I didn't handle that too well. It was a long day."

I look past him. The wall is white again. "You're starting over?"

"There is just no pleasing that guy."

"Hideki?"

"Yeah. I'd rather not get into it right now."

"I can't be grounded. What about my job?"

"I'll explain the situation to Mitsue. She'll understand. I'm not having a debate. Meanwhile, I'd better tell Kenji we're ready." He pats his pockets. "Now where is that phone?"

I take his cell phone out of my knapsack and silently hand it over.

KENJI'S PRIVATE DRIVER speeds through the streets of Roppongi, a ritzy business and entertainment district in the heart of Tokyo. The sky deepens to indigo blue. Enormous signs wink on, running vertically down the building sides. They brighten the sky and wash the streets in red, blue, green, and pink. The city gleams like candy.

"This is Roppongi Hills," Kenji announces as we approach a glass complex of connected buildings and walkways, which make me think of brightly lit ice cubes linked and stacked together. "Our restaurant is inside. This complex," he goes on, "was constructed by one of my company's top competitors, Minoru Mori. Hideki is planning a multi-use complex even greater than this. Restaurants, cinemas, offices, shops, and the most modern apartments. Assuming he can raise the necessary capital, it will be his first great project for the company when he is at the helm. A symbol of the new Japan, rising above the hard times we have experienced. A symbol of strength and hope. I have to admire his youthful ambition." He chuckles. "I just want to retire and run art galleries with my wife."

My dad's been gazing out the window, probably not listening as usual. But suddenly, he says in a flat voice, "Why don't you tell us something that really matters, Kenji?"

Kenji blinks rapidly. "I beg your pardon?"

"Fujikawa's men. Who do you suppose tipped them off about the FBI sting?"

"We do not know," Kenji replies. "Did either of you mention the operation to anyone or in conversation between yourselves? Perhaps you were overhead."

"I've talked to no one," my dad snaps. "Come on. You can't pin that on us."

Kenji looks at me. "Has anyone come to your hotel room?"

"Just the regular cleaning service. Oh, and room service." Then I remember gabbing away in Harajuku, trying to impress Reika with the mystery. "I might have mentioned the sting, just a little, to Reika," I mumble. "While we were shopping in Harajuku."

Someone must have followed us and overheard. It's my fault the sting failed. I should have been more careful about how and where I told Reika about it. Now I really owe it to the Yamadas to find that painting and put an end to this mess. I can't even meet Kenji's stern gaze.

"Another question," my dad says. "Are Fujikawa's men still in Seattle?"

"Customs in the U.S. and Japan have been alerted, but we still must use extra precautions," Kenji says. "Borders do not always contain them. Shinobu Nishio has used at least three aliases in the past. Kazuo Uchida has used five."

"Wait, what were their names again?" I exclaim.

"Kazuo Uchida. Shinobu Nishio."

I unzip my backpack and find the rubbing I did from Julian's notepad. I hold it up to the streetlight coming through the car window. It doesn't say "kazoo" at all. It says *Kazuo. 6:30.*

I hand the note to Kenji. "This is a rubbing I made from Julian's notepad the night of my dad's art show. I think Agent Chang might be interested in the fact that Julian knew Kazuo Uchida. Especially considering Julian was assaulted by Kazuo and now has quit his job."

"Julian!" my dad explodes. "I never trusted that guy. I'm not surprised he's got some kind of connection to these gangsters. Jesus, do you think *he* warned them about the sting?"

"I found this note before the FBI even planned the sting operation," I point out. "Julian and Kazuo must have been talking about something else. But yeah, I also wondered about Julian tipping someone off. I wondered if Margo told him about the plan, and then he leaked it to someone."

"Agent Chang investigated this possibility, after you mentioned that Julian quit," Kenji says. "I spoke with her about it today. She says Julian could not have known about the sting in advance. He never went back to work after he left the hospital. And Margo knew nothing of the sting. She was out of the room when it was being discussed. Margo swears she's had no communication with Julian Fleury since she saw him in the hospital. But I will certainly mention this note to Agent Chang, since she has been interested in what Julian might know about this case. We need to find out what Julian and Kazuo were communicating about and if Julian has any possible connection to Fujikawa."

My dad turns to Kenji and narrows his eyes. "Why do I get the feeling you're holding back information?"

"I beg your pardon?"

"I feel like you know more about Fujikawa than you're letting on. And I want to know what the Japanese authorities are doing about him, not just the FBI."

"I appreciate your concern. But Hideki prefers to keep this as a private family matter."

"What about *my* family matter? I've brought my kid here. I need to know if she's safe."

"I'm sorry, but I cannot reveal details about the situation."

"Tell me what's really going on!" my dad demands. "If I don't get all the facts, there's no mural. No art show. I'll pack my stuff and be gone in the morning."

"May I remind you, you are contractually bound to—"

"Contracts be damned. And you can keep your money!"

I can't help smiling. My dad's showing real *chikara*, standing up for us. For me.

"Yes, of course." Kenji motions to his driver to park. "I can understand. If I had a daughter, I would feel the same. I will tell you, my nephew and I prefer to settle this matter with Fujikawa by using our private resources. Without Japanese authorities."

My dad stares at him. "Are you telling me the FBI isn't working with the CIB and the Tokyo Metropolitan Police Department and all that?"

"That is correct. Fujikawa works with many people within law enforcement in Japan, paying them for protection. Not everyone is trustworthy."

"So you'll just pay this guy off, and he'll go away? Money solves everything, huh?"

Kenji sighs. "I wish it were so simple. Fujikawa is angry

about the sting. He has put forth an ultimatum. If I cannot produce the painting by July eighteenth, he will confiscate something of value from us."

"Not something. Someone! He's going to hurt you, Dad!" I explode. I can't believe Kenji won't just say it like it is. "I heard Kenji on the phone the other day. Fujikawa is going to kill you if that painting doesn't show up in eight days!"

Kenji looks at me with an expression I cannot read. I feel his body stiffen. I'm sure he's not thrilled that I was eavesdropping, and that I've now revealed this threat to my dad.

"He's not going to touch me," my dad scoffs. "I'm nobody to him. It's an empty threat."

"You are not nobody," Kenji says in a somber voice. "You are very important to the company. And to Mitsue and me. And I apologize, Glenn, for not telling you. I had my reasons." He shoots me another look, and this time the expression is clear. Displeasure. I've crossed a boundary; I've violated his trust. "But I had every hope he would accept our offer, Glenn," Kenji goes on, "and I did not wish to cause you alarm. I can tell you I have doubled the security staff at our building and arranged for undercover protection." He gestures to a car across the street and another parked in front of us. "You see, you are never alone."

"But your offer fell through. You got a Plan B?"

"Yes, I do. I intend to find that painting. Searching for it is my full-time occupation right now. My nephew's, too. We are making inquiries based on new leads." Our eyes briefly meet in the mirror. His look is a little softer this time. I guess he remembers that I'm the one who found Tomonori's sketch journal. I feel slightly forgiven. But only slightly.

24

It's Day One of my confinement. Still rattled from last night's conversation with Kenji, I collapse into a lounge chair by the pool to wait for Reika so we can go over the sketch journal again. Yoshi is already settled in three lounge chairs down, turning the pages of a baseball magazine. A man hoses down a walkway. Another rakes a gravel path. Another prunes flowering shrubs. It'd be almost peaceful here in the hotel gardens, except I trust none of these groundskeepers. I can't shake the feeling that the informant about the sting operation is someone in Japan, someone close to us.

An out-of-breath Reika flops in the lounge chair beside me. "Sorry I'm late. I had to ditch the 'responsible older cousin.' She's seeing her boyfriend. I'm free for six hours."

"Thank you for spending your furlough at the lovely Grand Prince Prison."

"There's nowhere I'd rather be. Any news before we get started on the pages?"

I quickly tell her about our ride with Kenji last night. "I'm sure it's my fault the sting failed," I conclude with a sigh. "I should have been more careful. The informant has to be in Japan because almost no one in Seattle knew about the sting—just the Yamadas, the FBI agents, my dad, and me. Somebody here in Japan overheard us. We were being followed."

Reika brushes away a tear. "It's not your fault. It's mine. I blurted out that stupid comment about the sting at the subway station, when I left you. This really cute guy was passing by, and I just wanted to get his attention. So maybe someone following us overheard me say that. I'm really sorry, Violet. Lots of people in Tokyo understand English, even if they don't speak it perfectly. I don't know what I was thinking."

"That's okay." I sigh. Reika is so smart, but I can't stand it when she does dumb things just to get some guy's attention and totally loses her focus. "Let's just take a look at this journal. We don't have much time."

Reika sniffs and nods. "Okay."

I look at my set of pages until my eyes hurt. The more I study them, the more straightforward they seem. Reika's translations of the captions and notes by each sketch make them seem even more ordinary, despite their beauty. And there's no story. They're just sketches of random things Tomonori saw and liked in his travels around Europe and Japan.

I take the twenty-five photo-booth strips and look at those to rest my eyes. There are a couple of silly shots where we're making goofy faces and peace signs with our fingers. But most are serious ones of us studying papers.

But looking at the sketch journal pages that are visible in some of the photos, I see how truly detailed Tomonori's drawings are. Way more detailed than any roughs I produce in my sketchbook. Otherwise they wouldn't show up so sharply in the photo strip—a photo from a photocopy, doubly removed from the original source. And the sketches Tomonori did of the woman must have taken a ton of time. Now that I've been laboring over backgrounds and other details in *Kimono Girl*, I can appreciate this. The kimono in his sketches shows a dragon, clouds, and flowers. The sculptures he sketched show filigree. The framed paintings he copied show the cracks in the wood. You don't just dash off drawings like that. It would take me two days to even attempt one of these pictures with my best fine-point pens.

I turn the photo strips sideways and upside down. Then I see a strange shape emerge in the base of a sculpture pedestal in one of the drawings. A black bird with a long, curved neck.

I snatch up my photocopied journal pages and rifle through them. When I find the corresponding page, I turn it upside down. Again, I see a black bird, its wings spreading out. It reminds me of the tattoo on Skye's shoulder. A cormorant, drawn to blend in with the pedestal.

I grab another journal page and turn it upside down. Now that my eye is trained, I'm quick to spot another cormorant within the frame of a still life. It wears a collar around its neck, and a dangling leash. In the corners of the frames are tiny *ayus*.

On the next page, I find another embedded sketch. This one shows a long boat embedded in a drawing of a stringed instrument called a *koto*. The boat has a basket attached to the front and something on fire. Could Tomonori have burned the painting?

I get faster at spotting these tiny hidden drawings, discovering at least one on each page.

In the folds of a Greek statue's skirt, I spot men on a boat, one wearing a strange grass skirt and a headband, another one casting a bunch of lines or strings into the water. In a sketch of a bowl of fruit, I find a drawing of a long, canoe-like boat with hanging lanterns on it; the lanterns blend in with grapes hanging over the lip of the bowl.

The last spread in the journal contains six sketches of a beautiful young woman in a kimono. The details are more on her robe than her face, though. And embedded in her kimono I find very small sketches that seem to tell a story. I number the pictures in a sequence that makes sense. It feels like trying to follow untranslated manga, using only pictures to guide me.

My heart beats faster as a possible story comes together. A man puts a painting on an easel. He puts another painting over it. He wraps up a canvas with the two paintings. Carrying a wide, flat object, he boards a train. Then a long boat. Or he takes the boat before the train—I can't decide which would come first. And embedded in the final kimono, still carrying the painting behind a painting, the man walks down a flower-lined path, approaching the door of what looks like an old house. A house like something in a folktale, with low hanging eaves and curved shingles. In one hand, he carries that flat package, and in the other, he holds what looks like a long walking staff or a stick.

"Reika. Check this out."

Reika snatches the pages from my hands, exclaiming over each picture I've circled in the kimono drawings and elsewhere.

"What's up with all these cormorants?" I ask her.

"*Ukai?*"

"Yeah, I'm okay. Why do you ask?"

"No, *ukai*. Cormorant fishing. It's an ancient sport. Though now it's really more of a tourist attraction on some of the rivers in Japan."

"Where? Here in Tokyo?"

"In Gifu, and in Nagoya. Oh, and just outside Kyoto, I think. In Arashiyama."

I almost drop my pages. I stare at her. "Hello? The Hiroshige print is called *Moon Crossing Bridge at Arashiyama.*

When we were talking about Tomonori's *ayu*, why didn't we think about cormorant fishing? Cormorants and *ayu* go hand in hand. Or, uh, wing in fin."

Reika groans. "I guess we were too focused on the small things to see the bigger picture."

I'm also kicking myself for not having shared *Kimono Girl* with Reika. Ever. If I'd shown her my story so far, or even talked about it, she might have seen my sketches of cormorants and made that connection sooner.

"Maybe the painting is hidden in Arashiyama," Reika suggests. "Maybe it's in a boat!"

"I don't think that would be good for the painting," I say, thinking of water damage, humidity, and other problems. I've learned a lot about art conservation in just a few days working with Mitsue, and I've seen how art can be ravaged by the elements and by time. "I think Tomonori would have found a safer place for it. Like in this building we see the man standing by here, whatever it is. But I agree, that painting must be in Arashiyama."

"Wait. I see something else." Reika points to a cluster of lines and crosses near one of the embedded bird drawings. "This is the *kanji* character for *akatsuki*. Meaning 'dawn.'" She turns the page and circles an identical mark. "Here's another! And another! He's written 'dawn' on almost every page. If this is a kind of treasure map, this word is like 'X marks the spot.'"

"We have to show this to Kenji right away. Maybe the building the man walks into has something to do with *dawn*. Maybe Kenji will know what that means."

Suddenly, a breeze blows a section of newspaper over to my chair. Bending to pick it up, I notice Yoshi is no longer in his lounge chair. His newspaper's been abandoned.

I spot him a few yards away, talking with a blond couple wearing fanny packs and Mariners caps.

"I could be wrong, but those tourists don't strike me as Japanese speakers," I say to Reika. "Come on. I want to hear this." We sneak behind a shrub and listen.

"Yes, I saw Ichiro play for Yomiuri Giants, three years ago, before Mariners bought him," Yoshi says in perfectly clear English. He swings an imaginary bat. "He is quite an excellent hitter. Do you know his batting average?"

Reika and I, wide-eyed, look at each other. We've just found our leak.

PART 3 KYOTO

**2
5**

Bells chime a tinny melody as the doors to the bullet train close. Moments later, the train shoots out of Tokyo station. Our first-class car glows orange from the rising sun. The *shinkansen* is nothing like the Amtrak from Seattle to Portland. After the gentle announcements of stations, in Japanese and English, it's almost completely silent. The train sways slightly; it never shudders or lurches. The ticket-taker bows and murmurs a soft greeting when he comes into our car. He bows again when he leaves. The sandwich-cart lady does the same thing.

The three Yamadas sit at the opposite end of the train car from my dad and me. They are studying the journal clues Reika and I showed them and a map of Arashiyama. Anyone might think they were ordinary travelers. But I know they're refining their search strategy.

My dad reclines the seat in front of me and snaps on a sleep mask from the hotel. "I'm going to catch up on some z's. Wake me when we get to Kyoto."

I glare at his seat back. How can he sleep now, of all times? Kazuo Uchida and Shinobu Nishio, reported masters of disguise, may be back in Japan already. Their boss, Hiroshi Fujikawa, lurks somewhere in this country, ready to take off with the Yamadas' favorite artist—my dad—if they don't deliver the van Gogh painting one week from today. I'm sure Yoshi's furious that Reika and I reported him as an informant and got him fired. What if he comes after us, too?

As the train glides into Shinagawa Station, where Reika is supposed to meet us, I scan the platform for her, my heart pounding. The platform's not so crowded this early, heading out of the city, but I don't see her anywhere. What if her aunt and uncle changed their minds about letting her travel with us? Or worse . . . what if Yoshi did something to her?

YESTERDAY, REIKA AND I figured out pretty quickly that Yoshi's "Engrish" was just fine. He had been listening to us all along and almost certainly tipped off Fujikawa about the sting operation, just in time for Fujikawa to get his men out of the way. When we figured this out, we ran to the nearest ladies' room in the hotel lobby and called Kenji on Reika's phone. Within a half hour, both Kenji and Hideki appeared in the hotel lobby and quietly sent Yoshi packing. How creepy, to think a trusted security official had really been a *yakuza* informant, that he'd been listening to my every word. Even creepier: now we were walking around with no bodyguards, since Kenji didn't trust any of his security staff anymore and let everyone go.

But mostly I felt sad. As Yoshi left the hotel lobby, our eyes met briefly. His face hardened. He hadn't been a friend. All those gallant gestures? They were just part of his act.

When Reika and I showed Kenji and Hideki the embedded drawings, Kenji's mouth dropped open. "I have spent hours poring over these drawings. They are the most subtle clues that Tomonori ever planted. And the *kanji* for *akatsuki*—I don't even know how you picked those fine lines out of these crosshatch marks. Oh, to have young eyes again!"

Hideki, too, said we'd done well. He just couldn't stop smiling, looking handsomer than ever. I thought he might even cry as he ran his hand over the journal pages. I just felt glowing, bursting with pride as he showered me with compliments. And I remembered the magical feeling of seeing my dad's murals back at his house in Fremont. It felt like I was glimpsing who he really was in private: a sensitive dreamer with inspired visions, despite his poorly primed walls. I wondered if Hideki felt something like that, if he could sense Tomonori in his personal art.

Then Hideki asked us if there was any chance that Yoshi had heard us discussing the clues or seen the pages.

"Oh, I'm sure he didn't," Reika said, sidling up to Hideki and edging me out of the way. "I remember when we were talking about cormorant fishing, I looked up and noticed him talking to that couple. He wasn't listening to us then."

Hideki seemed satisfied with her answer and then arranged a meeting. We all went back to the Yamada Building and into a private conference room, with my dad and Mitsue, too.

Hideki sat at the head and explained the plan. "My uncle, my aunt, and I will travel to Arashiyama for a few days. We know of a historic *ryokan* there, called the Akatsuki Ryokan. Mitsue has traveled there before, with her family."

"A *ryokan* is a traditional Japanese inn," Mitsue quickly explained to my dad and me.

"The Akatsuki Ryokan is completely inaccessible by roads or public transportation," Hideki continued. "It makes sense that my father would have hidden the van Gogh there, perhaps behind another painting as his pictures suggest."

"Hang on. You can't just leave us here," my dad protested. "Waiting around for gangsters to demand why you guys skipped town? No way. Violet and I are coming with you."

"Me too!" Reika piped up, shifting closer to Hideki and beaming at him.

Hideki leaned away from Reika. "I hardly think it's necessary to interrupt Glenn from his work on the mural," he said, twirling a pen in his fingers.

"The mural!" Kenji exclaimed. He turned to his nephew, eyes flashing. "The mural can wait a few days. Glenn is right. Everyone would be safer at this lodge. We will remain together. We will all look for the painting." He gave his nephew a long look. "I think you forget I am your uncle. I am still your senior. And I am still head of this company for two more months. I have let you make many decisions, but this decision is mine."

"Violet's friend must come with us, too," Mitsue added quickly. "Since she was involved in reporting Yoshi as an informant. We are safer in a group, in a secluded location."

Kenji outlined a plan while Hideki, his face clouded over from his uncle's rebuke, continued to twirl his pen. We'd have to leave first thing in the morning by train, traveling like regular tourists, to blend in and avoid being followed. We'd have to look for the painting discreetly; if we attracted attention from other guests, we might spark a scavenger hunt for the van Gogh, maybe even a media frenzy, and the painting could slip from our hands. Our cover? The Yamadas would be showing their foreign guests a relaxing time at a traditional Japanese inn. We'd inspect the property during times when the *ryokan* was quiet, and otherwise try to pass as regular tourists. My dad could paint. Reika and I could relax at the *onsen*, the spa and hot springs.

It all sounded like a pretty good time, if it weren't for the fact that a gang boss was breathing down our necks, threatening my dad's life for this painting.

But now there's still no sign of Reika at Shinagawa Station. A series of soft bells in the train car sounds huge alarms in me. This train is going to take off any second.

Without her! Yoshi's on the loose. Reika has no bodyguards or security at her aunt and uncle's house. What if he figured out where Reika lived, and kidnapped her as revenge for turning him in?

Suddenly, I see her running to the train, a Hello Kitty suitcase in tow. I bang on the window. Passengers stare. The old ladies sitting behind me frown. "Reika! Hurry!" I shout.

Seeing me, Reika picks up speed toward my car, her long, dark brown hair streaming behind her. As a conductor on the platform barks at her in Japanese, she sprints the final few yards and leaps into the train, two seconds before a melodic chime sounds and the automatic doors swiftly close.

The train glides out of the station.

Panting, Reika makes her way to my seat and shoves her suitcase in the overhead.

"I'm in shock," I say when she sits. "I thought your aunt and uncle changed their mind." I'm embarrassed to admit how worried I was that something far worse happened to her, and how scared I was that she was going to get stuck in the train doors.

"They're why I'm late." From her backpack, she takes out three paper bags filled with froths of tissue paper. "The Yamada name carries a lot of weight, and they weighed me down with all these gifts for them. They're probably on the phone at this very moment, calling up all the relatives, telling them what a lucky niece they have to travel with these executives. Look at all the *omiyage* they packed. Stationary. Sake cups. A chopstick set—like the Yamadas don't have a million of these things already. I could just die. Oh wait, what's this?" From a gift basket, she extracts a box of colorfully wrapped pastries. "Cool. *Wagashi!*"

"Looks like breakfast to me! The sandwich I had was so tiny. Can we eat this?"

"Of course! This is an insane amount of food." Reika's aunt and uncle have packed up the most generous basket of dazzling, sugary confections, shaped like flowers and animals. There are tiny cakes galore—pink, green, and white, covered with a delicate film of powdered sugar. My favorite are the small sponge cakes shaped like *ayu*, filled with a red bean paste.

As we eat, I gaze out at the industrial outskirts of Tokyo, which soon gives way to countryside. We pass lush, green rice paddies and little houses with shiny blue shingles. Fields of tea. Farmers and field workers wearing pointed hats. It's like traveling through a *ukiyo-e* print.

It's almost perfect. Except Reika's not the only one I was worried about.

"Hey, can I see your phone for a sec?"

Reika hands over her red, rhinestone-studded phone case. "Let me guess. Email? Edge?"

"I'm really worried. I still haven't heard back from him. What if something happened?"

I pull up my email. And there it is. One new message. From Edge.

> VIOLET! I'VE BEEN WANTING TO WRITE.
> THANKS FOR THE WARNING ABOUT THE YAKUZA.
> I HAVEN'T SEEN ANYONE SUSPICIOUS, BUT
> MOST DAYS I'M LOCKED UP IN THE STUDIO,
> EDITING. IT'S NOSE TO THE GRINDSTONE
> HERE, WORKSHOPS MORNING TILL NIGHT.
> ANYWAY, I'LL BE CAREFUL. THANKS FOR
> YOUR CONCERN.
>
> ACTUALLY, I'M WORRIED ABOUT YOU. PLEASE
> BE EXTRA CAREFUL OVER THERE. STAY IN
> TOUCH, OKAY? YOUR PAL, EDGE.

Your pal. Was that simply to say we made up, we're friends again? Or did he mean "Your pal, and not your anything else, not ever, don't even think about it"? And why didn't he say a thing about the fight we had? He's acting like it never happened. Like we didn't hurt each other's feelings. That's not right. That's a sloppy coat of primer. We can't repair our friendship or do anything else unless we acknowledge this fight. But I'm not brave enough to do it, either.

"Everything okay?" Reika asks.

I shrug and pass back the phone. "He's alive."

Reika unwraps a package of squid chips. "I wish you two would just get together. The two of you are like in episode seventy-eight of a manga series with no climax."

"What are you talking about?"

"It's so obvious you're into him. And vice versa."

"How do you know?"

"You guys just have this crazy vibe," she says through a mouthful of squid chips. "You're always laughing together and talking about creative stuff. Coming up with little stories."

I shake my head. "You're wrong. He's into Mardi Cooper."

"And? Did something happen between them?" Reika looks at me expectantly. When I don't answer—it's still too painful—she puts a hand on my arm. "Hey. You're supposed to be able to tell your friends about boy troubles, right? I know a few things about guys. Maybe I can help. And if I can't help, at least I can listen."

I take a deep breath. And I tell her what happened between us before I left Seattle. It feels good to tell someone about our fight and how I feel about Mardi and him. It's like I've been carrying around that ugly rock for so long. Finally, I can set it down. I can rest.

Reika licks salt off her fingers. "This is a textbook case. Here's the deal. Edge answered the siren's song because he got frustrated trying to figure you out. Mardi made herself available, and he went for it. Typical guy stuff. But his heart's not in it. It's you he likes."

"What do you mean, he got frustrated trying to figure me out?"

"Trying to read your signals. Or lack thereof. Maybe he couldn't find a door to your heart. You're been playing it too cool. He thought you weren't interested."

"But I was interested. I just didn't want to scare him off or wreck the friendship."

"Violet." Reika smiles. "If you don't even try to tell Edge how you feel, you'll never know if he feels the same way. You'll just spend the rest of your lives circling each other. Missing each other. You'll die alone."

"It's too late to tell him anything. Mardi's already got her claws in him."

"She doesn't have superpowers. He's not going to change for her. Believe me, as soon as this business with the painting is over, this is your next mission. Operation 'Get Edge Back.'"

"Yeah. Sure. Can we change the subject now? It's starting to depress me."

"Oh, guys can depress the hell out of you. Believe me, I know. Squid chip?" She reads from the package. "'It's plentiful tasty will deright and surprise.'" She shakes the bag at me.

"Thanks." I take a few chips. "Mm. Plentiful tastiness."

"So tell me about this supersecret graphic novel you've been working on."

"Uh, it's kind of a fantasy plus mystery." I stammer through the basic premise, but she doesn't shoot it down. She smiles encouragingly. The next thing I know, she's convinced me to let her see my sketchbook. I cringe as she turns page after page and doesn't say anything.

"It's so good!" she exclaims, beaming when she reaches the end of my story so far. "I'd totally buy this in a store! Here's my favorite scene." She flips to the page where KG hides in the woodblock print.

"Really? You think that works? I wasn't sure. . . ."

We lose ourselves in my fictional dangers for the next hundred miles or so, brainstorming ideas for how KG can bring the Cormorant down and recover the *Sunrise Bridge* painting. New characters and scenarios take shape. I start to see how *Kimono Girl* could be good. Like, contest-entry good. I think of that flyer Jerry sent me. Maybe after this whole van Gogh business is over, my next mission can be entering that teen manga contest.

WHEN REIKA EVENTUALLY nods off, I open my sketchbook. Before I know it, my pen is flying across the paper, sketching the next scene in *Kimono Girl*.

Kimono Girl emerges from the woodblock print she's hiding in and lands in the Cormorant's office. She inspects the painting on the drying rack. It's a still life, a fruit bowl and flower vase painted in acrylics. "I've got to go in," she mutters, crossing her kimono right over left. She flies into the canvas.

"Something's wrong!" she cries out. The fruit doesn't hold together well. It's sticky. It smells. Whenever she enters a work of art she feels a falling sensation until she gains some footing in the composition, gets her bearings again. But with this one, she keeps falling, in a sticky swirl of colors. She's drowning. She can't grab on to anything to anchor herself. Grapes pop. A banana squishes. She grabs a flower stem but it snaps apart. She falls farther.

And then lands. Hard. She blinks and opens her eyes. She's on a bridge, and a river runs beneath it. The colors are so bright they almost hurt. Sunrise pinks and oranges streak the sky, so thick it seems like she could reach up and climb the clouds.

She brushes her hand over the railing of the bridge and looks down into the water. The water is teal, choppy, moving fast. And she suddenly knows where she is. Only van Gogh uses such thick paint, such swirls in the sky and water. And the light. It's incredible. An eternal sunset that almost hurts her eyes. She's standing in the stolen painting *Sunrise Bridge*. In the ultimate cover-up: a painting over a painting.

I STARE AT what I've just drawn in the final panel. I think about Tomonori's sketches. A man—probably Tomonori himself—put a painting behind a painting, on an easel. I'd assumed that meant he slipped the painting behind another frame.

In the back of my sketchbook are the photo-booth strips from Asakusa, the pictures of Reika and me studying the journal pages. I didn't notice when we took the photo strips out of the machine, but now I see one picture has a nice clear shot of the page with the woman in a kimono. I zoom in on that and look hard at the last embedded kimono drawing. It's the one of a man, probably Tomonori, approaching the door of a building, carrying a flat package and a long stick. I notice a detail on top of the stick that I hadn't seen before. The stick is really a giant paintbrush. I shiver. Maybe Tomonori painted directly over the canvas to hide it!

I wonder how it would it feel to paint over a van Gogh. I'm not sure I could even put my fingers on a van Gogh canvas, let alone a paintbrush. Could Tomonori? Was he that desperate to get the canvas out of sight?

I think about this possibility until chimes ring and Kyoto Station is announced. I see we're on the outskirts of Kyoto, gray buildings looming ahead. I chug some Pocari Sweat from my backpack and notice my Sensō-ji fortune in my backpack pocket as I'm replacing the bottle.

I unfold the fortune, thinking I'll read it again for good luck.

I drop it like it's on fire. This is not the fortune I saved.

It's a paper cut to the same size and folded the same way. But on this one, there's just one sentence, handwritten in block letters.

IN JAPAN, WE HAVE SAYING. "NAIL THAT
STANDS UP GETS POUNDED DOWN." I STRONGLY
URGE YOU FOLLOW ANY RULES GIVEN. DO NOT
BE NAIL STANDING UP.

Arashiyama is only forty-five minutes from Kyoto by local train. But it feels remote and sleepy, steeped in humidity. It's a different humidity than in Tokyo. There's a freshness in the air, and a scent of grass and water, that makes me think of the dark green *matcha* we once drank at Kenji and Mitsue's house. The town itself is surrounded by lush, tree-covered hills—the same hills Hiroshige and van Gogh put in their art. Shop owners take their time unlocking doors, washing down walkways. Couples go out for morning strolls. Men in pointed hats pull rickshaws. I can smell breakfasts cooking: salty, pungent smells of rice and miso, seaweed and salty plums and pickles, staples of the savory Japanese breakfast. Nobody's in a hurry. Nobody but us.

Hideki leads us at a brisk pace down to the Katsura-gawa, a wide, green river that seems as unhurried as the town. At a boat launch, an old man hobbles over to us, and Kenji speaks to him in Japanese.

"That's going to hold all of us and our stuff?" I ask, eyeing a long, wooden boat with a canopy. It looks just like one of Tomonori's embedded pictures. I'm sure it's a part of his story.

"The *ryokan* sends this private boat for guests," Mitsue assures us. "They are accustomed to carrying luggage."

The floor is lined with *tatami* mats. We all remove our shoes, just like we would inside a Japanese home, and sit along the sides. Then our unlikely captain propels the boat with a long pole and surprising strength.

On the boat, while the adults talk or gaze at the scenery, I finally have a chance to show Reika that creepy note. I pass it to her. "Did you write this as a joke? On the train?"

"No!"

"Someone took out my Sensō-ji Temple fortune and replaced it with this."

"I bet it was Yoshi. Probably just after he got fired. Ugh. Throw it out."

I wad it up to the size of a pea and drop it into the water. Noticing this, the captain glares. Whoops, I forgot how much littering is frowned on here.

As we glide down the Katsura-gawa, I notice a long, wooden bridge before us. Its gentle arc looks familiar. "Is that the real Moon Crossing Bridge?" I ask Kenji.

Kenji nods almost curtly, his mind apparently far away.

"Yes. In Japanese, the name is Togetsukyō Bridge," Mitsue replies. "It is—"

Hideki interrupts her in Japanese.

Mitsue looks startled, then nods. "Hideki would like me to explain to the three of you how a *ryokan* works. There are a few procedures and rules to be aware of."

I look at him, his legs stretched out, his arm slung over the side of the boat. His posture is relaxed, but he looks upriver as if his burning gaze could power the boat faster. I can imagine how keyed up he must feel as he approaches a place his dad once visited, a place where his dad might have stashed an incredibly valuable painting.

"When we arrive, we will be greeted by the *okami-san*, the manager of the inn," Mitsue explains. "She will show us to our rooms and give us *yukata* to wear. Special summer kimonos."

"Men, too?" my dad asks.

"Oh, yes," says Mitsue. "It is traditional for both men and women to wear *yukata* on the grounds, to promote relaxation. And before dinner, it is customary to visit the *onsen*—the spa and hot springs—and bathe. You will also wear your *yukata* to dinner."

Reika and I glance at each other, smirking. I can't help smiling at the thought of my scruffy dad wearing some flowery robe.

"Most important, Hideki says you must remain on the inn property at all times," Mitsue adds. "We can't risk anyone following you and finding us at the *ryokan*. We cannot attract attention from other guests. You must look like you are happy tourists and not publicly discuss our true purpose in coming here."

"I'm a good actress. I can play happy tourist," Reika says, twirling a lock of hair and smiling at Hideki. But Hideki is still staring upriver, his face composed except for a vein pulsing at his temple and a twitch in his jaw as if he is grinding his teeth.

After a bend in the river, our geriatric captain pulls up to a small dock. We all get out, collect our bags, and walk a long gravel path through an elegant, landscaped garden. Blue and violet hydrangeas bloom everywhere.

My dad eyes them hungrily. "I can't wait to paint here," he says. "Mitsue told me that this inn has attracted many artists to it over the years. I can see why."

"Aren't you worried?" I ask.

"Worried?"

"This isn't a vacation. If the Yamadas can't find the painting, your life's in danger!"

"But this is a painter's dream."

"You mean you're really not freaked out by all this?"

"No." He shrugs and smiles wryly. "I feel like this is the real Japan. The one I wanted to see. I feel like for the first time since we've gotten here, I can really relax. Isn't that strange?"

"I guess." I must be doing the freaking out for him. Especially since I got that replacement fortune. It's beautiful here, but we haven't found the painting yet, and I'm still looking over my shoulder for Yoshi, for those *yakuza* from Seattle, for anyone suspicious.

We arrive at the main entrance to the inn. The *ryokan* is a sprawling, wooden building, old but in good repair, with heavy, dark beams and curved shingles on the roof. It's dark inside. The door looks similar to the one from Tomonori's picture.

Kenji goes to the door and calls out something in Japanese. A woman's voice calls back.

Then a woman comes to the door. Her face is etched with fine lines, her black hair streaked with silver threads, but there's something beautiful about her. She wears a type of kimono I haven't seen before: deep blue, with a transparent outer layer. With mincing steps, she comes out to a wooden porch, bows, and says something in Japanese. Her words sound warm, but her face is stone.

"The *okami-san* is greeting us," Mitsue explains.

The *okami-san* studies Kenji and Hideki. Her face, while still beautiful, looks hardened and suspicious. Slowly, she bows, bending from the waist. She says something in Japanese to all of us, and Reika jabs me in the arm.

"Ow! What?" I rub my arm.

"She just welcomed us to the inn," she whispers as we bend down to exchange our shoes for rubber slippers on a rack.

"Are you sure? She doesn't look very welcoming."

The stone-faced *okami-san* leads Reika and me down a long corridor. She shows us the room we will share. As soon as she leaves, I start sneezing, probably from the dust or the grassy smell of the *tatami* mats that line the floor. Mitsue said the place is supposed to be over a hundred years old. It sure smells like it.

My dad knocks on the door a few minutes later. "I'm just across the hall," he says. "They only had three rooms left— it's all booked for something called the Gion Festival that's going on in Kyoto this week. So I'm rooming with my man Hideki."

"Is he stressing you out?"

"Oh, it's not so bad. I thought he'd be on my case about the mural, but he's already busy. Off with Kenji, talking to the *okami-san*."

"Can we start looking for the painting?" I ask. "I saw a bunch of art in the lobby."

"Not yet," my dad says. "Kenji said to hold off for now. There are too many guests around. There's some kind of business retreat going on here, and the place is full of office types. Kenji says we need to lay low while they have the *okami-san* check the inn's records of art acquisitions. Apparently, a number of grateful guests have given art to the inn over the years, and inn has lots of art in storage, too. If they can't find a record of a gift from Tomonori in 1987, as soon as the guests clear out of the halls, we'll all start looking at the paintings to see if Tomonori hid the van Gogh behind one."

"*Yukata!*" Reika sings out after my dad leaves. She holds

out a box of two cotton robes. They're both deep indigo and white with a pretty bamboo pattern.

Changing into a *yukata* makes me think of Kimono Girl, as well as the young woman in Tomonori's sketches, with those detailed embedded sketches in her robe. I want to start looking for the painting right now. We could be sitting on top of a van Gogh painting! But the room doesn't exactly look full of hiding places. There's no art except a hanging scroll with calligraphy in one corner. And there's hardly any furniture at all—only a low table with two square, red pillows on either side of it, placed on the *tatami*. Reika tells me chambermaids will unroll our futons after dinner.

I go out to a small screened-in porch overlooking the Katsura-gawa and sink into a wicker chair. It's raining steadily now. I watch the drops pelt the river. It's a different rain from Seattle rain. Quieter, softer, like an unseen hand is scattering uncooked rice. It would be downright relaxing if we were actually here as tourists.

Reika joins me, a stack of manga in hand. She sits down and sighs, flipping through the latest issue of *Naruto* without really looking at it. "I don't think he's into me."

"Who?"

"Hideki. Have you noticed he barely looks at me now?"

"He has a lot on his mind. He's about to find out where his dad put this art. Plus, he's, like, twice your age! Of course he's not interested in you!"

"And he's moody, isn't he?" Reika goes on, ignoring my last comment. "Mitsue mentioned he's thirty-two and already divorced. No kids or anything. Sad, isn't it? I bet he's lonely. All this family drama with the art heist, and no one to comfort him."

"What's that?" I point to a brochure sticking out of a copy of *Naruto*.

"Oh, I snagged it at the reception desk." She hands me a brochure for the inn. "It has a floor map. Check it out. This place is pretty big. Two stories, and an east and west wing on either side of the lobby. That's eight corridors in each wing, and they all look to be full of artwork. And then there's the *onsen*, behind the guest rooms."

I study the map. "Great. We can note the location of anything suspicious. Then we can tell Kenji and Hideki where to go for a closer look."

"What exactly are we looking for, anyway? A painting that's sticking out in some way?"

"Maybe. If it's attached to another painting or hidden behind another frame. But I have a new idea about how it might be concealed." I show Reika the photo of Tomonori's sketch journal from our day at the photo booth, pointing out the man carrying a package and a stick. "Look closely. It's not a walking staff. It's a big paintbrush. It's out of sequence, but maybe he drew the brush here to suggest what was really going on with the painting cover-up in the earlier picture.

Maybe Tomonori painted right over the van Gogh."

"Wouldn't that wreck the original painting?"

"Not necessarily. My art teacher once showed us how some paints, like acrylics, dissolve with certain solvents. We tried removing a layer of paint in class, and it worked pretty well."

"But how would you know something was painted over? Don't you need some kind of fancy camera to detect that?"

"Yeah, infrared. But to the naked eye, the paint might look different. Heavier. Or you might see some original color bleed through."

"It's a plan, then. We'll look at all the art on the walls for anything suspicious."

"And keep our eyes peeled for any signs from Tomonori, like cormorants."

"And *ayu*."

We search for the painting in fits and starts because of that business retreat. The businessmen go from their rooms to a meeting room to lunch. We watch from cracked-open doors. When the halls clear, we all dart out and inspect the art. We run our fingers all around the frames, looking for signs of tampering. We lift paintings off the hooks to look behind them. We look at the walls in case plaster might have been cut away to create a hiding place for a painting. Reika and I look closely at the canvases for especially thick paint or any visual clues. We don't find anything suspicious, and there's so much art on the walls, our progress is slow.

At five, Mitsue tells us it's time go to the *onsen* and bathe before dinner. "We must keep up appearances," she reminds us when Reika and I protest.

The *onsen* is in a separate section of the inn, behind the two guest wings, connected to the lobby by a long, narrow corridor with squeaky floorboards. The hall smells like mineral water tinged with soap. These walls are strangely bare, except for one dark painting hanging near the door. It shows a river scene at night. My eyes linger on it. But Mitsue is ushering us through the door to the spa so I don't have time to inspect it. I make a mental note to return.

In a communal changing room, naked women are hanging up their clothes, brushing their hair, shaking out towels. The big wooden bathtub is communal, too. Five women are already soaking in it, steam swirling up around them.

Mitsue shows us wooden lockers where we can leave our house slippers and hang our *yukata*. She points out a wall lined with stools, buckets, and shower nozzles, for shampooing and rinsing off before going into the bath. She reads us a list of rules posted on the changing-room wall. "Do not go into the bath without rinsing. Do not bring the washcloth into the water. Do not wear toilet slippers into the changing area or the bathing area." I'm feeling more and more boxed in. I thought I'd find freedom in Japan, but there are so many rules. That creepy fortune was right. Wherever I go, I'm the nail sticking up.

"No way am I walking around naked in front of all these people," I mutter to Reika.

"It's no big deal. This is a traditional Japanese bath. Come on, this will be relaxing."

"Relaxing! Uh, hello, we're not really here to relax, are we?"

"Hideki told us act like tourists to keep their cover, right? We're actually helping."

With a sigh, I untie the canvas belt and peel off the *yukata*, one sleeve at a time. I feel enormous, exposed, sitting on the tiny bucket and soaping off with a shower nozzle.

As I walk toward the bath, I'm grateful for the thick mist in the air. It acts like glassine over a print, creating a screen, concealing bodies.

Mitsue and Reika are already up to their necks in the bath. "This is so much better than the public *sento* my aunt and uncle take me to," Reika says. "It's a natural hot spring."

I sit on the edge of the tub and dunk both feet in the water. It's unbearably hot. And something just feels so wrong about this. My dad's safety—his life—is at stake. We should be spending every moment looking for the painting that could keep us all safe.

I kick at the water, staring at my reddened feet. Kimono Girl wouldn't chill out in a spa when there was a mystery to solve. You don't see Superman stopping off for a haircut or a massage before flying to the toppling building.

I stand up and run to my locker, past the "no running" sign. I yank on my *yukata* and flee out of the *onsen* and into the west wing of the inn.

I find myself in a corridor similar to the one we're staying in, on the east side, and lined with woodblock prints. I doubt they're concealing a van Gogh. Even though they're framed, they're probably not big enough to disguise a painting behind them, and a print couldn't cover up a painting. Still, I walk the length of the hall, hoping I'll see something important.

At the end, a *shin hanga* woodblock print catches my eye.

It shows a solitary bather in an outdoor bathhouse, in the evening. A warm yellow lamp illuminates her contented smile. Outside, rain falls, but the bather appears at peace.

This print hangs next to a door that's cracked open. Room nine. I push on the door and peer inside.

Inside is a cedar box—a private bath—with so much steam rising up from it, it's as if a cloud is bathing there. Then a man slowly rises from the steam cloud, reaching for a washcloth on a ledge. His back is to me, and I see it is covered with an elaborate tattoo: a *samurai* warrior brandishing a sword. An orange dragon swooping down from one shoulder. It's as vivid and bright and detailed as any *ukiyo-e* print. Every inch of the skin on his back is colored.

I know, from manga I've read, that in Japan, where regular people don't get tattoos—especially as detailed as this one—that means only one thing.

The bather is a *yakuza*.

I should run, but my feet are rooted as the man reaches to open a nearby window to let in fresh air. He puts his washcloth on top of his head and sinks back into the steam.

Thought bubble: *GET OUT OF HERE! NOW!*

My legs move. I run back to the *onsen*, pausing to look at the painting by the women's entrance, that scene of boats on a river at night. Even in my freaked-out state, its beauty demands my attention. It's a dark painting, but I notice dazzling flashes of light: in hanging lanterns, in fireworks, in stars lighting up the night sky.

In the changing room, I ditch the *yukata*—no time for modesty now—and find Reika in the women's outdoor spring. Thankfully, she's alone there, a Seattle girl undaunted by drizzle. Mitsue must have gone back to her room. Steam swirls up around Reika, and she leans her head against one of the boulders lining the pool.

"Glad you could relax," I say, wincing as I slide into the scalding water. "I'm about to wreck your moment." I tell her about the bather in room nine. "He's got to be a yahoo."

"Could he be one of Fujikawa's henchmen? Could he have figured out we're here?"

"This guy had gray hair, so I don't think it was Kazuo Uchida or Shinobu Nishio. I guess it could be another guy who works for him." I shiver despite the scalding water. "Oh my God. Do you think it could it be Fujikawa himself? Keeping a close eye on our progress and waiting for this painting in person?"

Reika draws her knees up to her chin. "The only way he'd know we're here is if Yoshi heard us talking about the clues, made the connection to this inn, and told him that we'd come here. It's a long shot."

"Then the bathing yahoo is not Fujikawa. He's just some random gangster."

"Or we still have an informant."

We all eat dinner together in a private dining room, sitting on flat cushions on the floor. It's a traditional *kaiseki* meal that seems to go on forever. There's no chance to ask Kenji and Hideki how the search is going. The *okami-san* and the chambermaids keep sliding open the *fusama* door, dropping to their knees, and shuffling in to deliver and clear trays and to top off our cups of warm *sake*—rice wine—which, thankfully, my dad doesn't seem to notice Reika and I are drinking, too. We eat grilled meat, yellowtail fish, tofu as creamy as crème brûlée, miso soup, sticky rice, and magenta pickles called *shibazuke* that curl my tongue. I keep waiting for a lull in the courses or conversation so I can bring up the bathing *yakuza* I saw. Reika and I agreed before dinner that the Yamadas need to know about this guy. But it seems there is always at least one chambermaid in the dining room with us. Now I think everyone secretly speaks fluent English, and I don't dare talk in front of any of these women.

"*Kaiseki* should be six to nine courses. We are up to fifteen," Hideki grumbles. He glowers at the *fusama* sliding open, as the *okami-san* brings in another tray, the tiny, lacquered bowls clattering slightly as she drops to her knees, her eyes downcast.

Everyone sits back on their cushions, looking slightly ill. Finally, there is silence, and finally all the chambermaids and the *okami-san* are gone.

Reika glances at me. "Now," she mouths.

"Something weird happened before dinner," I announce. "I opened the wrong door by mistake and saw this guy with a huge tattoo all over his back." I describe it.

Kenji and Mitsue exchange a worried look.

"What's that look about?" my dad asks, watching them carefully.

"*Yakuza*," Kenji says quietly. He glances toward the door.

Hideki nods, but in a dismissive way. "He could simply be on vacation. They have benefits and time off, too. Their organizations are run like companies."

A vacationing gangster. This does not reassure me as much as I'd like it to.

"No doubt he chose a private room because of his tattoo," Hideki goes on. "Often they cannot go to public baths because they are not welcome there. The tattoos give them away, and the owners of public baths and hotels ban them, to avoid scaring off other guests."

Kenji frowns. "He should not be here. If there are *yakuza* here from one of Fujikawa's rival gangs, and if they hear what we are looking for, our investigation could take a wrong turn."

"I will inform the *okami-san* and have her dismiss him," Hideki promises.

"You don't think he's someone working with Fujikawa?" I ask.

Hideki smiles at Reika and me kindly. "You must not worry yourselves. There is no chance Fujikawa has sent men to follow us here. We have traveled discreetly and quickly."

His smooth voice reassures me a little. He will take care of this. The man will be dismissed. But my dad doesn't seem too happy.

"Rival gangs? A *yakuza* on the premises? I don't like it," he says, folding his arms. "Where there's one, there might be more. Girls, after dinner, go straight to your room. Lock the door. Stay there all night. Understood?"

AFTER DINNER, REIKA and I stagger back to our room. I keep crashing into the walls. "Ow. Who moved the walls?"

Reika laughs so hard she snorts.

Then I laugh and get the hiccups.

Somehow, despite the buckling floor and the blurry numbers on the sliding doors, we manage to find our room again. Two red futons are laid out for us, dressed with crisp, white cotton sheets. An electric fan purrs on the floor between them, stirring the soupy air.

The *tatami* smell is getting to me. I lay back on a futon to quiet my churning stomach.

Reika is giggling uncontrollably, somewhere in the room. "Have to stake awake! Stay awake! Stay . . . awake . . ." I hear her voice echo as the room tilts and rocks me to sleep.

I DREAM THAT I'm inside a *ukiyo-e* print. In a long wooden boat, propelled by an enormous silver salmon that pushes it from beneath the water. Two *ayu* trail behind us. I'm chasing after a boat up ahead, but I can't see who's on it. I just know I have to catch up. I shout at the salmon to swim faster, faster. I near the other boat, and the sole passenger turns and looks at me. In the moonlight, I see him. It's Edge. A lost look in his eyes.

My boat pulls up beside his.

"Help me," he says. "I can't get off. I want to get off."

I find a pole on the boat, and I hold it out to him. "Grab on! I'll pull you over here."

He reaches, but the pole is brittle, dead wood. It snaps.

My salmon driver does not stop. My boat glides on. Edge is left alone on his, holding half of a stick and watching me go with the saddest eyes I've ever seen.

I WAKE UP drenched in sweat. Somebody turned off the lamp and the fan. I sit upright and check my watch. Almost midnight. Oh my God. When did I fall asleep? How much time did I waste on that horrible dream? "Reika?" Her futon is empty, her sheets hardly disturbed.

I stand, still reeling from the *sake*. Maybe someone kidnapped her! Maybe the bathing yahoo in room nine! I run into the hallway. No light shines from under from under anyone's doors. Through the paper-thin walls, I can hear snoring, shifting, settling.

I first check the women's restroom at the end of our hall. Empty. I walk back up the hall. Unlike the Grand Prince Hotel, with its fake cricket sounds and perpetual artificial lighting, the cricket song here is real, leaking in from outside, and the corridors are almost completely dark. As I tiptoe toward the lobby, I keep tripping over house slippers that other guests have set out in front of their doors.

The air is hot and close, and thick with a thousand ghosts. I have a strong sensation of not being alone. Am I being watched, perhaps by someone from behind a cracked-open door? Or am I being observed by a ghost, perhaps the mournful van Gogh, wanting his painting to be brought out to the light of day? Or by the spirit of Tomonori Yamada, urging me forward?

The lobby is lit by pale moonlight slicing through bamboo by the window. No one works the front desk at this hour. A mosquito whines by my ear. The lobby walls are decorated with some paintings, woodblock prints, and Japanese artifacts—musical instruments and what looks like old fishing equipment—but I can't stop to inspect anything. I need to find Reika first.

I head toward the *onsen*. Something seems different by the women's entrance. Absent. Maybe it's the dark, playing tricks on my eyes.

I run on, back to the hotel area, around another corner of the west wing rooms. Fear rises up in my throat, a choking sensation, as I approach the room where I spotted the bathing yahoo. But no light glows from beneath the door of room nine. I don't know if he's sound asleep or if the *okami-san* sent him packing.

I head down another corridor. That's when I hear shuffling and scraping sounds. Bathing yahoo on the loose? I flatten myself against the wall, then peek around the corner.

Hideki is a few yards away from me, lifting a large, framed picture off the wall. In the moonlight, his skin has a cool blue glow, and his dark eyes seem to glitter. I fight the urge to run. I keep my eyes fixed on him. Has he found the painting? Is that why he looks so intense?

He lays the painting on the floor facedown and inspects it carefully with a flashlight. He runs his hands over the entire frame. Then he rehangs the painting and moves on to another.

I take a step forward, thinking I'll offer to help him. Then I step back. The look on his face is so determined, it's almost fierce. I'm afraid to interrupt and break his concentration. He obviously can't rest until he finds his dad's art. This must be like a spiritual quest for him.

I tiptoe back to the lobby, then up the stairs to the second floor. There I notice a faint glow beneath an unmarked door. A door with no house slippers lined up in front of it.

I push open the door and shield my eyes as a light shines in my face.

"My God, Violet, you scared me!" The light lowers.

"Reika! Why didn't you wake me up?" My relief at finding her quickly shifts to annoyance. "How long have you been here? Where did you get that flashlight?"

She motions for me to close the door. "I brought the light from my aunt and uncle's house. Thought it would come in handy. And I did try to wake you up. That *sake* went right to your head, you lightweight. We are seriously going to have to work on your drinking skills."

There's no time to stay mad. "I saw Hideki in the hall, inspecting paintings. By himself."

"Me too," says Reika. "Do you think that's kind of weird?"

"Not really. Kenji's old. He probably can't stay up so late. And I'm sure Hideki can't sleep till he finds his dad's painting."

"So I found this storeroom on the map. Take a look." Reika shines the flashlight around.

The room is like a museum—though a disorganized, cluttered one—filled floor to ceiling with art and antiques, including a suit of armor on a stand, old swords, and a wooden canoe hung by the ceiling. There are also lots of matted woodblock prints and framed and unframed paintings, stacked and leaning against the walls. Reika points to the unframed canvases. "I just started going through these."

"I can't believe the door was unlocked. There's valuable stuff in here," I whisper.

"Hey, kick that blanket under the door crack, will you? Oh, and it wasn't unlocked," she adds as I maneuver a gray wool blanket on the floor. "I picked the lock with a nail file."

"Where'd you learn to do that?"

She doesn't answer. Instead, she sets the flashlight down between us, and we work in silence, dividing up the stacks of art, flipping through canvases and matted prints.

I'm getting discouraged, but then at the end of the second stack, the last canvas makes my heart pound. I've seen this painting before.

Reika shines the flashlight on the painting. The canvas, set in a heavy, dark wood frame, is about two feet by three feet—the same dimensions as van Gogh's *Japonisme* paintings. It shows a scene from *ukai*. "Cormorant fishing," Reika observes.

"This was the painting outside the women's entrance to the *onsen*! I thought something looked different when I walked by the bath just now. Somebody moved it."

"You think the *okami-san* took it down and hid it here?" Reika asks.

"Yeah, maybe that's why our dinner took so long. She needed time to hide the painting!"

"And are you sure it's the same painting?"

"Positive." I inspect at the canvas more closely. "Not only that, but I can tell you the artist. It's Tomonori Yamada."

"No!"

"Take a look. Some of the images in this scene are right out of his sketch journal."

The more I stare at it, the more those separate embedded sketches from his journal now come together to make one beautiful, harmonious painting. I point them all out.

A nighttime scene on a river, a long boat in the foreground. Three men stand on the boat, all wearing dark blue robes. One man maneuvers the boat with a long pole. Another beats the water with a wooden paddle. A third, wearing a kind of apron, holds five or six leashes in his hands. A wire basket with flaming logs hangs from a pole off the front of the boat, illuminating an area of water where you can see what is on the ends of those leashes: black cormorants, with collars clamped around their slender necks. The diving birds strain at their leashes.

And in the lower left corner, in gray paint, is a circle with two *ayu* coiled together. The same image from the box where his journal was hidden. "There's his 'signature.'"

"You're right," Reika says. "Man, what a gorgeous painting. He's captured cormorant fishing perfectly. I saw this two summers ago, in Gifu. See here, this guy with the pole stirs up the water, and this other guy beats a drum to bring the river trout to the surface. Then they let the birds go in to catch the fish."

Dark hills, furred with forests, rise up behind the river. To the right is the graceful arc of a long, low bridge, which can only be the Moon Crossing Bridge. In the background, arranged in a semicircle, other boats drift: long boats with raised roofs, dotted with glowing lanterns, and filled with the silhouettes of spectators.

In the passenger boat closest to the fishing boat, one figure catches my eye: a woman in a pink kimono with red-and-white flowers, leaning over the side to trail one hand in the water. I can't see the features of her face very well, as her hair, falling out of a clip, partially obscures it, but I get the distinct impression she is a beautiful, young woman. How strange that she would be painted with such a level of detail, since she's part of the background. Or is she? The more I look at her, the more I feel like the painting is really all about her.

"It's sad. Tomonori Yamada could have been a great artist," says Reika.

"I know. He died too young. Nobody knew his potential. Maybe not even himself. And you know what else is sad? If there is a van Gogh painting underneath this, Tomonori's over-painting will have to be removed. This guy's one painting will be lost forever in the recovery of the van Gogh. Just so we can give it to a gang boss."

"You really think the van Gogh is under here? The frame doesn't look old," Reika says.

"Any canvas can be reframed." I touch the paint. It feels thick, applied more heavily in some places than others. "I can't say for sure. We need special equipment to see beneath."

"Or we need Kimono Girl." Reika sits back on her heels. "Too bad you made her up."

"Wait. There's someone who can help us. Skye."

"Your dad's ex? In Seattle?"

"I could call her. She might know someone who could help us here, someone with one of those infrared camera thingies."

"And you trust her?"

I consider this. An unanswered question still lingers about her. The issue of her "cash windfall." If she wasn't trafficking in stolen art, where was her windfall coming from? Still, she'd been right about one very important thing: the men Edge and I caught on film did turn out to be *yakuza*. She'd been right to warn me to be careful. "I trust her. And Skye has knowledge of art and restoration work that we don't."

It's now one in the morning Tokyo time. Skye should be at work by now. We look up the SAM number on Reika's phone. I call, and reception transfers me to Skye's direct line.

"Violet? What a surprise to hear from you. Are you guys back in Seattle already?"

"Nope. We're in Kyoto. Arashiyama, actually, just outside the city."

"Arashiyama? What are you doing there? Wait—is something wrong? Is Glenn okay?"

"He's fine," I say. "I mean, considering he might be kidnapped or killed in a week. . . ."

I hold the phone away from my ear because Skye's shriek of alarm is so painful.

"And I think my friend Reika and I have just found *Moon Crossing Bridge*."

"The drawings?"

"The painting. And now we need your help." I describe what we've found.

"This had so better not be a prank call," she says after a long pause.

"It's not. I swear. I can take a picture of the painting we found and email it to you."

"No, I believe you. But you guys are in way over your heads. I'm calling the FBI."

"No! They'll communicate with Japanese law enforcement, and Kenji doesn't want that. He says that Fujikawa seeks revenge every time Kenji calls in the authorities. Besides, we don't know for sure that this painting is concealing the van Gogh. That's why we need you."

"Can't you just give the art to Kenji? This is his problem, not yours."

"It is my problem. My dad's in danger!" I feel dizzy. It's not the *sake* this time. It's panic. "Please. Help us." I swallow hard. "We need someone with the right equipment to see if the van Gogh's underneath the painting we found."

"Okay," Skye relents. "I do know someone who might be able to help out. A woman named Natsuko Kikuchi. I went to grad school with her. She's a conservator at the Kyoto National Museum. I'll call her and set something up. But you have to trust Kenji. Tell him what you found."

Do I trust Kenji? "You said he was a cheater," I cautiously remind her.

"Oh, that." Skye sighs. "Yeah, he hit on me. Maybe he'd had a beer too many after work. One slip doesn't make him a womanizer or a pathological liar. Go easy on him. I don't even think about it anymore."

I hadn't thought of it that way. Along the same lines, maybe one emotionally charged public scene with my dad doesn't make Skye a crazed, revenge-seeking art thief. Maybe one comment about Mardi's tastes in movies doesn't mean Edge is in love with her. I've always wanted people to see there's more to me than meets the eye, but I forgot that can work both ways. Who knows what I've missed by slotting people into boxes so quickly, framing them with my expectations?

"Violet, are you still there?"

"Yeah. I was just thinking about what you said."

"Look. Adults are just complicated and, well, *weird* sometimes," says Skye.

"That's what people say about teenagers."

Skye laughs. "So maybe we're not all that different. But seriously. Tell Kenji. And while you're at it, you might want to pass on some breaking news about Julian Fleury."

"Julian?"

"After he quit his job at Margo's, suddenly no one could reach him," Skye says. "Police even got a search warrant to enter his apartment. His neighbors said he hadn't been there for days. Then Federal agents caught up with him this morning at a real estate agency in Tacoma. I guess Kenji called in a tip about some phone number Julian had on his notepad at work, and that's how they tracked him down there. Anyway, Julian showed up with a big fat check, hoping to buy a gallery space right by the Chihuly Glass Museum. That's prime real estate."

I catch my breath. That part of the investigation happened because I did that notepad rubbing, and because I gave the information to Kenji!

"It's all pretty bizarre, since Julian's hardly wealthy," Skye goes on. "He's been up to something, all right. They're just trying to find out what."

"I'll let my dad know. And thanks again for your help."

The instant I hang up, the door to the storage room flies open. The doorway frames the T-shaped silhouette of a woman in a dark blue *kimono*. For a moment I'm sure I'm looking at a ghost.

Then a light switches on, revealing the *okami-san* glaring at us.

3
0

The *okami-san* marches into the room, shuts the door behind her, and points to Tomonori's painting, which we have propped up in front of an antique bureau. She says something in Japanese, practically spitting.

Reika looks terrified. "She's going to get your dad and Kenji—who she thinks is my dad—unless we can explain what we're doing here."

I think fast. "Let's let her think we suspect *her* of having something to do with the missing van Gogh. Make her nervous. Get some information."

"What, interrogate her? She's in charge here. We have to humble ourselves."

"As nice as it is to follow Japanese customs, this just isn't the time. Ask her if she moved this painting from the wall outside the *onsen*."

Reika asks the question in Japanese.

"*Hai*," says the *okami-san*. *Yes*. Her eyes flit from Reika to me to Reika.

"Now ask her if she moved it because she was trying to keep the painting away from the Yamadas."

"Hai," the *okami-san* replies again warily. Then she addresses Reika in Japanese.

Reika translates: "She wants to know why we are interested in finding a painting."

"Fine. Let's tell her what we think Tomonori Yamada painted over."

"Eh? Tomonori Yamada?" The *okami-san* pounces on that name.

Reika says something in Japanese. I catch the name *van Gogh.*

The *okami-san* sinks into a chair, one hand on her chest, fingers splayed.

"Ask her to tell us about this painting," I tell Reika.

The *okami-san* gazes at us for a long time, searching our faces. I meet the *okami-san*'s eyes and stare right back. I haven't come this far to let myself get intimidated. I'm feeling a wind rushing through me. *Chikara.* Confidence. Power. I sit up straighter and let it fill me.

The *okami-san* pulls up two other wooden chairs and gestures to us to sit down. Before I do so, I shove the blanket back under the door crack and turn off the light. We all sit facing each other, illuminated only by a trickle of moonlight leaking in.

In that soft light, the *okami-san* doesn't look so scary. She speaks slowly and indicates with a graceful gesture that Reika should translate for me.

"She says she'll tell us what she knows about this painting," Reika says. "Since we told her why we're looking for a lost painting here. She appreciates our honesty."

"Arigato gozaimasu," I whisper, bowing my head.

The *okami-san* explains, pausing every few sentences to let Reika translate.

"The people you are traveling with did not check in with the family name Yamada. They used the name Ueno. So I was surprised to hear Yamada," Reika interprets. "When the men told me they were searching for a painting that was possibly left here in 1987, I became frightened. I thought these people might be art thieves, though I did not understand why they'd be traveling with *gaikokujin*—with foreigners.

"In fact, a guest did leave a painting at the inn back in 1987. The painting you see before you. During dinner tonight I removed it from the wall until I could determine what these people might really be after. It took a great deal of time, as the person who gave me the painting instructed me to bolt it firmly to the wall, rather than hang it, because of the heavy frame."

"Did you know Tomonori Yamada personally?" I ask through Reika.

The *okami-san* freezes for a few moments, then nods. She looks deeply sad.

"The name gave me a start when you mentioned it," Reika translates after the *okami-san* speaks again. "I had not heard it in many years. Yamada-san—Tomonori—was a frequent guest here in the 1980s. He came here to relax and to draw. I was a chambermaid, still a young woman, and my mother was the *okami-san*. I served his meals. I set out his futon in the evenings. I was curious about the drawings in his room, and I looked at them one day. I got in the habit of looking through them every evening when I laid out his futon. Then I saw myself in them."

The *okami-san* falls silent. I hardly dare breathe, for fear of breaking the spell. But she goes on, as does Reika's translation.

"My mother trained my sisters and me to be invisible, as chambermaids. But my curiosity got the better of me. I confronted Tomonori. I asked him, why draw me? 'Because, Hanae, you are as beautiful as the flower you are named for,' he said."

I poke Reika, and she clutches my arm. I'm sure we're both thinking of the same thing. The woman he sketched on the two-page spread, whose kimono held the story of how the painting came to the inn. That wasn't his wife. It had to be this woman, the *okami-san*, when she was younger. Now I see what is familiar about her. A way she tips her head and looks at us sort of sideways. A graceful flourish of her left hand.

"He asked me to pose for him one day," Reika translates the next segment. "I knew it was inappropriate, but I agreed to it. Tomonori was compelling and very handsome. And, to be honest, I was fascinated by seeing myself on paper. I had never thought much of myself or my looks before then. It is hard to explain, but I felt as if I were coming to life on the page.

"Soon I was posing frequently. Our relationship deepened." At this, the *okami-san* reddens slightly and looks down at her lap. "I knew he was married and had a young son. I knew he was a businessman in Tokyo. I knew he lived another life. Yet here, at the inn, it was like we escaped to another world. Our own world. Our floating world."

I point to the woman in the pink kimono in the painting. "This is you?"

"Yes," Reika translates as the *okami-san* smiles. "This was our happiest evening together. I slipped away from the inn with him and went to the *ukai* show." The *okami-san* frowns, and Reika—unconsciously, I think—frowns, too, before going on. "Of course, that was all an illusion. The next day, he went back to Tokyo. I received an angry letter in the mail the next week, from Tomonori's wife. She had seen her husband's sketchbooks, and found repeated images of me, with my name written there, and a business card for the *ryokan*. Most Japanese women know when their husbands have affairs, she said in the letter, and they just look the other way. But she was not going to do that. Not when the family business, and her son's future, was at stake. She said she destroyed the journals and sketches she found. Tomonori would not be returning to the *ryokan*, and I must not communicate with him. She had threatened to leave him if he saw me again. Divorce would cause public scandal at a terrible time, just as the Yamada Corporation was expanding overseas. 'You will not steal my husband from me. We will all put this affair behind us,' she said. 'We will erase it. It never happened.'"

The *okami-san* dabs at the corners of her eyes.

My own eyes are watering. I know what it feels like to have a relationship erased. With a blank stare. Or with an accusation, hurled in fear.

"I was hurt, of course," she continues through Reika. "Hurt that Tomonori gave in to his wife's demands so readily. Hurt that our dream world disappeared in an instant. But I did not wish to cause trouble for him. If he truly loves me, I told myself, he will send a message. And our love will live on, growing more powerful, if only in our hearts and minds.

"You see, many Japanese people have a certain vision of love. They believe impossible love is the strongest type of love there is. Now I suppose I see it differently. Now I can see I have lost all those years. In my faithfulness to the ideal of impossible love, I have lost the chance to love anyone else in reality. I have even lost the chance to become a mother."

"So you never heard from him again?" My God. This is the saddest story I've ever heard.

The *okami-san* shakes her head after Reika conveys my question. "Only once. He came here to the inn in the middle of the night. He knocked softly on the door and called my name. My room was near the door, and I was awake anyway, watching a dragonfly trapped in a paper lantern, and thinking of Tomonori. So I heard him and I came to the door, afraid that my mother or sister would answer the door instead. 'You cannot stay here,' I told him, speaking through the crack in the door. 'Your wife is very angry. I cannot cast more misery upon your household.' He looked agitated. He was frowning, not smiling. He was not himself. In the moonlight, I could see the sweat on his forehead. I wanted to throw open the door and wipe it away. I resisted.

"He held up a large package wrapped in brown paper and said it was a parting gift, something he had made. 'The frame is heavy,' he said. 'You must affix it firmly to the wall.'

"I thought he had lost his mind. He had traveled all the way here from Tokyo, in the middle of the night, just to give me an unwieldy picture? To talk about frames? Without one gentle word, without one tender look? I refused to take it. I told him to take his picture and go.

"But he practically snarled at me. 'You must take this gift, Hanae! You must take it immediately! People are waiting for me. I cannot stay long here.' He glanced behind him. He was acting very strangely. I looked into the darkness behind him and saw no one. I could not understand his extreme agitation. I was angry that his distress didn't seem to have anything to do with me or our situation.

"I heard my mother stirring in her room, so I reached

for the package and grabbed it. It was very heavy. I nearly dropped it. Tomo's fingers brushed mine as he passed the package to me. Only after I had the package with both hands did he look into my eyes. 'Good-bye, Hanae,' he whispered. 'You are the woman who stole my heart. I am so glad you did. Nothing that happens will ever change that.' He leaned in as if to kiss me. But the heavy package I still held was awkward—he could not get close—and then a rustling in the bushes startled us. It was only a cat. Tomonori turned away and ran to the river, where I saw him get into a waiting boat.

"I was so dismayed by this visit, and his confusing behavior, that I slid the package into the back of a closet and did not open it. Two weeks later, I heard Tomonori Yamada's name again. In the newspapers. He had committed suicide off a Tokyo subway platform. The paper showed a picture of his shoes neatly placed on the platform, beside his briefcase. I wept in my room for hours. Then I took out that package. I ripped off the tape, tore off the brown paper. It was the painting you see here. He had sent me the message I'd hoped for. I had been a fool, I thought. The painting was about me and our love. Since then, I have displayed it near the *onsen*, where all guests must pass by, so that his work may be seen. My mother died without ever knowing that the painting was not just an anonymous gift from a grateful guest. Our story has been hidden for all these years."

"Did you believe Tomonori killed himself then?" I ask through Reika.

The *okami-san*, through Reika, replies, "For years, I flattered myself thinking he had killed himself because of his impossible situation. He couldn't be a professional artist. He and I could not be together. He lived his life in a box, one that was getting smaller all the time. But as time went on, I became less certain that he killed himself because of his love for me. Maybe that was my own selfish thinking. He had mentioned, on occasion, some work he did on the side to make extra money. Something about buying art for a wealthy collector, someone he'd met through a project his company was doing for a fish processing company in Kyoto."

Fine Ayu Food Products. Maybe Fujikawa was involved in that somehow—either in the company or as an investor who pulled out last minute and caused the whole thing to fall through.

Reika resumes her translation. "That collector was someone with *yakuza* associations, but he learned this only after he started buying for him. Then he did not wish to work for this man. But the man threatened him and said he would harm his family if Tomonori were to leave his employ."

Reika and I exchange an alarmed glance. So Tomonori did buy the painting on behalf of someone else. She has to be talking about Mr. Fujikawa! "Maybe the painting really is Fujikawa's," I whisper.

"And that makes Tomonori really the thief!" Reika whispers back.

"But it's so hard to believe. He cared about art so much!"

The *okami-san* continues her story, so Reika does, too. "I did wonder if he had angered this man for whom he bought art. That was the only reason I could think of why someone might have killed him. Especially so soon after his trip to Paris. But I did not dare to voice these thoughts. I was supposed to be invisible. And I also worried if I spoke up, the man he worked for would come after me. This is why I was so frightened tonight. I thought Kenji Yamada was that man, and I thought this was the time. It took me a long time—an entire fifteen-course dinner, in fact—to determine that Kenji was not this man. He did not show any signs of *yakuza* affiliation."

I nudge Reika. "But there is a *yakuza* here at the inn. Ask her if she got rid of him yet."

The *okami-san* looks startled when Reika tells her this.

"She wasn't aware the man in room nine was a *yakuza*," she says. "And he's still staying here."

"So Hideki didn't tell her yet. What is he waiting for?"

The *okami-san* looks hard at us. "Now tell me," she asks through Reika. "What leads you to believe Tomonori painted over a van Gogh and hid it with me?"

Just then I hear floorboards creaking. Footsteps pause before the door. The handle shakes. We hear a painting being lifted off the wall outside the door. A scrape as the painting is replaced. The footsteps continue on, fainter now.

I let out a long breath. "Ask her if she'd be willing to take the painting to the Kyoto National Museum first thing tomorrow to be analyzed. Tell her what Skye's friend can do. Make sure she knows it won't hurt the painting just to look at through it with special equipment."

Reika conveys all this, and the *okami-san* thinks. She shakes her head no.

"Please," I say. "People are in danger because of this. My dad's in danger. If Fujikawa doesn't get the painting in three days, I could lose my dad. If there's a van Gogh under here, it will save him. Aren't lives more important than art?"

As I wait for the translation and response, I blink back tears. My dad thinks art is more important than life. He's not even too concerned about his own right now. I wanted to think art was more important than life, too. I wanted to solve this mystery and recover the art even when I knew I was in over my head. But now, the thought of losing my dad—flawed as he is—makes me dizzy. I get that pulsing ache in my chest. I want to reveal this van Gogh and hand it over to the *yakuza*. I want my dad to live.

"There has been too much loss and sadness around this painting. I do not wish to be the cause of more," Reika translates for the *okami-san*. "I will do as you suggest."

There is nothing like a traditional Japanese *ryokan* in the middle of the day for finding monk-like solitude and silence. Or for driving you out of your freaking mind.

It's our fifth day at the inn. Fujikawa expects the painting in two days. And we're still waiting for the results of our lab analysis. It turns out Skye's conservator friend, Natsuko Kikuchi, has been honeymooning in Hokkaido. When Skye finally reached her at a remote *onsen* and told her how urgent the situation was, she came rushing back. The *okami-san* left an hour ago to deliver the painting to the museum lab in Kyoto, accompanied by all three Yamadas.

It's been tense, meanwhile, even though the bathing yahoo from room nine was dismissed by the *okami-san* the morning after we found that painting. The deadline for the painting handover looms. And Hideki is acting strange.

Hideki was definitely glad we found the painting as soon as we told him about it. But he hasn't taken the delay in the analysis well. With every passing hour, he sounds more skeptical that the painting is the real deal. He continues to search the inn, in case the one sent to the museum turns out to be hiding nothing. He's looked at every piece of art, including the art in two storerooms. Now he's checking loose floorboards and feeling the wall panels. He's almost given up any pretense of a normal vacation. His hair is unkempt, his face unshaven, his *yukata* stained with food and sweat. There's a wild look in his eyes. He looks like my dad when he's on an art-making binge. Guests are beginning to whisper.

Meanwhile my dad, strangely, looks more and more normal. He's started spending less time in his room sketching, and now brings a portable easel and palette outside. His skin is getting ruddy from the sun, and it glows from the daily dips in the *onsen*. His eyes shine a brighter blue. At breakfast this morning—which he actually showed up for on time, sitting across from me at the low table—he smiled at me. "*Ohayou gozaimasu.*"

"How can you be so calm? We just have two days left!" I said. "How long do you think we can hide out here before Fujikawa finds us? Finds *you*?"

"I don't know, Violet. I guess I tend to trust that this situation will work out. We probably have the painting now, so he'll have no reason to hurt me. Anyway, you don't hear of foreigners, especially emerging artists from Seattle, being killed by *yakuza*, do you?"

"Yeah, but, that doesn't mean it can't happen. An art gallery assistant in Seattle was assaulted by *yakuza*. I'm sure nobody saw that coming."

"We have time. The painting will be delivered. Kenji and Hideki have convinced me. Meanwhile, have you tried this *miso*? It's been cooked on a magnolia leaf, over this little pot with a flame. Magnificent!" He scoops some up with his chopsticks, which he proudly mastered last night.

While I'm glad to see my dad becoming more relaxed, a coal inside me smolders. If my dad's not worried about his own safety, I guess he's not that worried about me, either.

While Hideki's unraveling, and my dad's having some kind of spiritual conversion, Kenji is still searching for the painting, too, just in case. But the strain is taking its toll. I worry about his health. Mitsue does, too, bringing him water, wiping his brow with cool washcloths.

I've finished reading all the manga I've brought and all of Reika's. Other than the electric thrum of cicadas and the scrabbling of Hideki's hands feeling the walls outside my room, all is quiet at the Akatsuki Ryokan.

While Reika writes poetry, I flip through my sketchbook, which I've neglected since the train ride from Tokyo. Kimono Girl looks beseechingly at me, one hand outstretched as she reaches out of the covered-up *Sunrise Bridge* painting. *Finish my story*, she whispers. *I want to enter the teen manga contest.*

But I can't. Not now anyway. Because another story is taking up space in my head.

I draw the *okami-san*'s story in twelve panels, imagining youthful versions of her and Tomonori. It's the first time I've ever attempted to write or draw a love story. And it's a perfect explanation for how the painting could have been hidden all these years. If no one but Tomonori's wife knew of his secret love, and if this secret love would hold on to anything he gave her, with all her heart, what better place to hide it?

Then I turn to a fresh sheet and think about the real van Gogh mystery. Julian's been on my mind ever since Skye told me he tried to buy his own gallery. Talk about a cash windfall. If he were a middleman, like Sockeye in my story, he might get some money, but probably not that much. Not as much as if he sold it himself. An idea, a possible real-life story, starts to take shape, and I sketch it out in panels.

Shinobu Nishio and Kazuo Uchida, under Fujikawa's orders to get the van Gogh drawings, arrive in Seattle. They know that the Yamadas are buying Glenn Marklund's works, so they track down Margo since she represents my dad. They show up at Margo's gallery, seeking information on the Japanese collectors. They find Julian, find him willing to talk, and pay him for information about where the Yamadas keep the drawings. Then Nishio and Uchida break into the Yamadas' house one evening and make off with the drawings.

Next panel. Julian counts his cash. Then he visits a real estate office in Tacoma to inquire about buying a gallery space in Tacoma. He's dying to branch out and do his own thing, away from Margo, who doesn't appreciate him.

I stare at a blank panel. There's still a missing piece. What made the *yakuza* think the van Gogh painting was in Seattle? I draw a question mark. Could Julian have given them misinformation? Would he say anything for the right price?

After a while, I give up on the real-life mystery and turn back to the made-up one. Unlike the real-life mystery, I suddenly know how this one will end.

THE CORMORANT RETURNS to her studio, catching Kimono Girl just as she's emerging from the covered-up van Gogh. KG confronts the Cormorant. "I'm here to return the painting to its rightful owner. Now tell me where I can find the solvent that will remove this acrylic layer."

The Cormorant holds up a small vial. "Heh heh heh. This is my special formula—I invented it, and this is all I have. The oils beneath would surely be damaged if an ordinary solvent is used. Use anything but this, and you'll lose the van Gogh."

KG draws her sword and demands the Cormorant apply it to the canvas.

The Cormorant laughs and transforms into her bird form, then lunges at KG, trying to peck her with her beak. The two fight, causing chaos in the studio. Paints and solvents topple off shelves. Bottles break. Frames and canvases are crashed into and broken. KG dives for the van Gogh and grabs the canvas. The Cormorant spears her hand with her beak. Blood spurts everywhere, but KG holds on to that canvas with all her strength. Then she lunges for the vial of special solvent, which is now rolling toward the door.

As the Cormorant comes at her one last time, wings raised, KG slashes at her with the sword. She nearly cuts the canvas, missing it by a millimeter, and clips one of the Cormorant's wings instead. While the Cormorant recoils and cries out in pain, KG escapes from the studio with the canvas. And the solvent.

BY ONE, MY fingers are cramped and I have a crick in my neck. Reika's snoring softly; she's fallen asleep in one of the wicker chairs, and her poetry notebook has slid to the floor.

I look out the window and see my dad on the bank of the Katsura-gawa. He's set up his tripod and easel and is painting on a small canvas. With his wide *yukata* sleeves fluttering and his expansive arm movements, he resembles a wizard. A strange wizard with a messy ponytail and sneakers peaking out the bottom of his robe instead of the ridged wooden flip-flops—*geta*—that all the other guests borrow to wear outside.

There are no women's *geta* at the inn to fit my size-nine feet, so I find my Converse high-tops among the other guests' outdoor shoes by the front desk. I feel vaguely ridiculous, walking around the tea garden in my *yukata* and high-tops. I follow the winding gravel path.

I stand behind my dad for a while, watching him paint, careful not to startle him.

"Everything okay?" my dad asks after a few minutes.

"Yeah, sure. I just thought we could, I don't know, hang out or something."

"And do what?" His hand does not stop moving. His watercolors are light and delicate—different from his usual, splashier work—but his lines are sure.

"No, when you hang out, you don't really *do* anything. You just . . . never mind."

I turn to go. Then a shiver passes through me. I remember what it felt like to talk to the *okami-san*, to demand that she reveal what she knows. I had been full of *chikara* that night. I turn back to my dad now and stare at him hard, feeling that power surge through me again.

Feeling the force of my stare, I assume, my dad sets down his brush and turns to me. "What's on your mind, kiddo? Is it this gangster business?"

I nod, but surprisingly, what comes out of my mouth has nothing to do with that. "Why did you hide me?"

"Sorry?"

"You didn't tell Skye about me. Or Margo. I was so embarrassed at your reception. Nobody had a clue who I was."

"Oh." My dad sits down on the riverbank. "Yeah."

I sit, too, leaving a good three feet between us.

"I'm sorry. I hadn't told Margo because, well, that's a business relationship, and it simply never came up. And as for Skye, well, it's complicated. See, she wants children someday. We haven't sorted that out yet. I know I'm not a great parent. I haven't been there for you over the years. So I kind of froze up about the issue with Skye. I didn't know how to tell her about you. The longer I waited, the harder it got. I'm sorry it ended up embarrassing you."

I nod. I don't really get why the issue of having kids has to be so complicated. But at least I feel like he's telling me the truth. And at least he wasn't keeping me a secret because he's embarrassed about me.

A long wooden boat drifts downriver, poled by a young man standing up at the prow. He wears a dark blue *yukata* and a pointed hat, like the rickshaw drivers in town.

Grateful for the visual distraction to make up for our sudden silence, I make two Ls with my fingers. "Hey. Frame Game." I show my dad the image captured between my hands, following the boat as it moves. "What do you think?"

"Nice composition."

"Remember we used to play that when I'd visit you on Capitol Hill?"

"Sure. I didn't have a TV or video games or any stuff to keep a kid entertained. I was always in a panic about what to do with you. This seemed to do the trick."

"It was fun. Why'd we stop playing it?"

"Oh, I imagined you thought it was silly as you got older. I remember you once said, 'Couldn't we just get a camera? Then we'd always have the pictures we found.' I couldn't argue with that logic."

"Huh. Okay." I don't remember saying that at all.

"Any other questions, as long as I'm on the stand?"

"Yeah. Why'd you leave that house on Capitol Hill? With all those artists living together, talking about art all the time—it seemed really cool. I liked visiting you there."

"Did you?" My dad stares at the river. "Funny, isn't it, how kids and parents can see the same thing so differently. You know, Violet, that really wasn't such a great place. Bunch of wannabe artists and slackers. All talk. They'd rant about not wanting to sell out, not wanting to get real jobs, but meanwhile we were barely making rent." He sighs. "Unfortunately, I got sucked into their lifestyle. I made a few choices that I now regret. And one day I looked in the mirror, and I didn't even recognize myself. I'd lost my way. I knew I had to get out of there and clean up my act if I was going to make it as an artist . . . or as a person. Anyway, I guess that's why I sort of kept my distance from you the past few years."

"Really?"

"Yep. I didn't want you to think of me like I thought of those losers I lived with. I wanted you to have a better opinion of me, even if it was just an illusion. If I could do it all again, I'd have handled it differently. I didn't mean to mess up your life."

"It's okay. I'm not completely damaged."

"I hope not," he says in a serious way. Then he grins at me. "Grab your sketchbook. I'm not very good at hanging out, but we could work together if you want."

"Yeah, that sounds fun." I run to my room, where Reika's still dozing, and get my black book. On the bank of the Katsura-gawa, side by side, we work together in silence. At the end of an hour, we show each other what we've been working on, and my dad actually says my Kimono Girl drawings are good. "You have an excellent eye for detail."

"Thanks!"

"But what's this?" As he hands my book back, a page falls open to my sketches about the real van Gogh case. He sees the ones I did this morning when I was working out my theory of Julian's role. "Do you really think the *yakuza* paid Julian for information about the drawings?"

"I know it's crazy, but—"

"It's not crazy. Now that I see it storyboarded here, the way you have it, it kind of makes sense. Julian had been to the Yamadas' house more than once to help out with a print appraisal."

"So if he led the thieves to the drawings and got a ton of money for it, why would he get beat up later?" I wonder aloud. "Do you think he led them to believe there was a painting, too? And that either Skye had it, or you did?"

"It wouldn't be out of character. I bet once he made some money on the side, for the information about the drawings, he got inspired. Or greedy. For more money, toward buying that art gallery he always wanted, he might have gladly answered questions about the painting."

"And I bet that's why the *yakuza* beat him up and trashed your art. They trusted him after the good lead on the drawings, but when the painting didn't turn up, they retaliated."

My dad takes his cell phone out of his paint box. "I'm calling Agent Chang."

"But it's the middle of the night in Seattle now."

"Good thing she's not there, then."

"Where is she?"

"Here, in Japan."

"No way! Why?"

"She's pursuing some new leads that turned up in the case. She should be in Kyoto by now. I've been keeping her up to date ever since you told me about Fujikawa's threat." My dad talks to Agent Chang for a few minutes. "Natsuko Kikuchi has news for us," he says after hanging up. "There is something behind that painting."

"I knew it! Is it the van Gogh?"

"Agent Chang doesn't know yet. Something turned up on the infrared, and she's going to go see it in person. She'll be at the Kyoto Museum at seven thirty this evening, with the Yamadas and the *okami-san*. We should go, too. You and Reika should be there, too. I mean, since you've done so much on this case, you might as well see the result of your work."

He looks at me with a funny expression. It takes me a moment to recognize that it's pride.

In the late afternoon, my dad, Reika, and I are sitting in the wicker chairs on the porch, drinking green tea, when there's a tap at the door. Mitsue glides in, laden with shopping bags. Smiling. I've never seen her smile so much. She suddenly looks ten years younger.

"I just heard the news that there is a meeting at the museum lab tonight," Mitsue says. "It sounds very promising. Finally, this terrible situation can be settled. Violet and Reika, as an expression of gratitude for your help, this is for you." Mitsue hands us each a slick purple bag that says TAKASHIMAYA on the side. I know that's one of the fanciest department stores in Japan. "I would be honored if you would accept this gift from Kenji, Hideki, and me."

Reika and I dive into our bags and pull out layers of tissue.

"Summer kimono," Mitsue says with a smile as I pull out a long, red garment. "Actually it's a fancy *yukata*, but we also call it a summer kimono. Girls wear these out in the streets for the summer festivals. And tonight is *Yoiyama*, the festival night before tomorrow's *Gion Matsuri* procession. All the girls in Kyoto will be wearing kimonos like these."

"Gion Matsuri?" my dad asks as Reika and I exclaim over our kimonos, and the other items in the bags: wooden *geta*, split-toed socks, and paddle fans with floral patterns.

"The Gion Festival takes place every July in Kyoto," Mitsue explains. "It was originally a purification ritual to eliminate the plague. It is one of Japan's oldest festivals. The big parade is tomorrow, but the floats—portable shrines, called *yamaboko*— are all on display tonight. You can view many beautiful textiles and other art on the floats. Some people call them 'mobile art museums.' I think you and the girls would greatly enjoy seeing them."

I'm holding the kimono up to my body, stroking the soft fabric in disbelief. "Oh my God. Mitsue, this is gorgeous. Thank you. But it's too much." It's made of the softest cotton, unlike the stiff, starchy ones the chambermaids set out for us here at the inn. And it's the most beautiful red. The colorful fireworks pattern dances and dazzles my eyes. And Reika's, mint green with white morning glories, is equally stunning.

The label says TAMURA-YA. "That's a big-name designer," Reika whispers to me. I hate to imagine how much this cost.

"There's more in the bag," Mitsue says.

I reach back in and pull out a long yellow sash. An *obi*. Way nicer than the one I turned into a scarf and wore on the night I first met the Yamadas. Reika's *obi* is candy pink.

I love the clothes. But something is off. "You said these

were for the festival tonight. But there's a meeting at the museum lab. Are we going to the festival after that?"

Mitsue's smile fades slightly, though her voice remains cheerful. "Actually, Hideki has asked me to take you girls to Kyoto for *Yoiyama* this evening, instead of the meeting," Mitsue says. "Glenn, too. In fact, it was actually Hideki's idea to purchase the festival attire so that you would enjoy yourselves at the festival even more."

"That was nice of him. But I'd rather go to the meeting," I say.

"Me too," says Reika.

"To tell you the truth, I would rather go as well," Mitsue admits, her smile fading. "But Hideki insists. This matter is deeply personal to my nephew, and he wants only himself and Kenji in attendance. And the *okami-san*, since the art was found on her property, of course."

Reika and I exchange a sad look.

My dad sighs. "It's probably for the best that we're not there. If there's any chance Fujikawa caught wind of what's going on and shows up, that's the last place we need to be. I vote for the festival."

"Yes, we will manage to have our own little adventure," Mitsue says. "Girls, why don't you try on your outfits in case we need to make any adjustments?"

Reika and I go into the women's restroom down the hall.

"I can't believe, after all the work we did to find this painting, Hideki wants us out of the picture," I grumble as I slip my arms into the wide sleeves. "There wouldn't even be a meeting tonight if we hadn't found the canvas or figured out that it was painted by Tomonori. We wouldn't even be at this inn if it weren't for our sleuthing! What? What is so funny?"

Reika grins. "Look at you. You're so passionate about this mystery now."

I glimpse my face in the mirror. I do look a little different. My cheeks are flushed, and there's a spark in my eyes. I almost look fierce.

When we swish back into the room in kimonos, Mitsue's face lights up. "You girls look beautiful. Just like models." But it's me she is looking at. "May I?" She takes an end of my *obi* and unwinds it to its full length, until it spreads out like a piece of pulled taffy. Then she lays it flat on my belly, comes behind me, and begins a complicated process of winding and tucking, tugging tight in the back, then securing it further with a red cord, until I'm wrapped up tight.

There is no mirror in the room, but I can see myself in my dad's eyes as he smiles at me.

I actually feel pretty. I raise my arms, and the long sleeves flutter. I stand straight and tall. The *obi*, tied properly, makes me feel like I'm all held in, like I have a slender waist and a firm back. I feel simultaneously graceful and strong, despite a growing awareness of the red cord cutting into me and a slight inability to breathe.

I turn and find Mitsue beaming at me. "You may know how to make and wear kimono scarves," Mitsue says. "But this, Violet-chan, is how you wear a kimono."

I wish we could just go out tonight and enjoy the big party in Kyoto, and just be normal tourists. I wish that changing your feelings was as easy as changing your clothes.

We all take the local Japan Rail train together from Arashiyama back to Kyoto. At Kyoto Station, Mitsue stands up and beckons to my dad and Reika and me to follow. Kenji, Hideki, and the *okami-san* are going on to Shichijō Station, across from the Kyoto National Museum of Art.

We stand on the platform, waving at them while the door chimes, signaling departure. "I can't believe the *okami-san* gets to go to this meeting and we don't," I grumble, as Kenji, Hideki, and the *okami-san* wave back.

"It is her painting, technically, until we know otherwise," my dad reminds me. "They can't do anything to it without her permission. My advice? Let go of things you cannot control. That's Zen for 'take a chill pill.'"

Mitsue smiles. Reika giggles. I die a little inside. I've always been jealous of my friends' dads and their geeky dad humor, their bumbling attempts to bond, but this is just not the time.

Mitsue and my dad start walking to the exit. The train slowly pulls away. As the car passes, I notice a man's face that seems familiar.

"Reika, look! See that gray-haired guy in the train, about five rows back from the Yamadas? Reading manga?"

Reika looks. "Yeah. What about him?"

"He looks like that bathing yahoo from room nine!"

"The tattooed guy whom the *okami-san* banished?"

"Exactly! Reika, I'm almost sure that's the same guy."

We jog a few yards after the train, trying to glimpse him again, but the train picks up speed and we lose him.

We stare at each other. "It could be him. Following the Yamadas to the museum," I say.

"Or maybe you're just being a little bit paranoid," says Reika.

"Maybe."

Mitsue, in her plum kimono, turns to find us. "Girls! This way!" She points to the exit.

"We could ditch your dad and Mitsue. Make a run for it," Reika suggests. "Get to the museum and see the van Gogh unveiling, and warn them about the bathing yahoo, just in case that was him."

"Run? Are you kidding? I can barely walk in this thing." And with the split-toed socks and the wooden *geta*, I can only take mincing steps. "I'm going to have to totally rethink the way Kimono Girl gets around in my story. Besides, my dad will be really worried if we just disappear. Plus, if he is a yahoo after the art, he'd be pretty dumb to just walk into the museum lab. I'm sure the place is crawling with security. Agent Chang must have some backup there."

At least slowing down in this outfit lets me see stuff I might otherwise miss. As we leave the station and walk into the city, I notice the sunset. It's one that van Gogh would have loved to paint: the richest orange and yellows, the clouds like swirls of paint. And I notice the Kamo River, and the couples who line its banks. They sit with perfectly even distances between them, as if they all agreed to serve as units of measure.

Suddenly, the opposite bank of that river seems so far away. I wonder if I will ever sit next to a boy like that. Will I kiss someone at sunset? Will I even hold someone's hand? The world is full of happy couples. It seems so easy for other people to get together.

Maybe Edge is sitting like that with Mardi right now, his arm slung around her shoulders. I wish he could see me now, in this beautiful outfit. Reika's done my hair in a twist and helped me with makeup. I'm wearing contact lenses. I'm me and yet not me. I'm a different version of me. He might like what he sees.

But I can't daydream about some faraway boy now. I'm tangled up in an art heist. The idea of trying to get Edge's attention feels so foreign. Even the things I used to worry about, like running into Mardi and her gang in the halls, or being called Manga-loid, no longer really matter.

My dad calls to us. We hurry, as best we can, shuffling quickly to catch up.

"Stay close," Mitsue cautions. "We are approaching the festival streets, which are quite crowded. I don't want you girls to get lost."

We follow Mitsue onto Shijo-dori, a wide street roped off for pedestrian traffic and vendor stalls, and merge with a river of people. The street is congested with festivalgoers. The music, flutes and bells, is droning, almost eerie. It sounds somber to my ear, yet everyone looks so joyful. People buy *yakitori* and *mochi* and balloons on sticks. Girls our age swish past us in summer kimonos, laughing, snapping pictures of each other, without a care in the world.

I scan the crowds as if I might glimpse the *okami-san* and Tomonori, still young, still alive, still in love. Or as if I might see Edge running to find me.

The crowds thicken. The sharp sounds of flutes, the jangling of bells, and the metallic staccato of small *shime* drums makes my heart beat faster. Or maybe it's my sudden thoughts about Edge.

"Girls, you see these carts?" Mitsue points out the enormous wooden carts lining the main drag and tucked away on side streets. They look like houses with sloped roofs, and incredibly long poles—some decorated with bits of trees or ribbons. They rise two stories high or more, and glow with strings of hanging paper lanterns. "These are the *yamaboko* floats for tomorrow's parade. They are hundreds of years old. Tomorrow, teams of men will take those ropes and pull these carts along the parade route, just like in medieval times. Shall we take a closer look?"

Close up, the float looks nothing like the Seattle Seafair parade's tacky floats with pirates and clowns. The wooden wheels of the carts are taller than the men standing next to them, which means that the bottom of the shrine is way above my head. The sides are draped with dazzling tapestries, and atop the roof, a pine tree rises up to the darkening sky. Lanterns decorated with *kanji* characters illuminate the tapestry art.

The musicians, dressed in identical blue-and-white *yukata*, sit high in the shrine, beneath the sloped, pagoda-style roof. They play flutes, beat small drums, and pull bells on long tassels.

"This shrine honors Minami Kannon Yama," Mitsue tells us. "Goddess of Mercy."

"Kannon—she sure gets around. Wasn't she at Sensō-ji Temple, too?" my dad asks.

"Yes. Here, people pray for safety during tomorrow's procession. Shall we buy some *omamori* amulets for good luck?"

"No thanks," I say. "I'm still trying to figure out the fortune I got from her in Tokyo." Not to mention the creepy note that somebody, likely Yoshi, replaced it with. I'm pretty much done with fortunes and symbols. They don't seem to work for me.

Reika shrugs and follows Mitsue to the vendor's amulet display.

My dad and I circle the float, marveling at the tapestries.

"Frame game." He holds his hands up like Ls and winks at me. "Pretty amazing, huh?"

"Sure. But I'd still rather be at the meeting."

"I know, kiddo. It's tough. But to be enlightened by all things is to be free from attachment to one's self and others."

I stare at him. "Huh?"

"I'm just saying, we must live by dying, by shedding egoistic delusion and finding our natural face."

"What are you talking about?"

He holds up his cell phone. "I finally learned how to use this thing, and I found an app that sends me a Zen saying every day. I'm learning a lot. For example—"

But I can't hear his next words because suddenly men start shouting.

The noise comes from outside a bar a few yards away. Six men, dressed in suits, are in some kind of a shouting match in Japanese. Suddenly, one man shoves another man, and in the next moment, two men are scuffling on the ground.

"Bunch of drunk businessmen, I guess," my dad says. "At a festival! This is crazy."

But I notice something else. People all around us are

leaving. Couples are grabbing hands and running. Parents are picking up children. One child wails for a lost balloon drifting away. His mother shushes him and holds him tight against her chest as she follows her husband. The musicians on the float have stopped playing. They're jumping over the side. Running off.

Reika and Mitsue run up to us. "Yahoos!" Reika hisses.

"We should leave the area at once," Mituse urges.

That's when shots ring out. From more than one gun.

We duck, and my dad frantically gestures for all of us to hide under the *yamaboko* float. We cower together, pressed up against one of the big wooden wheels. I cover my face as a few more shots ring out, then peer at the alley through my fingers. No police sirens wail. In fact, two police officers are running away from the alley with the rest of the festival-goers. Finally, three men in the alley run away, and then three head off in the opposite direction. One guy clutches his side and limps. He looks like he's been shot.

"Rival gangs," Mitsue says in a shuddery voice. "There have been other incidents like this lately. Gang tensions have been escalating around Kobe and Nagoya, and now, it seems, here in Kyoto."

Mitsue is shaking. Reika is crying softly. I lean against the float, so dizzy I feel like I might pass out. I've never seen real guns before or heard them, except on TV. My left ear won't stop ringing. The image of the guy clutching his side won't leave.

"Violet, what time is it?" my dad asks.

"Twenty of eight." My throat is parched, my voice raspy.

"Time to crash that meeting. Let's get out of here."

3
4

I'm guessing Mitsue told the taxi driver to step on it when she barked an order in Japanese. First, the driver gapes at us in total bewilderment, no doubt trying to make sense of us as a combination: a white girl and a *haafu* girl wearing festival kimonos, a *gaijin* man in jeans and a T-shirt, and an elegant Japanese woman in a plum kimono. But then Mitsue barks at him again, and the guy lays rubber.

I grip the seat, terrified we're going to hit someone, and close my eyes until he pulls up, brakes screeching, in front of the Kyoto National Museum.

The museum, an enormous brick building with classic architecture, resembles a fortress. "And of course it's closed," my dad moans, pushing the front door.

Mitsue manages to reach Kenji on his cell phone and tell him what we just witnessed. A security guard comes to the door and escorts us to the Conservation Center.

Kenji greets us first. He speaks with Mitsue in Japanese, softly, and then gives her a quick embrace. Then he asks if we're all okay.

"Been better," my dad says. "A little rattled. We wanted to get out of the streets."

"Of course." Kenji shakes his head in dismay. "I am terribly sorry you had to witness such a frightening event. Kyoto used to be so peaceful, and now gang tensions have spilled over here. Well, follow me to the lab, where everyone is now assembled."

In a lab in the next room, Agent Chang, Hideki, the *okami-san*, and a Japanese man and woman I've never seen are already seated in folding chairs around a covered easel.

Agent Chang and the man come over to us. She greets us and introduces the stout, somber-faced man as Inspector Mimura.

I look at Kenji, confused.

So does my dad. "I thought you didn't trust Japanese law enforcement. You know, because of the risk of media leaks or internal *yakuza* connections. What gives?"

"When we heard that Glenn was directly threatened in the ransom note, and the safety of an American—and children—was at stake, we had to make other decisions." Agent Chang glances at Reika and me. "The situation had to be monitored. My team has worked with Inspector Mimura, and he is absolutely trustworthy. I insisted on his presence this evening."

"I can understand," Kenji says. "I only wish my nephew

felt the same. He is firmly against Japanese authorities getting too close to the situation. He doesn't want to risk Fujikawa seeking revenge."

I glance at Hideki, slouched in his folding chair, staring stony-faced at the covered easel. For some reason I think of a sulky child. I figure he and Kenji have had some words, and Kenji's put him in his place.

The Japanese woman comes over to us now, and Inspector Mimura introduces her as Kikuchi-san, Skye's old friend. She doesn't look like someone whose honeymoon was abruptly interrupted. She's dressed professionally in a business suit, her hair neatly pulled back in a ponytail, her makeup impeccable.

"Please, call me Natsuko," says the woman, shaking our hands in turn.

Sitting in a chair, still as a statue, is the *okami-san*. She wears street clothes, slacks and cardigan, not the special *ro-kimono* uniform I'm used to seeing her in. She looks tense, with her legs crossed and her purse clutched to her chest. She nods a greeting as we take our seats.

Inspector Mimura stands before us. "Thank you, everyone, for coming here this evening. First, we have some important news. Thanks to the efforts and bravery of these two girls," he says, glancing at Reika and me, "and thanks to Glenn-san's timely communications with the FBI, we are closing in on Hiroshi Fujikawa, one of Japan's most notorious gang bosses. Three days ago, thanks to your tips, we apprehended two of his henchmen, Shinobu Nishio and Kazuo Uchida, at the Canadian border. They were trying to cross into Canada, hoping to fly to Tokyo from Vancouver. They were taken into custody yesterday."

Reika squeezes my hand. "Nice work," she whispers.

"And there is more news from the American front," Agent Chang says. "When interrogated, Uchida and Nishio confessed that they had consulted with Julian Fleury on several occasions. They paid Julian for information about the van Gogh drawings. They also paid for information related to the painting. His lead on the painting, of course, was false. But for a while, Uchida and Nishio were happy to pay for Julian's tips. In fact, they were so convinced that Skye had taken the painting to Glenn's house, and put it in one of his art studio cabinets, that they broke into his house to search for it."

My dad's eyes widen. "When was that?"

"The day of your art show reception. Around four in the afternoon."

My dad looks at me in awe. "You were right!" he says. "So it wasn't petty vandalism!"

My mind is buzzing. I always felt there had to be a connection between the Yamadas' break-in and my dad's broken window. Now I understand how that window, that rock, led back to Julian. Motivated by greed, he'd sent those guys following a trail of crumbs that led there.

"Julian Fleury has confessed that he did receive payments

for information," Agent Chang continues. "Furthermore, the police report he gave at the hospital after his assault was not entirely true. A security camera from outside a bar in Pioneer Square showed that *he* destroyed Mr. Marklund's paintings, in the alley behind the Margo Wise Gallery, *before* Uchida and Nishio arrived and assaulted him."

My dad closes his eyes and presses his hands to his temples. For a moment, it looks like he's praying. "Jesus. He trashed my paintings with his own hands. Why would he do that?"

"He got scared," Agent Chang replies. "He knew he was in over his head. Uchida and Nishio were trying to get their hands on the van Gogh painting, based on all his false leads. He felt he was being followed when he left Glenn's house. Apparently, they had the idea that he would be delivering the van Gogh painting to them personally. Which, of course, he couldn't. His lies had to come to an end. He wanted to make the *yakuza* think that he had been intercepted in transit, and that somebody else stole the van Gogh. They didn't buy it. He is now being charged with conspiracy to commit a crime, as well as property damage."

I let out a long breath, letting this information sink in. So there hadn't been a reason to warn Edge about the *yakuza* on the loose. They hadn't seen us filming back in Seattle, and he was probably never in danger. I feel a little ridiculous for dashing off that email now. But I also feel relieved, knowing Edge is totally safe.

Now Mimura holds up a yellow-and-red courier envelope. From it, he removes a single piece of crisp, white stationery, with a few lines in *kanji* characters typed on it. "Here is the latest correspondence from Fujikawa-san. It was sent to Kenji at the Akatsuki Ryokan this morning." He reads it first in Japanese, then in English. "'I have received intelligence that you are in Arashiyama. What a lovely time of year to be there. I hope that while hosting your American guests you have found some time to locate my painting. I have business scheduled in Kyoto, at the Gion Festival, this weekend. I can easily make a side trip to Arashiyama to collect my property in person.

"'However, the last time I made arrangements with you, you attempted deceit, with American agents in hiding. Therefore, this time I will receive my painting on the Katsura-gawa, since there is no place for people to hide on the river. Bring the painting to the *ukai* show at seven tomorrow evening. Hire a boat. A colleague of mine owns a snack-vending boat. We will come by your boat to collect it. I would strongly urge you to come alone. My enforcers will be alert to the presence of any undercover agents you might wish to bring. Remember, if I am deceived again, the *gaijin* artist will be erased. This is your second chance to comply.

And your last. I look forward to seeing you on the river. Hiroshi Fujikawa.'"

The room falls silent for a moment as everyone lets the words sink in.

All I can think about is the *gaijin* artist being erased, and the "source." Someone told Fujikawa that all of us were here. I don't know how Yoshi would know this, but I can't think of who else could tip him off.

"That guy has some nerve," my dad says. "How can he think these paintings are his?"

"Actually," says Agent Chang, "some documents have turned up at an appraisal firm in France. In March 1987, an appraiser in Tokyo did in fact authenticate the drawings and the painting as van Goghs. However, the appraiser indicated in his personal notes that the client, Tomonori Yamada, paid the equivalent of twenty-five thousand dollars to devalue the art, and to destroy any documents related to the appraisal. The appraiser took the fee and kept quiet all these years, mostly out of fear of retribution. But he also kept the documents. I came to Japan to confirm this information."

"So I guess that means Fujikawa really is entitled to the painting," I say slowly. *And Tomonori Yamada was kind of a criminal himself,* I add in my mind. I think of the impish, gap-toothed boy in the photo. That boy did not look like a future art thief. But what else could he be? Yes, Fujikawa is a gangster, but he paid for that art. It doesn't seem right for Tomonori to have hidden it away.

"That remains to be seen," says Agent Change. "We're looking into sales records from this Paris dealer. Some of his art has turned out to have falsified documents attached, indicating that thieves have tried to leak looted art back on the open market through him. Since these van Goghs were unsigned and not known to the world, it's very possible the dealer did not know what he had. But Fujikawa might have had his suspicions. And Tomonori certainly had more than an inkling that the paintings were valuable."

There's one thing I still can't wrap my mind around. "Why didn't Tomonori deliver that art?" I wonder out loud.

"Perhaps when he realized its value, Tomonori thought he could hide the art, and tell Fujikawa it was stolen from him in transit," says Inspector Mimura. "After Fujikawa eventually died, Tomonori could sell the works for a much higher fee than the commission he would have received."

Kenji shakes his head. "No. That does not sound like my brother at all."

The *okami-san* slowly stands up. She says something to Reika, and Reika nods. The *okami-san* speaks, and Reika translates.

"I knew Tomonori. He was . . . a personal friend of mine. I know he purchased art for other people who valued his keen eye. I know he purchased art for a man with *yakuza* connections, who I presume is Fujikawa. One night, the second-to-last time I saw him, I went to the *ukai* show with Tomonori. On the boat, he confessed something to me. He said some art he purchased in Paris had more value than his client thought. He knew Fujikawa was going to arrange for false documents to go with the papers and pass them off as works by a significant artist. He also knew Fujikawa would use the art as currency with other gangsters. When Tomonori discovered the drawings and painting were valuable, he didn't want them used for this gangster's purposes. He couldn't bear the thought of a crime boss using van Goghs to secure loans for illegal activities. He did not know how to save the art.

"I told him to hide the art and pretend it had been stolen from him. It was not a serious remark. I was young. I occasionally said reckless things. I never assumed he would do such a thing. He would be risking his life, angering a dangerous client. But after he died, I gradually came to suspect this is what he had done. When I think of how passionately he used to speak about art, and how carefully he listened to my wild suggestion that night at the *ukai* show, it now makes sense to me."

The *okami-san* takes a deep breath and continues, with a faraway look in her eyes as Reika translates for us. "I suppose that for most people, lives are more important than art. But to Tomonori, art, great art, was something worth dying for. If he could not stand up to his father and become an artist himself, at least he could save art from getting into the hands of real criminals who didn't appreciate it."

I wish the *okami-san* had told us all of this in the store-room the other night. It might have been helpful to know the extent to which Tomonori was tangled up with Fujikawa. But I guess she wanted to try to protect her lover as much as she could, as long as she could.

I glance at Hideki to see how he's taking this disturbing information about his dad. All this time he has sat with arms folded and legs crossed, his foot tapping in an agitated way. Now he is glaring at Inspector Mimura.

"Regardless of my father's motives, the evening is getting on," says Hideki. "We are wasting valuable time. If there is no painting beneath this one, we have only twenty-four hours to locate and deliver the painting. May we now see Kikuchi-san's results?"

His harsh words jolt me, but I can kind of understand why he sounds upset. The investigators and the *okami-san* have just revealed a new perspective on Tomonori. His taking the van Gogh out of Tokyo and hiding it in a remote inn was a kind of heist in itself. Tomonori might have had high values about art, but technically, he bought the van Goghs on behalf of Fujikawa and never delivered them. That's stealing.

"Yes, let us now see what Kikuchi-san has found," says Inspector Mimura.

Natsuko goes to the easel and flips on a powerful light

directed at the canvas. It connects to a computer screen, which shows shapes and shadows beneath Tomonori's painting.

"Usually, this technology would reveal an underpainting or drawing quite clearly," Natsuko explains. "Now, on this canvas, we can see some shapes here, and some faint impressions of what may be hills, a bridge, and a river. However, they are not clear 'ghost images' in the way that typical underpaintings appear. This leads me to believe that there is something else beneath this canvas. To find out, with Ogawa-san's kind permission, I must remove the back of the frame."

She looks at the *okami-san*, who nods.

Natsuko lifts the painting off the easel and moves it over to a table. She removes the screws and pries off the staples that hold the back of the frame together. Finally, she removes the canvas on its wood stretcher and sets the frame aside. She looks startled. "I must do more," she murmurs. "I am going to separate the canvas from the wooden stretcher." She brings out more precise tools and removes staples from the stretcher and canvas.

When all staples and tacks are out, she slips on a pair of white gloves and peels the canvas edges off the stretcher, working her way all around it. She pulls apart . . .

Two canvases.

"I thought so!" Natsuko exclaims. "This is a double-stretched canvas. Yamada-san put another canvas beneath his. Then he fitted the double-stretched canvas into the exterior frame. That way he did not need to apply paint directly. I am relieved to see this. I feared we would find an impossible situation here."

"You mean there's no special solvent that would just take off an over-painting?" I ask.

Natsuko shakes her head. "Some solvents can remove some kinds of paint, yes. But applying paint, and later a solvent, to a canvas and oil painting from the 1800s would certainly damage the original art."

There goes my whole theory about the over-painting. I guess Tomonori's picture of the man with the big paintbrush must have been a symbol of his own painting, and the scene with the easel and two canvases must have meant exactly what it looked like. A painting slipped behind another painting. I'm a little disappointed. It was a good theory, and it worked out well in *Kimono Girl*. But I guess life isn't always like manga. Still, I'm glad I came up with the over-painting theory because it did make me look more closely at all the canvases in the inn. I might otherwise have missed Tomonori's *ukai* painting, both in the *onsen* corridor and in the storeroom.

Natsuko has finished laying out the two canvases on a table, side by side. Now she ushers all of us over to look. Next to Tomonori's canvas is another one. Van Gogh's *Moon Crossing Bridge*.

I can't even describe the feeling of seeing the van Gogh painting in real life. The colors—blues, browns, greens—are vibrant and thickly applied. The brushstrokes are vigorous, with the artist's characteristic swirls and chops; the river actually looks like it's moving, as do the clouds in the sky. This painting is alive. It's hard not to reach out and touch it.

"Is it in good shape?" my dad asks.

"Much better than I expected," says Natsuko. "The top canvas concealed the painting from exposure to elements that might have caused damage. Though it is never advisable for one painting to nestle against another, with canvases touching, and I detect some cracking in the paint. I will need to conduct further studies to determine the extent of restoration work that is needed and the—"

"There's no time for restoration work," Hideki says, cutting her off. "And for our purposes, it does not matter what shape the painting is in, only that we have it. I need you to package this canvas for transportation. Make sure it's in something that keeps it safe from the water. And while you're at it, I could use some kind of waterproof tube for the van Gogh drawings Fujikawa-san will bring."

"Waterproof? I'm afraid I don't understand," says Natsuko.

Hideki sighs. "In case the art falls into the river or gets splashed during the exchange."

"Oh, we'll nab Fujikawa just before the exchange takes place," Agent Chang assures him. "I don't think there will be time for the works to be damaged in any way."

Hideki gives her a hard look. "Thank you. But that will not be necessary," he says. "We will exchange the painting for the drawings, as he demands, and then he will leave."

"You can't obstruct justice!" says Agent Chang. "This guy is behind the Seattle van Gogh heist, and he's a suspect in several other international art crime cases. Not to mention an enormous public safety threat. I learned from one of my associates here that his gang is behind some of the turf wars that have been erupting lately. I think all the boats need to be filled with undercover agents, and we need to take this guy down tomorrow night."

Inspector Mimura looks embarrassed. "Actually, Agent Chang, I have looked into the possibility of a covert operation, given Fujikawa's history with drug and weapon sales, but there is not enough of a link to this art heist to justify mounting a sting operation. Setting him up on the river tomorrow, well . . . it is kind of impossible. It violates Japanese law. I am sorry."

Agent Chang paces, clearly annoyed. "This is so frustrating. He's right within our reach."

Hideki shakes his head. "Do you really want to put a foreigner at risk here?" He looks at my dad. "Fujikawa has clearly been threatening Glenn-san in his recent letters. Even if you take Fujikawa into custody tomorrow evening, he'll have someone else carry out orders."

I swallow hard and look tearfully at my dad, who is picking a hangnail and frowning. He's not looking so Zen right now.

"I have a better solution," Hideki says. "Keep your agents far from the river. I will go with my uncle and my aunt to deliver the painting and collect the drawings at the *ukai* show."

"Not your aunt," Kenji says. "There is no need for Mitsue to be anywhere near this scene."

"I'm not leaving your side," Mitsue insists, and she says a few words to him in Japanese.

"After Glenn leaves Japan, we can work together to make another arrangement," Hideki continues to Agent Chang. "I will help the FBI, Interpol, any agency, in any way possible. I will lure Fujikawa to the United States, where you could then bring him into custody. Please, let me settle this business between Fujikawa and my father."

Agent Chang looks disappointed, but she shrugs. "If that's what you wish, I'll get out of your way. I've done all I'm authorized to do here."

Natsuko clears her throat. "Excuse me. I am ready to package the van Gogh for transport. But what about the other painting?" Natsuko gestures to Tomonori's *ukai* picture.

Hideki looks at the *okami-san*. "Ogawa-san shall have it," he says. "It was a gift to her from my father. It is rightfully hers."

Natsuko picks up the van Gogh and heads for another room. I catch a strange expression on her face, an expression I can't quite read. An odd look of determination.

"Where are you taking that?" Hideki demands.

"My wrapping supplies are in another room. It will be ready for you in twenty minutes."

As the door closes behind her, the *okami-san* picks up Tomonori's *ukai* canvas and replaces it in the frame, with a grateful glance at Hideki.

July 18, the day of the painting handover, arrives with a van Gogh–worthy sunrise. I stretch luxuriously in my futon, in the warm yellow light, feeling well-rested for the first time in days. The painting's been found. Fujikawa will be satisfied. The Yamadas will get the van Gogh drawings back. And my dad will be safe.

The mood is lighter at breakfast, too, when we gather with the Yamadas in the private dining room. My dad shares some quotes from his Zen phone app, and I'm actually not annoyed. The wrapped-up canvas rests against a wall near the head of the table, like a guest of honor; Kenji swears he won't let it out of his sight until the art exchange on the river this evening.

Hideki, though, is strangely quiet. He retreats to his room soon after breakfast, with apologies. "I have ignored some important work for the office for too long."

Kenji and Mitsue leave soon after, taking the canvas back to their room. They each pick up a corner of it and ease it out the door, as if carrying a napping baby.

My dad, Reika, and I take the train to Kyoto and watch the *Gion Matsuri* parade. We spend the day touring the Gion district, visiting some famous temples and shrines, and walking *Tetsugaku no michi*, the Philosopher's Path. We visit a crafts museum and watch a demonstration on how to make woodblock prints. I watch one man carve a waterfall scene into a cherry block. He uses his delicate knives and chisels so expertly, it looks like he's drawing in a hunk of cheese or butter.

When we finally leave the crafts museum, my dad hands me a package. It's a cherry block and a rolled-up bundle wrapped in rice paper. When I unwrap it, I find a leather pouch, and inside that, a starter set of wood-carving knives.

"These are beautiful!" I exclaim. The blades glint in the afternoon sun. "Thank you!"

"Enjoy them, kiddo," my dad says with a smile. "I know you think drawing's your thing, but it's always good to flex your muscles and try another medium. Mitsue tells me you have a good eye for prints. Who knows, maybe there's a printmaker in you waiting to come out!"

We roam around Kyoto for several more hours. Even though the memory of last night's gunshots still reverberates in my head, and my left ear still rings, the streets feel safer in daylight. I feel like a normal tourist. We stay in Kyoto for an early dinner before hopping the train back to Arashiyama.

As the boatman poles us back down the river to the *ryokan*, the sky turns pink with the first blush of sunset.

"Those must be people getting tickets for the *ukai* show

already," I say, pointing to a line of tourists at the dock that we're leaving behind.

"It's a beautiful night. A good night for seeing *ukai*," Reika says a little enviously.

"Don't get any ideas," my dad says. "We'll go another time, when gangsters aren't out on a boating excursion. Hey, when we get back to the inn, let's go to the riverbank and watch the sunset. That's kind of a show, right?"

Back at the *ryokan*, the three of us put on our regular *yukata* and meet up again by the river. My dad brings a sketchbook and colored pencils, and I bring my new wood-carving set. As the sky turns a deeper pink, and then orange, my dad sketches. Reika writes a poem in her Hello Kitty notebook. I outline a simple shape of an *ayu* in pencil on my cherry block and begin to cut my pattern with a knife. It's not nearly as easy as the man in the crafts museum made it look.

While I labor over my tiny cuts, I position myself so I can see the door to the *ryokan* in my peripheral vision, and I look up about every minute. I want to see the Yamadas leave for the boat launch with the painting. Maybe for a sense of closure. It's so weird that nobody's talked about the painting or the art exchange since breakfast. It's almost as if the past two and a half weeks never happened.

Suddenly, my dad groans. "Oh, no. Sunflower yellow."

"What about it?" I ask.

"It's a colored pencil I need. I left it in my room. I'd love to finish up this sketch before we lose the light."

I glance at my watch. It's twenty of seven. The Yamadas should be leaving any moment. Maybe if I get the pencil I'll bump into them in the hall. Besides, my hand is getting tired from cutting. "I'll get it," I offer, shaking out my cramped fingers.

"I'll come, too," says Reika, closing her notebook.

"Here, take this, in case Hideki's left already." My dad hands me the silver room key. "Oh, and this tablet of paper could go back, before the evening damp sets in," he adds, handing me a large drawing tablet and a case of fine-tipped pens.

My hands are really cramped from woodcarving; I think I'm done with that for the day. My progress feels so slow. So I roll up my knives and chisels in the little leather pouch, and tie the string of the pouch to my *yukata* belt, freeing my hands to carry my dad's stuff.

As we enter the *ryokan*, Reika remarks, "It's so quiet. Where is everyone?"

"The business-retreat people left today. And everyone else is probably going to the *ukai* show," I grumble. "I totally think we could be there watching this from afar."

"There's not even anyone at reception," says Reika, pointing at the empty desk. A phone rings instantly, and no one comes running. The door to the *okami-san*'s private office is closed.

"The chambermaids are probably cleaning up dinner stuff, and maybe the *okami-san*'s helping," I suggest. "We're usually in the dining room now, so maybe it's always this quiet."

"I guess. It's just sort of eerie. Let's get this pencil and go."

We tap on the door to my dad and Hideki's room. Nobody answers. I insert the key in the lock and slowly slide open the door.

It's easy to see which side of the room is Hideki's. His black suitcase is open in one corner, all his clothes neatly folded and stacked. My dad's clothes and art supplies are strewn around the floor. I spot the sunflower-yellow pencil with some other pencils on top of his portable easel. I also find his cell phone on top of a T-shirt, in the *tokonoma*, the sacred alcove where you're not supposed to put stuff. Not wanting the *okami-san* or the maids to take offense, I pick those things up.

Reika gathers an armful of button-down shirts from Hideki's suitcase. She holds them to her face and inhales. "I just love Hideki's cologne." Reika smiles. She looks almost drugged. "Why do high school boys wear that cheap Rite-Aid crap? Here, smell this."

I back away. "I am not smelling Hideki's shirts. Let's go."

Then I notice something in the suitcase, which is exposed now that she's taken out shirts.

Two red-and-yellow courier envelopes. I think of the day I saw Hideki take one of those in his uncle's office. And the one Inspector Mimura opened last night at the meeting. My feet propel me forward, as if I'm remote controlled, and I take those envelopes out. From each envelope, I shake out a document: crisp, white paper with typed *kanji* characters. I ask Reika to translate.

She reads both letters silently. "Oh, Violet. Something is way off. These letters are signed by Fujikawa, and demand the painting. But they don't say a thing about your dad."

"They don't? Then what do they say?"

She translates. In the first letter, dated last week, Fujikawa expresses anger about the sting operation in Seattle, and demands the van Gogh by July 18. "I understand your company is facing an audit from the Osaka Securities Commission, to investigate possible past dealings with *yakuza*. Rest assured, I will use all my media contacts to make it known that your brother once worked for me, and that your company has made numerous payoffs over the years. Your company will not survive. Your nephew's promising career will be destroyed."

The second letter sounds almost exactly like the one Inspector Mimura read to us last night, detailing how he will collect the painting in exchange for the drawings on the water. But again, no mention of the *gaijin* artist being erased if he's deceived. Instead, these words: "Do not attempt to deceive me again, or your history will be made known."

"These are blackmail notes!" I exclaim. "Not death threats. Hideki must have intercepted these letters and changed them, adding stuff about my dad, before passing them on to Kenji!"

"But why?"

I stop and think about it for a moment. "Reika, I think that Hideki wants to get his hands on the art. The drawings and the painting. He wanted to scare Kenji into thinking my dad might get hurt, to make him—to make *all of us*—work even harder to find the painting. Which we did."

"I don't get it," says Reika. "Isn't Fujikawa the villain here?"

"He's a villain, all right. He might have murdered Tomonori Yamada, and he ordered those two *yakuza* in Seattle to steal the drawings. And he's done awful things to the Yamada Corporation. But he's not the only villain. Don't you see? Hideki's the real mastermind!"

Reika stares at me, almost tearfully. "No," she whispers.

"He is taking advantage of Fujikawa's greed. He wants to get the drawings and the painting in one place so he can take off with them!"

Reika starts pacing, staring helplessly at the letters. "I don't know, Violet. If Fujikawa doesn't get the art, then it belongs to Kenji and Mitsue, right? Tomonori left Kenji all his art in his will. The only way that Hideki could possibly get it is if—" She claps her hands to her mouth and stares at me.

"If both Kenji and Mitsue were dead," I finish. I take a

deep breath. "Reika, I think the bathing yahoo from room nine is working for Hideki. I think he might be . . . a hit man."

"What would Hideki do with the van Goghs?" Reika asks.

"Sell them. If they were 'discovered,' and legally inherited, he could sell them at auction and get way more money than he could selling them on the black market. And Hideki could use the money," I add. My mind is racing now, memories flashing. I think back to that drive with Kenji through Roppongi Hills. The Mori Tower complex. "Hideki's dream project is to build something greater than the Mori Tower. Some huge business and entertainment complex. He'd need a lot of dough."

"But how can Hideki sell the painting if it probably belongs to Fujikawa?"

"He has to get rid of Fujikawa, too. I bet it was Hideki's idea for Fujikawa to come here and collect the painting in person. That way he could get all three people with claims to the painting in one place and eliminate them at the same time." I lay out the letters, take photos of them with my dad's cell phone, in case something happens to the originals I'm about to steal. I set down the cell phone on Hideki's suitcase while I slide the letters under the lapel of my *yukata*. I put the empty courier envelopes back in the suitcase.

Meanwhile, Reika arranges Hideki's shirts as neatly as she can, cursing herself for having moved them. "I'm not sure if these blue ones were on the left or the right of the suitcase," she mumbles. "Are you really going to take those letters out of this room?"

"Yes. We have to tell the Yamadas not to get on that boat tonight, and we'll need these as proof to convince them. And we have to get them to Inspector Mimura as well. But first, let's go tell my dad what we found."

We race back to the river and show the letters to my dad. Reika translates them for him.

"We have to tell Kenji and Mitsue not to go to the river tonight!" I exclaim when she's done. "We only have fifteen minutes to make sure they don't get on that boat!"

"But Kenji and Mitsue already left the inn," says my dad.

I look around. "What? When?"

"They took the painting down to the boat launch right after you guys went inside. You must have just missed them."

Reika and I exchange an anguished look. The Yamadas are drifting toward doom right this moment. "Were they with Hideki?" I ask.

"No. When I said good-bye to them, they told me Hideki was staying behind to take care of some business. Something about an international conference call. I did think that was odd, considering how invested he was in finding this art. You'd think he'd want to see the exchange. I guess now it makes sense. He's got to stay out of the way so a hit man can do his job."

"You have to call Agent Chang!" Reika says.

"I think she's already on her way back to Seattle," my dad says. "She said there wasn't much that Inspector Mimura could authorize her to do here."

"Then how are we going to reach the Yamadas and Inspector Mimura?" I moan.

"We could call Kenji on his cell," Reika suggests. "Since Hideki's not with him yet. And we could call the police and ask them to help us reach Inspector Mimura."

"Good plan!" My dad looks around the grass at his belongings. "Now where's my cell?"

"I have it. It's right—wait." I look down. My hand is clutching the stupid yellow pencil, not the phone. "I left your cell in your room. Oh my God. I left it right on Hideki's suitcase after I took pictures of the letters! If he sees it, he'll figure out we were looking through his stuff."

We all look at each other and then start walking quickly toward the *ryokan*.

Suddenly, I hear thrashing in the hydrangea bushes on the path behind us. Before I can turn around, strong hands grab my arms and wrench them behind my back. Reika screams. The next thing I know, my wrists are bound together with twine. The twine cuts into my skin when I try to squirm free. I try to twist and kick my captor, but he holds my arms fast. The last thing I see, out of the corner of my eye, is two men grabbing my dad and Reika from behind. Then what seems to be a burlap sack is thrown over my head.

I feel like I'm drowning, choking, and I'm not even in water. I'm aware that we're all being pushed downhill, down the path toward the river and the *ryokan*'s small dock.

I'm shoved onto some kind of moving platform. I fight to keep my balance, and lose. I fall, hard, on my side. A moment later, I hear Reika and my dad fall down next to me. Reika is trembling right by my side, my dad is breathing heavily next to her, and we all seem to be lying facedown. Then I realize we're on a boat. I can hear the lapping of water. I can feel the *tatami* beneath my bare feet. I can smell grass on the river-bank. And a sweet, musky smell. Hideki's cologne.

Wild hope seizes me. Reika once said she doesn't read *kanji* as well as she speaks Japanese, and she didn't use a dictionary when she translated the letters from Hideki's suitcase. Maybe she misread the letters. Maybe Hideki's not such a bad person. Yahoos have captured us, working off misinformation, and Hideki's our only hope.

"Hideki! Help us!" I call out. My voice sounds so muffled from the sack over my head, I'm not sure he can hear me. I call out again.

"Help you?" says Hideki. "After you went through my personal belongings? Why should I help you?"

Something sinks inside me. He knows we know. He's the one behind our abduction. These thugs are working for him.

"We didn't go through anything!" I hear Reika protest.

"Lying will not help you," Hideki says. His voice is

as smooth as ever. "I found Glenn's phone on my suit-case. I saw the pictures you took. Pictures of my personal correspondence."

"The girls were just playing around with my phone," my dad protests. "If they found anything of yours, I'm sure they didn't read it."

I wince. *Nice try, Dad.*

Hideki speaks in Japanese. I feel the boat rock as some of the men get off. At least two men; I can hear their footsteps as they leap onto the dock. That leaves one of our abductors on the boat, which lurches as he moves toward the front. I hear something slap the water. The boat begins to move, turning slightly. I guess the man is poling the boat away from the dock.

"Where are we going?" I call out, in case Hideki's still with us.

There's a pause, then Hideki answers. He must be sitting just a couple feet away from us. "You are on a *ukai* show spectator boat."

"Are we going to the show?" Reika asks in a wavery voice.

"In a sense," Hideki says. "Though I doubt you will have the opportunity to see much of it. I'm afraid you don't have the best seats for viewing."

"Enough of this!" my dad snaps. I can feel him thrashing next to me, trying to loosen his bindings. "Untie us right now!"

"This will all go much more smoothly, and be more comfortable for everyone, if you remain silent and if you do not struggle," says Hideki.

"Tell us what's going on!" my dad barks. "We have the right to know."

"I can understand your position," Hideki says. "I can tell you this much. In a few minutes, this boat will stop a few yards behind my aunt and uncle's boat. Fujikawa, in a snack boat, will tie up to my aunt and uncle's boat. At the time of the art exchange, my associate here will take out Fujikawa, Kenji, and Mitsue, and then the three of you. Then I'll collect the drawings and painting, and I'll be on my way."

"Take us out—we're going to be killed, too?" my dad asks.

My limbs have gone completely numb. I don't know if it's from the ropes or from terror. Of course he's going to kill us. We know too much. Even if the art exchange goes through, we have enough information, and the letters we found, to launch an investigation of Hideki Yamada. Hideki's worked too hard on this plan to inherit the art. He won't risk having us mess it all up.

"If you kill us, the FBI will be on you in an instant," my dad says.

"You think because you are Americans you are going to get special treatment?" Hideki laughs softly. "Your FBI already could not prevent this moment from taking place. Agent Chang has given up and returned to Seattle. Your deaths will be considered casualties of *yakuza* warfare. You will be killed in the dark, far from the shore, with no witnesses. *Gaijin* travelers in the wrong place, at the wrong time."

"It'll make the news," my dad says. "You can't cover up something like this."

"Yes, it will certainly make the news," Hideki agrees. "The headlines will read that the Yamada Corporation CEO and his wife, and three *gaijin*, were caught in the crossfire of a gang turf war. These unfortunate incidents happen, and investigators do not bother looking closely into gang warfare incidents here in Japan."

"Your mural isn't done!" my dad protests. "Your dignitaries will be welcomed by an empty wall!"

"That is a pity, I agree," says Hideki. "But it cannot be helped. And now, I must insist on silence. No more talking, please. Keep your heads down. I apologize for the scent of this canvas tarp. It may be a bit unpleasant. But at least your time beneath it will be brief."

I hear a scraping sound, and then something that sounds like a flag snapping. In the next moment, I'm smothered by a heavy material that smells like mold and covers me head to toe. He must have thrown a big tarp over all of three of us, to conceal us from any passing boaters. I can feel Reika beside me, twisting her head to get air, and to the left of her, I can hear my dad sneeze.

The boat glides down the river. *Should I yell? Are we near any other boats, anyone who can help us?*

No. Too risky. All Hideki's hit man has to do is show his gun. People will think he's a yahoo and get right out of the way.

I have to get my wrists free. There's no way to take action otherwise. I twist my hands around and feel the twine gradually loosen. A little. But not enough.

While I'm shifting and twisting, I feel something jab my waist on my right side. The leather pouch with my wood-carving tools. I tied it to my *yukata* belt earlier! It contains three knives that are small but have supersharp blades. If I could get just one knife from that pouch, we could cut the twine off each other's wrists. Under the tarp, in darkness, our escape might not be detected. *Can I do this? Can I do it blind?*

I roll to shift my weight to my right side and move my hands, behind my back, toward my left side. My wrists are bound, but my fingers can just grasp the pouch. I twist my torso as far as I can, but I can't get enough leverage to pull up the pouch flap and open it up.

"Reika," I whisper. "My carving tools. They're in a pouch on my *yukata* belt. Can you reach the pouch?"

Reika maneuvers slowly, writhing along the bottom of the boat until she's positioned a few inches higher than me. She fumbles and grasps the pouch. "I got it!" she whispers, and tugs until it opens. After a little more fumbling, she extracts something from the pouch. "I'll try to cut your bindings."

"Quiet," my dad cautions.

Reika saws at the twine around my wrists, but nothing seems to be happening. "I don't think this is a knife," she whispers. "It's not cutting at all."

"It's probably a gouge," I say. "It's not sharp enough. Go back in the pouch and grab another tool. Hurry!"

Reika rummages again and extracts another tool. "Ow!" she mutters. "This one's a knife, all right. I just cut myself." She saws at the twine, timing her knife movements with the sounds of the bamboo pole hitting the water. She can't see what she is doing, since the burlap is still over her head. I pray she doesn't press too hard and hit my skin with the blade. But after about ten slices, I feel the twine slide off my wrists. I take the sack off my head, reach for the knife, and cut her free, then my dad.

Untied, we huddle under the tarp, which smells overpoweringly of mildew. "I wonder where we are?" Reika whispers. "Should we jump out and swim for shore? Or stand up and yell for help? Maybe the *ukai* show passengers would hear us."

"I'm assuming these guys are armed," my dad says. "Let's lie low, at least until we figure out where we are."

I raise myself onto my elbows and lift the edge of the canvas, just enough to see out. The sky has darkened to indigo. We're on a long passenger boat for the *ukai* show, complete with cheerful glowing lanterns dangling from the roof, each one decorated with a black cormorant. Hideki is sitting at the front of the boat, looking intently ahead, while an older, gray-haired man poles the boat forward. When he turns to the side, I recognize him as the bathing yahoo. Shaking, I lower the canvas. "We know the hit man," I whisper. "It's our old friend from room nine."

"Look again," Reika urges. "Do you see other boats? Anyone we could ask for help?"

I gather all my courage and raise the canvas again. Now I can see we've passed under the Moon Crossing Bridge already, and the *ukai* show is about fifty yards up ahead.

Twelve spectator boats just like ours form a graceful arc, the passengers silhouetted in the dark. One boat lingers some distance behind the others. I figure it contains the Yamadas and the van Gogh, and some poor boatman who's about to get caught in the middle of a mess.

A bit closer is the *ukai* fishing boat. Fire crackles inside the wire basket hanging off the boat, making the water glow orange. With that light, I can make out the three men standing on the fishing boat, and the bobbing heads and flapping wings of cormorants, still tied up, eager to dive. One man slowly beats a drum. "The fishing boat's only about twenty yards away," I whisper. "Maybe we could communicate with them somehow."

I watch as one fisherman tosses the birds into the water, then leans way over the side of his boat, struggling to keep control of the leashes as the birds dive down. Then he pulls the birds back on the boat and extracts fish—the *ayu*—from their beaks. I wish I could set them all free. They're working so hard and don't get to keep their rewards. They strain at their leashes. They squawk in protest and flap their wings.

Is that how Tomonori felt, collecting art for a gang boss? Is that why his journal clues and his cover-up painting all related to *ukai*? Or was it just that the *ukai* show was located near the love of his life, who would keep the van Gogh painting safe as a symbol of their undying love?

Suddenly, I hear the whine of a motor. A wooden boat with an outboard motor slowly approaches the Yamadas' boat. It's the snack boat. Which Fujikawa is on.

The bathing yahoo—our boatman—poles us faster toward the snack boat. Reika is squeezing my hand so hard it's going numb.

"What's going on, Violet? What can you see?" my dad asks.

"The bathing yahoo—the hit man—is poling our boat, standing up on the end, and Hideki's sitting right by him. And I can see the snack boat moving toward the Yamadas' boat."

A man on the snack boat cuts the motor as he pulls up by the Yamadas. This could be Fujikawa himself. He looks old enough to be the famed gang leader; he has a slight stoop, and his hair glows silver in the moonlight. Yet he doesn't look as scary as I thought a gang boss would. He wears a black windbreaker and a baseball cap, like some old guy going to a sporting event. But since he's old, and not so physically strong, I'm guessing this has to be Fujikawa and not one of his henchmen.

Now he's holding up a long tube. Kenji reaches out for it. I suck in my breath. "Fujikawa's just handed over the drawings," I whisper to my dad and Reika. That means we're minutes, or seconds, from gunfire.

Think, think, think. Tears sting my eyes. I'm not Kimono Girl. I have no superpowers. I can't fly over to that boat and stop this exchange from continuing.

They say your entire life flashes before your eyes when you're about to die. For me, it's all forty-three episodes of *Vampire Sleuths*. Scenes of Kyo and Mika thwarting bad guys. And suddenly a scene from episode five flashes into my mind and sticks. Kyo and Mika were on a boat not unlike this one. A canoe. An armed villain crept onto it, and they threw all their weight against the side to knock him off the boat. This *ukai* spectator boat is wider and longer, but maybe if three of us rocked the boat hard, we could cause Hideki and the hit man to topple off.

Back under the canvas, I quickly whisper the plan to my dad and Reika. "Hideki and the hit man are right on the front of the boat. Hideki's perched on the edge, and the hit man is standing up with the pole. It shouldn't take much effort to throw off their balance."

"But how can we rock this boat?" Reika asks. "If we all stand up, they'll see us and shoot us."

"We can stay under the tarp. We'll roll really hard and make the boat lurch." I'm surprised at how steady my voice is. There's no time for fear. Only action. "Go right, then left. On the count of three. One. Two. Three!"

We roll right. The boat tips. I hear a splash. Then another. We throw off the canvas, and I see both men in the water, thrashing and coughing.

The bathing yahoo's hand reaches up for the boat. He's going to climb back on.

"Quick, girls! Swim toward the *ukai* boat!" my dad shouts, jumping off. Reika follows.

And I, too, slip over the side of the boat, into the dark, cold water of the Katsura-gawa.

The *yukata* fabric weighs me down and sticks to my legs. I tread water, gasping, pushing the fabric away. My dad and Reika are stronger swimmers, and don't notice I've gotten tangled up and fallen behind.

While I loosen my *yukata* belt so I can move in the water better, I see the bathing yahoo and Hideki both climbing back on the boat we've just left.

I look at the Yamadas' boat. Startled by the commotion, the Yamadas are looking toward us. Mitsue points to my dad and Reika swimming toward the *ukai* boat.

The bathing yahoo stands on the prow again and raises one arm. He points a gun. Not at the Yamadas, but at my dad and Reika. The *ukai* fishermen fight to control the agitated birds as my dad and Reika approach.

Hideki barks something at him in Japanese. The bathing yahoo turns and aims in the direction of the Yamadas and Fujikawa instead. This is it, then. The moment when he kills Fujikawa, Kenji, and Mitsue. I close my eyes.

Fujikawa starts the motor of his boat, and I open my eyes again. Passengers on spectator boats, figuring out what's going on, start to scream. Boatmen struggle to turn their boats around and flee.

The bathing yahoo fires the gun. Twice. I can feel the hot rush of air as the second bullet screams past my head. Instinctively, I dive under water. I stay there, holding my breath.

When I emerge, gasping, I see my dad and Reika are being hauled up onto the *ukai* boat. They're safe, for now. But I can't see Kenji and Mitsue. Did the bathing yahoo kill them?

No. They're standing up. Kenji picks up the wrapped canvas, the painting, and hurls it into the water, and then he hurls the tube with the drawings, like a javelin. Then he and Mitsue jump overboard and swim for shore.

The painting! The drawings! Why did Kenji throw them into the river? Maybe he wanted to distract the gunmen, send them away from him and toward the art.

Another shot rings out. This one comes from the snack boat. From Fujikawa himself, now crouching and pointing his gun. So the hit-man didn't kill him yet, either.

The bathing yahoo teeters on the edge of the boat for a moment, as if hesitating, and then falls backward into the water with a loud splash. He does not come up for air.

In the next instant, Hideki dives overboad. He must swim underwater a long distance; I can't see where he went. I don't know if he's armed. I don't know if he's going after his aunt and uncle, Fujikawa, the van Goghs in the water, or me. And

Fujikawa is now scanning the water, his arm with the gun outstretched as he searches for his next target.

I have to get to the *ukai* boat, to my dad and Reika.

A white paper lantern with a cormorant painted on it drifts by; it must have fallen off our boat when we rocked it. Without a light in it, it slips easily over my head. It's amazing it hasn't disintegrated yet; the paper must be treated. I'm now at a part of the river that's shallow enough for me to touch bottom. From a distance, in darkness, I might look like a lantern bobbing on the water and avoid detection by Hideki or Fujikaya. I poke a hole in the paper so I can see out.

Halfway to the *ukai* boat, my fingers brush something. A stick? I scoop the object toward me. A black plastic tube. I clutch it with both hands. This has to be the drawings! I grab the tube and frog-kick through the water, trying to glide without making a splash or a sound.

As I near the *ukai* boat, I can see the last bird has been hauled out of the water. My dad and Reika are anxiously looking out over the water for me. "Violet!" my dad calls. "Violet! Where are you?" His voice is hoarse, his eyes wild.

A few feet from the boat, I rip the lantern off my head and wave the plastic tube at him.

"Violet! Thank God, you're there!" my dad calls. "Swim over here, kiddo! Hurry!"

A fisherman tosses me a rope. I reach for it, but in doing so, I drop the tube.

Somebody grabs the end of it.

Hideki. I didn't even hear him swim up behind me.

I grab for the tube with one hand and manage to get my fingers around it.

"Give. Me. That." Hideki tugs hard on the tube as he spits out his words.

I hold on firmly with one hand and cling to the fisherman's rope with the other.

"You are a troublesome little *gaijin*," Hideki snarls. "You seem to be always in the way." He lunges at me and tries to push me under.

I kick him off and resurface. *Chikara* fills me head to toe. If I were in Miyazaki film right now, a great wind would be stirring up and the water would curl into waves. My voice, when it comes, sounds so commanding I hardly recognize it. "Your dad would be so disappointed if he knew what was going on here!"

"You know nothing of my father. What do you know about anything? You are a typical American child—an interfering, spoiled, disobedient child," he hisses. He grabs the tube with such force it slips out of my hand.

I grab it back and hold it close to my chest.

"I do know things," I shout at Hideki. "I know that if you kill your aunt and uncle and Fujikawa, and then sell this art, you can build your stupid business complex, and the world can enjoy the lost van Goghs. But the world won't have Kenji and Mitsue. And I know that people are more important than art."

I feel the rope tugging at me. All three fishermen are pulling now, dragging me toward the boat. Hideki splashes after me. His fingers graze my sleeve, but I manage to snatch it free.

Just as I reach the side of the boat, Hideki makes one last grab for the tube. I summon all my strength, let go of the rope, take the tube in two hands, and hurl it onto the *ukai* boat. It comes dangerously near the basket of fire, but lands safely on deck.

The next thing I know, strong arms are pulling me up. I flop onto the boat deck, gasping. The cormorants in their cages squawk wildly. As my dad and Reika throw towels around me, I see that the fishermen have managed to get a rope looped around Hideki's leg. They are pulling it tight while he thrashes and shouts. It's their biggest catch of the day.

I look beyond him to the snack boat, whose motor is sputtering and spewing smoke. Something seems wrong with it. Fujikawa frantically tries to fix it. Then I see someone stand up from behind the counter of the snack boat and approach Fujikawa, pointing a gun.

I stifle a scream when I see who it is. It's Yoshi!

Fujikawa turns around. Slowly, the crime boss raises his arms in surrender.

Then a police boat zooms toward the scene. Someone calls out through a megaphone. The police pull up to the snack boat, board it, and handcuff Fujikawa, as Yoshi, gun lowered, stands to the side.

"Yoshi must have snuck onto Fujikawa's snack boat," I say to my dad and Reika, through chattering teeth. "I bet he did something to mess with the motor, and then he threatened Fujikawa with the gun and forced him to surrender."

My dad frowns. "I don't get it. I thought Yoshi was an informant."

"Yeah, wasn't he tipping off Fujikawa?" Reika asks. "Like about the Seattle sting?"

"I'm sure Yoshi was an informant," I say. "But I think he was working *against* Fujikawa all this time. Not for him." A new piece of the puzzle slides into place. I smile. "Which means he didn't tip anyone off about the Seattle sting after all. He wasn't the leak."

Reika stares at me. "He didn't? Then who did?"

"Hideki. I bet he's had his own little private communications with Fujikawa all along."

Another motorboat, carrying more policemen, speeds over to the *ukai* boat. The officers move fast, hauling Hideki out of the water, into one of their boats, and handcuffing him. He's no longer a handsome movie-star man, and not even a crafty mastermind anymore. He looks more like a scrawny drowned rat, and the firelight reveals his true expression. Bitter. Defeated.

Then police help my dad, Reika, and me off of the *ukai* boat and onto the police boat. One officer drapes a wool blanket around my shoulders. I'm grateful for the gesture as much as the warmth.

We speed back to the dock at Arashiyama. Two police help us off the boat, and Hideki is led away.

I hear footsteps approaching. I turn and see Agent Chang approaching us with a smile.

"I thought you went back to Seattle!" I exclaim.

"I couldn't leave. I only said that to pacify Hideki. This art exchange tonight was too important," Agent Chang says. "Kenji and Mitsue are on their way here by boat. Officers picked them up on the opposite shore."

I reach into my *yukata* and pull out the letters from Hideki's suitcase. I hand the two soggy papers to Agent Chang and explain what they are as we unfold them. The ink, though blurred, is legible.

"This will be very useful for the Japanese detectives who will interrogate Hideki," says Agent Chang. "You're one brave young lady," she adds. "You saved lives. And the drawings."

"Thanks. But the drawings might be wrecked. And the painting—that fell into the river, too, and I'm sure it's completely waterlogged by now."

"The painting is fine."

I shake my head, not understanding. "But I saw the flat package on the Yamadas' boat. And then I saw Kenji throw it, along with the drawings, once people started shooting."

"It was blank," Agent Chang says. "The real van Gogh painting is safely in a vault in the Kyoto National Museum. Natsuko Kikuchi told me privately, at the meeting last night, that she had a funny feeling about Hideki."

So that explained the odd look the conservator had on her face when she hurried away to package the van Gogh, out of Hideki's sight.

"Ms. Kikuchi couldn't bear to send a real van Gogh out on the river like that," Agent Chang continues. "I told her that while we couldn't formally mount a sting operation in Japan, due to the laws forbidding undercover operations, it was not against the law for an art conservator to make an independent judgment, an ethical decision. And it was not against the law for an FBI agent, concerned for the safety of some American travelers she knows, to monitor a brewing situation and line up some officers from the Organized Crime Bureau. Now, shall we have a look at those drawings and see if they survived submersion?"

I hope the plastic tube has done its job, and the drawings aren't water damaged.

We follow Agent Chang to a police station down the road, where we can safely open the plastic tube without tourists and onlookers watching. As Agent Chang uses a razor to slice through a laminated seal, I have a horrible thought. Maybe Fujikawa tricked us with an empty tube. I hold my breath.

Agent Chang pries off the lid and carefully shakes out three dry papers. My dad and Reika look over my shoulder.

"Nice job, kiddo," says my dad.

It's the three van Gogh drawings of *Moon Crossing Bridge*, safe and sound.

38

My dad and I stand before the Yamada Building in a gentle rain, waiting for Reika. We're holding the same clear plastic umbrella as everyone else in the streets. It's like we're all standing in bubbles. I want to draw this. As soon as my dad's mural is revealed, I'll take out my sketchbook and capture this scene. I haven't had much time to draw just for fun lately, and I want to get back into that.

It's been hard to find spare time since we left Arashiyama two weeks ago, with all the interviews Reika and I have been doing. My dad gave a few interviews in the beginning, too. ("It's good exposure for you," Margo insisted to him on the phone.) But it became clear that both the Japanese and the American media were more interested in the two American girls than they were in some middle-aged artist. TEENAGERS HELP RECOVER VAN GOGHS. AMERICAN SWEETHEARTS EXPOSE CORPORATE CORRUPTION; HIDEKI YAMADA BEHIND BARS. GAI-KOKUJIN GIRLS PUT NOTORIOUS GANG LEADER IN PRISON.

I also have so much going on these days at the Yamada Museum, where I'm learning from Mitsue how to assess prints for damage. I'm helping to set up an exhibit in Mitsue's show, to show the connection between modern manga and *ukiyo-e* prints. Kenji and Mitsue also replaced my set of wood-carving tools, since my set floated away in the river. My *ayu* is coming along nicely, and Mitsue knows a printmaker in Seattle who can help me to ink and print it when I get back.

In between work and media interviews, Reika and I have been doing a lot of brainstorming on *Kimono Girl* together. I've decided to enter that teen manga contest back in Seattle, and the deadline is coming up fast. I knew I needed to make the story stronger, and to rewrite it so it didn't end up framing Skye. Reika has turned out to be a huge help. She has really creative plot ideas, which include adding a little romance between KG and that handsome *samurai* in the print.

"You'd better get inside and get ready," I tell my dad. "I'll wait out here for Reika."

"Okay." But my dad seems unable to get himself through the revolving door. He stares at it, scratching his neck.

"They're going to love it," I assure him, even though I haven't seen the completed mural myself. I don't even know what he decided to do about it in the end, if he put a bridge in it or not. But I can't imagine anyone not loving his work. And Hideki has no say about it anymore. He lost his position at the company and is awaiting trial. Kenji and Mitsue have disowned him.

"I hope so," he mutters. "I've knocked myself out trying to get it done in time. The paint's not even dry."

"Ganbatte." I give him a thumbs-up sign. "Do your best."

He smiles back. "See you inside, kiddo."

I turn to Yoshi, my wingman. "I'm okay on my own now," I tell him. "I don't see any reporters or paparazzi hanging around here."

"All right, I'll see you in there," Yoshi says, winking at me as he pushes the revolving door. I'm so glad Kenji hired him back as personal security after Inspector Mimura confirmed that Yoshi was working for the Organized Crime Bureau in a long-standing effort to keep tabs on Fujikawa. Hideki confessed, in custody, that he was the real informant about the sting, not Yoshi. My suspicion was correct. Hideki had sent an anonymous note to Fujikawa to warn him about the FBI's sting operation. It was yet another part of his master plan to capitalize on Fujikawa's interest in the van Goghs.

The only information Yoshi tried to leak was to me, in a hastily written note that he put in my backpack pocket. That weird "fortune" about the nail standing up. Knowing Hideki was dangerous, he was just trying to tell me not to take unnecessary risks. He couldn't tell me directly that he was monitoring the situation all along.

Reika jogs up the steps a minute later, holding a huge, hot-pink umbrella, not a clear one. "Violet, you look *sugoi!*" she gushes.

"Thanks." I'm wearing my latest Harajuku find: a gauzy, green sleeveless blouse, a pair of slimming pants—black, with some kind of shiny fabric—and a pair of totally *sugoi* sandals, with thick heels, black straps, and gleaming silver buckles. Yes, I finally found my size, confirming my suspicion that you can find anything in Japan, even size-nine sandals, if you just look hard enough.

In the lobby, my dad and Kenji stand before a curtain that has been hung across the big wall. The crowd of office workers gathering around looks eager and happy, maybe because of the impending unveiling, but maybe also because the temperature in the building has finally returned to a comfortably cool setting, now that the mural is done.

The crowd quiets as Kenji steps up to a podium. My dad and Mitsue stand off to the side.

Kenji makes a brief speech in Japanese. I don't have a clue what he's saying, but he seems proud. When his speech ends, everyone applauds. And Kenji pulls back the curtains.

The crowd breathes as one, gasping in awe at the mural.

It's stunning.

It resembles a triptych of woodblock prints, with three long panels, spaces between them. Almost like a comic book sequence. Each panel focuses on a different image from *ukai*, with the sky progressively darkening as the evening goes on. In the first panel, a river runs wide and shallow. A row of canoes tied up by the bank patiently awaits passengers. In the second panel, the boats make their way to the center of the river, lanterns glowing. In the third, they gather around the *ukai* fisherman as they toss the birds into the water.

The painting reminds me of van Gogh's, of course, as well as of Hiroshige's print. But it reminds me most of Tomonori's painting, especially that third panel, with the passenger boat almost stealing the scene because of its level of detail. What a great way to bring Kenji's brother's vision to a wider audience. I'm so proud of my dad in that moment, for paying attention, for honoring him.

And yet the mural isn't just some copy. Its style is uniquely my dad's. Those are his colors, his details, his way of capturing light and air.

I glance at Kenji's face, and then at Mitsue's, to see their reactions.

They're both staring hard at the panels. Kenji is frowning. Oh, no.

I take a few steps closer to hear what Kenji is saying to my dad. "Sorry, but Glenn, where is the bridge?" he asks quietly. "I thought surely any revision you came up with would include the key element that everyone had agreed on."

He's right. There is no bridge.

"Well, Kenji, if you look closely," my dad says, "you will see that there is, in fact, a bridge. It's right there, in this boat."

"A bridge in the boat? How could that be?"

"Take a look," he says, pointing to the front passenger boat in panel three.

In the boat are four young people—Japanese teenagers, boys and girls—eating snacks, holding sparklers, smiling. They look like any of the young people we saw in the crowds at the Gion Festival, before chaos took over that night. The kids are talking with two girls sitting opposite them, one in a red kimono with a yellow *obi*, and one in a green kimono with a pink *obi*. American girls. And not just any American girls. It's Reika. And it's me. I'm sitting right where Tomonori had painted Hanae. One of my hands is trailing in the water, just like hers.

I now get what Hanae, the *okami-san*, meant about seeing herself in a drawing. Feeling invisible, and then finding out you were seen all along.

"This is my concept of a bridge, now that I've spent some time in Japan," my dad says. His voice grows louder, more forceful, as he speaks. "See, a bridge isn't just something we build out of wood or steel. A bridge can also be the people that connect our past to our present, or the people that connect one country to another. And making or sustaining a bridge can be as simple as people talking. It's people making connections."

So he not only saw me, he heard me. My dad used the seed of my idea.

Kenji turns back to the mural, hands clasped, and studies it in the same way he looked at the lone madrona tree the very first time I saw him in Margo's gallery. A slow smile spreads across his face. Mitsue, also smiling, comes up beside him to study the painting up close.

"Yes," Kenji says. "Yes, you are right. I can see the bridge. And I feel my brother here, too. Your painting, for me, is a bridge to him. Thank you." He turns to my dad, his eyes glistening. He bows. Then, surprisingly, he turns toward me. "And Violet-chan," he says. "I think I have not properly thanked you. *Go-kuro-sama deshita.* Thank you for going out of your way." He bows deeply to me, and Mitsue does, too.

"*Domo,*" I murmur, bowing back.

"Hold still, Violet." Reika jabs a bobby pin into my head.

"Ow. You're making me a human pincushion."

"I know what I'm doing. There. You're done. Take a look."

I lift my head and look in the ladies' room mirror. She's done wonders. Half a tube of gel and one million bobby pins later, my hair is slicked back in a tight bun, at the nape of my neck. My makeup is perfect; she's applied everything from foundation to mascara in a way that looks natural. And my new glasses—thinner ones, with delicate rims—look elegant. You'd think we were back in Japan, not in a ladies' room at the Seattle Asian Art Museum.

"I love it. You look like a brainy geisha," Reika says. "Let me just fix your *obi*."

"It's my work on exhibit, not me," I remind her, but I let her tighten the sash. It feels good to wear my Tamura-ya summer kimono again, for the first time since the Gion Festival.

I have to stand by the bristol board versions of *Kimono Girl*, with final inking, and talk about my work to anyone at the Seattle Asian Art Museum Teen Manga Show who's interested in learning what the third place winner—me— had in mind when I created my story.

Reika inspects her own makeup in the mirror and wipes a lipstick smudge off her teeth.

"Who's coming tonight? Edge'll be here, right?"

I shrug. "I don't know. I told him about it. He probably has plans with Mardi. I haven't even seen Edge since I got back from Japan."

"You're kidding! I thought you guys made up."

"We've talked on the phone, emailed a lot, talked about our creative work. But I've been so busy. Anyway, that's fine if he's not here," I add, almost believing myself. "I have more than enough people coming tonight. My mom's here, and my dad is coming. And Skye."

Reika raises an eyebrow as she applies her mascara. "Is that going to be weird?"

. "There is a high probability of a weird factor."

My dad decided, sometime in our last days in Japan, that he was going to give things with Skye another try. On the plane ride home, he told me that he was really touched at Skye's concern for my safety throughout this whole ordeal, and by what she'd done behind the scenes to help out on the case. After we found the art, her name was cleared. And her "windfall" of money she talked about? When I asked him, he laughed at the idea I thought it came from stolen art. It was a small inheritance from a grandfather who recently died.

Not a ton of dough, but enough that if they combined their resources, they could fix up the Fremont house better. "We could add some nice touches," he said. "Get some real furniture. Make it more livable for two people and an occasional guest. We both hope you'll be coming over a lot more. And we'd love you to paint a mural in the guest room."

Reika leans in toward the mirror and asks, "And the Yamadas? Will they come?"

"No. They're still in Japan, taking care of a bunch of legal stuff. Hey, Reika . . . I've been meaning to tell you . . . thanks."

"For what?" She paints her eyelashes with a practiced flick of the wrist.

"For helping me fix *Kimono Girl*. It's a lot better now. But more than that, thanks for coming with me to the show this evening."

"It's the least I can do. You saved me, you know."

"What do you mean?"

"By letting me hang out with you and letting me help find the painting. I was totally depressed in Japan, I could hardly get out of bed. I couldn't write any poetry. I was just dragging through the days."

I'd saved *her*? I never thought of it that way. I guess in a way we saved each other.

"You're a good friend," I tell her.

She punches my arm lightly. "Your friendship worms my heart."

"Thanks for the heartworming sentiment."

"Well," she says, "they're going to open the doors. We should probably get to the show."

We enter the gallery on the ground floor, which has been turned over to the Teen Manga Art Show. Manga-influenced drawings and paintings hang on the walls, and sculptures rise up from tables in the center of the room.

"Violet!"

I turn to see Margo Wise waving at me, her scarf light and loose around her neck. I can't believe I ever pegged her as a villain type. Not only did she come to see my work today, when she must have a million other things to do—including training her new assistant—but she's major sponsor of this show. I saw her gallery listed in the program.

She comes over to me and pats my shoulder. Thank God I changed the appearance of the Scarf character in my last revision. Now she looks nothing like Margo.

"I must tell you, your graphic novel looks very engaging," Margo says. "Your characters are precisely and consistently drawn, and you have a real eye for details and landscape."

"I do? Th-thank you." I wait for her to compare me to my dad. To say something like, "Maybe one day you'll be as great as Glenn." But she doesn't. Instead, she pats my shoulder again and says, "Stay with it. Keep honing your vision. While I can see the manga influence in your work, you have a style that's all your own beginning to emerge.

Cultivate that originality. Be true to your vision. You'll go far."

I'm still tingling from her words as I join Reika at my exhibit area.

The gallery is quickly filling up with kids, parents, teachers, strangers—some of whom come up and congratulate me and Reika on finding the van Goghs, recognizing us from TV interviews or newspapers. But I feel a pang in my chest. There are two gaping absences. I'm missing Edge. Powerfully. And my dad isn't here yet, either.

I start to get a sinking feeling. I've expected too much, thinking my dad will show up.

He's started a new project since we got back from Japan—a series of paintings inspired by our stay in Arashiyama—and he's probably locked up in his studio, lost in time, oblivious to the outside world and all its responsibilities and demands.

"Hey." Reika pulls my sleeve. "Isn't that your ex-boss coming this way?"

I look up and see Jerry from Jet City coming toward us. "Am I dead or something?" I whisper to Reika. "Is this my life flashing before my eyes? What is he doing here?"

"Hey, Violet," says Jerry.

"Hey," I say, instinctively backing away. I figure maybe he's come to seek revenge and bawl me out for quitting.

"So you're famous now."

"More in Japan than here."

"Still. That's cool."

"What are you doing here?"

"I saw your name mentioned in the paper. Not just about the stolen art and the gangsters, but in an article about this show. That's great you got into this. Third place! That's something."

"Thanks, Jerry. And thanks for telling me about the contest."

"No sweat. I'll expect you to come back to the store and do a big signing of *Kimono Girl* when you get it published someday." He coughs. "I don't suppose you'd have any interest in coming back to work? Now that you're a celebrity and all? I was thinking you could take the whole back wall, build up our manga section."

"You mean that?"

"Yeah. You could do the ordering—I'll teach you how—and maybe plan some events around manga, to help bring people into the store."

"I'll think about it. I'm not sure if I'll have time. . . ."

"Yeah, sure. Let me know. Anyway, if it doesn't work out for you, drop by all the same. I'll still give you your employee discount. See you around."

"See you around." I stare at him in wonder as he walks away.

Before I know it, I have a big crowd gathering at my exhibit. Kids are studying my storyboards, asking questions about how I did certain drawings, how many techniques I borrowed from manga and which were my own. But I don't know if I can completely explain how I created *Kimono Girl*. It was so tangled up in my attempts to solve the real-life mystery; it was hard sometimes to keep track of what was real and what was not. It's why I had to write and draw the whole thing over again. Twice. But maybe not everything about art has to be explained. My dad likes to say that part of the process of making art is always a mystery, and now I think that must be true.

Reika helps by holding up or pointing to various poster boards as I talk. "In this one, I tried to give a sense of movement, so I used extra speed lines here. And here, I had Kimono Girl bust through this panel and into the next one to interrupt the boundary between . . ."

My words trail off as I notice the door to the gallery opening. Could it be my dad?

It's Edge. Wearing his most dapper, vintage pin-striped suit. And Mardi, less dressed for the occasion, in blue sweatpants and a Crestview High hoodie.

Edge catches my eye, smiles and waves. Mardi looks away and yawns.

I finish my sentence, then ask Reika to hold down the fort. "Back in a second," I murmur, and I hurry over to Edge and Mardi. I'm going to welcome Mardi as a part of my friend's life. Suddenly, I understand that fortune from Sensō-ji. That person with the open heart, awaiting me at the end of my journey. That was me.

"Hi, guys, thanks for coming!" I make a special point of grinning at Mardi, even though it feels like smiling through a mouthful of really gross food.

"Of course! Crikey, I wouldn't miss your big debut for the world," Edge says.

Am I imagining it, or does Mardi look just a teensy bit annoyed?

"There's food over there. Help yourself. Walk around, enjoy the show. There are a lot of great exhibits here. I mean, if you like manga and anime stuff." I look at Mardi and shrug.

Mardi rolls her eyes, then turns to me. "Congratulations on finding that art," she says. "I saw the *Today* show interview."

"Thanks, Mardi." It's funny; I thought outdoing Mardi would feel amazing. Violin music and triumphant drumbeats. But that's not the case. I guess I'd feel better if she acknowledged not what I did but *who I am*. Edge's friend. Her own former friend. A manga fan. An artist. A regular, decent human being with feelings. But she says nothing else, and when her gaze drifts to look at the refreshments table, I realize that's as far as I'm going to get with her. And I suddenly feel really sorry for Mardi.

The revised *Kimono Girl* ends with Sockeye and the Cormorant both stuck in their animal forms, so deeply entrenched in their evil, underworld selves that they lose their ability to return to their original shapes. They've lost their way. Mardi's a bit like that, too, I see now. She's not a villain out to get me. It's more complicated than that. She's like a shape-shifter who transformed in order to survive in her new world—a rich-kid neighborhood—and never got back to her original form.

"I'm going to get some food. I'm starving," Mardi announces. "You coming, Edge?"

"In a second." As soon as Mardi wanders off, Edge grabs my arm. "Can we talk?"

"I can't just leave my exhibit. I'm talking to—"

"Please? It's really important."

Reika seems to have things under control, explaining some of the storyboard sequences.

"Okay. But make it fast."

It's a beautiful evening, the sunset sky stained pink and orange. Edge and I walk out of the museum, past the greenhouse filled with exotic plants, and into Volunteer Park. We find a boulder in a grove of trees. Madrona trees, like the one my dad painted. But in real life, these trees don't stand apart. They lean toward one another. Their branches reach out, touch, and meld together, as if the trees are holding hands.

Edge gestures for me to sit down on the rock, then takes a seat beside me. "So how does it feel to be a celebrity?" he asks.

"It was fun at first. Especially seeing my picture in Japanese newspapers. But then it got kind of old. Reika and I got recognized everywhere there. People took pictures of us and followed us around. We actually needed a bodyguard the whole time we were in Tokyo."

"I can't believe you found *both* the painting and the drawings," says Edge. "And now you're rich, right? Did they give you the reward money?"

"They did. My parents had it put in a trust for college.

Honestly, though? I'm glad it's all been put away for the future. I didn't even want to take it at all, but the Yamadas kept insisting."

"Really? You didn't want a hundred grand?"

"It didn't feel right, after all we've been through together. And to be honest, I'd feel more thrilled about our success if the van Goghs were actually displayed somewhere."

"Where are they?"

"In a vault while a bunch of lawyers fight over who owns them, and some art detectives research their history."

"Isn't it technically that gang boss's painting? Since he paid for it?"

"It's complicated. There's this thing called statute of limitations. In Japan, it's two years."

"What does that mean?"

"Tomonori's crime is too old to prosecute. Agent Chang says that, legally, the *okami-san* at the inn we stayed at may be the owner, since the art was found on her property and was underneath something she legitimately owned, as a gift from Tomonori." I still remember how brightly the *okami-san*'s eyes shone when the FBI came to tell her that she could be the owner of a van Gogh worth millions. She could never have the man she loved. He'd given her just brief moments of happiness in her life, and mostly a lot of sadness and misfortune. But in the end he may have given her something worth so much money—underneath a painting that symbolized his true feelings. A double gift, and a sign that he really did love her.

"Well, I'm just glad you're all right," Edge says. "You had me so worried." He's looking me right in the eyes now. "I have to tell you something," he says.

"Sure."

"It's not working. This thing with Mardi."

"You haven't been going out that long." I try to keep my face neutral. "Give it time."

"Going out? I don't know that I would use that term. It's like we're in this gray area. We just had this one ambiguous weird kiss thing at a camp party. But the thing is, I don't even know who this girl *is*," he goes on, leaning forward and putting his elbows on his knees. "On one level, she's really smart and interesting. She sees stuff in film I've never noticed. Her work at camp was brilliant. She won a camp Academy Award."

"But?"

"Camp ends, we're back in town, she starts going to soccer practice, swim team practice, student government meetings, getting all caught up with her friends—who completely ignore me when we're with them, or who laugh when I'm not trying to be funny—Violet, I think you were right. She just wanted me to help her look good at film camp."

"It's not about my being right. Look, I'm sorry that things

got so confusing with Mardi. I'm sorry because you're obviously not happy with her."

He sighs. "I don't know what I was thinking. I guess I was really flattered that someone like her would even pay attention to me."

"So what are you going to do?"

"Stop hanging out with her, I guess. Even though she's taking video production this semester, and things are going to be awkward. I just don't know how to tell her."

"Are you asking me for advice? Me, the great relationship expert?" I laugh.

"It's not funny. I feel stuck. And I have to do this tonight. It's killing me." He kicks at a patch of grass.

I study the green grass marks on the white part of his spectator shoes. I remember buying those shoes with him at a vintage shop in the U District last year. How we laughed that day, trying on outfits. And then I remember how we chased Skye all around downtown at the beginning of the summer, how we had so much fun together before all these complications set in—with the mystery, and with Mardi.

The fundamental fact, beneath all the layers of complications, is that I really, really like this crazy guy. He may not be perfect, but who is? And I love that there's nobody like him. No one comes anywhere close to Edge.

"What happened with us anyway?" he asks in a soft voice. "Before camp, before Japan?" He reaches over and plays with a loose thread on my kimono sleeve. He's not even touching my skin, but my whole arm tingles from how close he is.

"I don't know." I look down at my feet, my face burning. "You said I wasn't listening to you. You might have been right about that."

"Oh, that." He sighs. "I'm sorry I said that. I think I was just getting so much attention from that video on the Internet, which was cool at first, but it made me overthink things. I wondered if people were just talking to me because of what I'd done, not because of who I am."

I nod. "I can understand that. It's weird, you think you want to *do* things, important things, to stop being invisible, and to get people's attention. Then you get that attention and you still worry that nobody sees you for who you are. You can't win."

Edge looks at me. "I see you. I always saw you, Violet."

I swallow hard. *It's now.* "I have one last idea to help you out with your Mardi situation," I tell him. "It's a crazy one, though."

"Crazy is good. Tell me."

I take a deep breath and lift my gaze from his shoes to his eyes. "You could just tell her your girlfriend would rather that you didn't hang out anymore."

"My girlfriend? The person I'm looking at now?" His voice is low and quiet.

I'm falling into his eyes. "If you want. I mean—I'd really

like that." I know, in that moment, I'm done hiding things. From now on I'm going to be more open about my art. My passions. My feelings. "I really like you."

And suddenly, Edge's arms are around my waist, and mine are around his shoulders, and it feels completely natural and amazing. And then he's kissing me, and I'm kissing him back, and I'm startled by the softness of his lips and the strength of his arms. I'm so shocked at what a great kisser he is that I don't even have to worry about whether I'm any good or not.

It's like being in a woodblock print, I want to tell him. Time stands still. We're in our own world, under our tree, the sunset pink and orange bathing our faces.

But I don't tell him this. I don't say anything. All I have to do in this moment is be here.

After a while, we break apart and just hold each other. I rest my cheek on his shoulder.

"I have wanted to do that for a very long time," he murmurs into my hair.

As we're sitting there, through our screen of madrona trees I notice a red Honda Civic drive into the museum parking lot. My dad and Skye get out. Skye gives him a little push and says, "Hurry, Glenn!" and they run up the museum steps.

I shrug and smile. My relationship with my dad, like any relationship, is a work in progress. Today, showing up late to my show—but showing up all the same—I guess that's progress.

"My dad just got here," I say, reluctantly extracting myself from Edge's embrace. "And I've got to get back to my exhibit. I can't let Reika do all the talking for me."

"Right." He moves a stray curl from my face and tucks it gently behind my ear. "You've got your adoring fans. I suppose I'd better get used to sharing you with the world."

Holding hands, we leave the shelter of the madrona grove behind. We walk back to the art museum to join the people there.

AUTHOR'S NOTE:
ABOUT *MOON CROSSING BRIDGE*

The Moon Crossing Bridge at Arashiyama is a real print by the famous Japanese *ukiyo-e* artist Ando Hiroshige (1797–1858). The print is from a landscape series called Famous Views of the 60-Odd Provinces. The van Gogh drawings and painting in *Tokyo Heist* that are based on this print are fictitious. However, I like to imagine that his renditions of Hiroshige's print could exist. Here is why.

Hiroshige created over 5,400 prints in his lifetime. There's no record of whether van Gogh owned a copy of *The Moon Crossing Bridge at Arashiyama*, but it's entirely possible he possessed it, saw it, or at least knew of similar prints in Hiroshige's masterpiece series, Fifty-Three Stations of the Tokaido (scenes from the highway connecting Edo [Tokyo], to Kyoto). Woodblock prints were inexpensive and plentiful in the nineteenth century, and reproductions, often exported to Western countries, were widely available.

In Europe, many Impressionist and Postimpressionist painters were fascinated by all things Japanese. They were part of an aesthetic movement that became known as *Japonisme*. Vincent van Gogh (1853–1890), as a collector and student of

Japanese woodblock prints, was a part of that movement. He lived and breathed Japanese prints. Almost literally, he inhabited *ukiyo-e*: they papered the walls of his studio in Arles, France. He directly copied the prints in order to understand their composition and use of perspective. In fact, as his mental health deteriorated, he actually imagined he was in Japan, not in France. In his correspondence, he told friends that all he needed to do was open his eyes and paint what he saw; he didn't need to copy from Japanese prints anymore.

Van Gogh transformed three of his Japanese print copies into major paintings. *The Bridge in the Rain* and *The Flowering Plum Tree* were directly based on Hiroshige's print designs and given van Gogh's special touches: elaborate borders and decorated frames (with his version of Japanese *kanji* characters), heavy brushstrokes, and richer or more contrasting colors than were used in the original prints. The third *Japonisme* painting, *The Courtesan*, was copied from a print by Keisai Eisen. Eisen's *Courtesan* originally appeared on the cover of *Paris Illustré*, a popular nineteenth-century magazine. Today, all three paintings hang in the Van Gogh Museum in Amsterdam and can be viewed in their virtual gallery: www.vangoghmuseum.nl.

What if van Gogh really did a series of sketches and a painting based on *The Moon Crossing Bridge at Arashiyama*? Wouldn't such works have surfaced long ago? Not necessarily. Van Gogh was a prolific artist who did not enjoy great success or sales in his lifetime. His brother Theo acted as his art dealer, yet there are a number of paintings and drawings that were not sold through traditional means, both during and after van Gogh's short life. Some art was given away, put into storage, left behind in a house, or otherwise not accounted for. Van Goghs have turned up, over the years, in surprising places all over the world, even beneath other paintings on canvases reused by van Gogh or by other artists.

Who knows how many van Goghs are out there, waiting to be found?

Acknowledgments

Writing *Tokyo Heist* has been a long, exciting journey. I'd like to thank the many people who helped along the way.

I feel incredibly lucky to have Kirby Kim as my agent. I am grateful for his keen editorial eye, his enthusiasm, and his belief in Violet's story. Kirby found the perfect publisher for this book and, with Ian Dalrymple, expertly steered me through the publishing process.

Enormous thanks to the Viking/Penguin team. Specifically, I'd like to thank Regina Hayes and Leila Sales. My writing is forever improved from working with such talented editors, and I am particularly grateful for Leila's help in reshaping the story. This book is what it is today because of her attention to detail. I am grateful for the keen eyes of Susan G. Jeffers, Janet Pascal, Jennifer Tait, and Abigail Powers. Also many thanks go to Kate Renner for creating the cover design of my dreams, and to Catherine Frank, who initially acquired the novel.

I owe so much to my writing group: Steven Lee Beeber, Clare Dunsford, Eileen Donovan Kranz, Patrick Gabridge, Vincent Gregory, Edward Rooney, Heather Totty, and Deborah Vlock. Fearless readers and steadfast friends, for years they donned hard hats and stepped into the construction zone of my novel. They rescued me from shaky scaffolding, plucked me off of falling beams, and cheered me on to the end. I've learned so much from these talented writers. I hope we all write together for many years to come.

I owe thanks to other talented writer and editor friends: Marc Foster, for early feedback; Julie Wu, for title help and library companionship; Elizabeth Hale, for plowing through an unwieldy draft; Lisa Borders and Lisa Nold, for consulting on manuscripts and helping me find my story. Kira Gabridge and Naomi Shwom read drafts and offered their perspectives on teenagers and *otaku* culture.

Arigato gozaimasu, Kyoko Shiga. Thank you so much for reading, for consulting on Japanese culture and language, and for fielding questions on everything from *wagashi* to footwear to the depth of the Katsura-gawa. Any errors are my own. *Arigato gozaimasu,* as well to Bill and Yuko Hunt, who opened so many doors in Japan. You may have thought you were merely giving travel advice and entertaining, but in fact you were setting me on the long path of writing this novel.

Many people in law enforcement and in the art world offered assistance with research. Among them, Special Agent Robbie Burroughs of the Seattle FBI fielded questions about art theft. Sarah Thompson at the Museum of Fine Arts in Boston gave me a crash course in Japanese prints, access to their *ukiyo-e* collection, and the opportunity to shadow an art conservator. Elizabeth English and Sarah Gurney consulted on art collecting and art conservation. Brigid Alverson helped me to navigate manga. Sam Garland taught me how comic book artists work. And I'm grateful to my former employers and colleagues at Golden Age Collectibles in Seattle, who introduced me to the world of comics, manga, and anime back in the 1990s.

The Writer's Room of Boston provided the ideal writing space during early drafts. Later, Tricia Gaquin and Andrea Lyons, babysitters extraordinaire, helped me to carve out time.

I'd like to thank the Apocalypsies, as well as my partners in crime on the Sleuths, Spies, and Alibis blog, for their support, wisdom, encouragement, and inspiration.

I am so grateful for the boundless support of my entire extended family, especially my parents (all of them). My stepdaughters, Sarah Nager and Rachel Nager, read drafts and offered encouragement at a most critical time. My son, Gabriel, gave me the gift of long afternoon naps.

The biggest thank-you goes to my husband, James Nager, who enthusiastically traveled in Japan with me, and who supported my long, odd working hours. Thank you for waiting so patiently on the other side of this novel.